Karen King is a bestselling author of fiction for both adults and children and has also written numerous short stories for women's magazines. *The Cornish Hotel by the Sea* was an international bestseller, reaching the top one hundred in the Kindle charts in both the UK and Australia.

Karen is a member of the Romantic Novelists' Association, the Society of Authors, the Crime Writers Association and the Society of Women Writers and Journalists. She lives in Spain with her husband Dave and their two cats, Tizzy and Marmaduke.

By Karen King

Romance titles
I do? or do I?
The Millonaire Plan
Never Say Forever
The Cornish Hotel by the Sea
The Bridesmaid's Dilemma
Snowy Nights at the Lonely Hearts Hotel
The Year of Starting Over
Single All the Way
One Summer in Cornwall
The Best Christmas Ever
The Spanish Wedding Disaster

Thriller titles
The Stranger in My Bed
The Perfect Stepmother

Karen King

The Spanish Wedding Disaster

ACCENT

First published in paperback in 2022 by Headline Accent
An imprint of HEADLINE PUBLISHING GROUP

1

Cataloguing in Publication Data is available from the British Library

ISBN 978 1 4722 7875 3

Typeset in 11.25/15.25 pt Bembo by Jouve (UK), Milton Keynes
Printed and bound in Great Britain by Clays Ltd, Elcograf S.p.A.

HEADLINE PUBLISHING GROUP
An Hachette UK Company
Carmelite House
50 Victoria Embankment
London
EC4Y 0DZ

www.headline.co.uk
www.hachette.co.uk

For my dad who instilled in me a love of reading and writing, and my mum who passed on the strength and determination needed to build a writing career.

Chapter One

Sophie

'Maddie!' Sophie shouted, as she spotted her best friend about to go into the café where they'd arranged to meet, recognising her instantly even though her shoulder-length hair was now bright purple rather than the luminous green it had been the last time they'd met. Sophie never knew what colour hair Maddie would turn up with, or what colour eyes for that matter. Her friend had glasses with a variety of frames and also often wore contact lenses, though not always the clear kind that showed her natural hazel eyes, but turquoise, honey, pearl ones – and once she even turned up with tiger eyes.

Maddie turned at the sound of Sophie's voice, her hair blowing in the March wind as she moved to the side of the door and waited for Sophie to catch up.

Now she'd turned around, Sophie could see that she was wearing huge, red-framed glasses today. Only Maddie would be able to wear such a rainbow of colours – a three-quarter length blue, red and white striped coat over orange and black striped jeggings tucked into black Doc Martens boots decorated with hand-painted red roses – and pull it off. Sophie grinned and increased her pace, the wind biting her cheeks. It was bitterly cold today and she was glad of the warmth of the fur-trimmed hood of the cream parka she was wearing, over a thick pastel-blue jumper, indigo jeans and black boots.

Maddie was shivering slightly, hands thrust deep into her coat pockets as she waited for Sophie to join her.

'It's so good to see you again. It's been ages!' Maddie wrapped Sophie in a big hug.

Whenever they met, no matter how long had elapsed, it always felt like they'd only seen each other yesterday, Sophie thought as she returned the hug. 'I know. I don't know where the time goes.'

'Let's go inside and have a quick catch-up while we wait for Steve.' Maddie pushed open the door of the café and scanned the room, her gaze resting on an empty table for four by the window. 'That's perfect.'

Sophie followed her, wondering what new tales Maddie had to tell. Her work as a publicist for a media agency meant a lot of travelling and meeting interesting people, whereas Sophie worked in a local florist, and while she loved the job it wasn't as exciting as Maddie's – something that Sophie was very pleased about. She preferred a quiet life. She was happy living with her boyfriend Glenn in their one-bedroomed flat in Worcester near the river, but she still enjoyed listening to Maddie's tales.

The café was waitress service, so they both pulled out a chair and sat down on one side of the rectangular black table, leaving room for Steve to sit opposite.

'I wish Kate was coming too, we haven't seen her for a while,' Sophie said, hanging her bag on the back of her chair. She left her coat on, still feeling a bit chilly even though the café was warm and cosy.

The three women had been friends for years. Sophie and Maddie had hit it off as soon as Maddie had parked next to Sophie's blue Fiesta in her purple and yellow psychedelic Beetle in the college car park and they had got talking. They hadn't been on the same course but had met for lunch in the canteen and quickly become good friends. Maddie said they were 'Yin and Yang' and that Sophie was good for talking Maddie out of some of her madder schemes, whilst Maddie was great at coaxing Sophie out of her 'safe zone'. When Kate, an old school friend of Sophie's, had moved back to the area after working abroad, Sophie had introduced her to Maddie and the three women had all got along well.

Sophie had been intrigued when Steve, Kate's partner, had messaged her in the week to ask her if she could meet him here today. He'd said he was inviting Maddie too, and asked her not to mention it to Kate as he was planning a surprise. Sophie had immediately called Maddie, who confirmed that she'd had the same message from Steve and had been about to call Sophie. They had both speculated what it could be about. It wasn't Kate's birthday until the end of the year and she'd be thirty-three so it wasn't a big one that Steve might be planning a party for months in advance. Curiosity, and the chance to meet up with each other, had prompted them both to agree to go.

'I know, it would be great to have a catch-up with her. What do you think Steve wants?' Maddie asked. 'I didn't think that he was the type for surprises. Didn't Kate say she was the one who organised everything? She even booked their holiday to Spain for this June.'

Sophie cast her mind back to the last time they'd all met for lunch, just after the New Year. Kate had told them she had just booked a two-week holiday on the Costa del Sol for herself and Steve and was really looking forward to it. 'I can't wait to chill out on the beach with a cocktail in my hand,' she'd said. Sophie and Glenn hadn't got around to booking any holidays yet but had talked about getting a last-minute deal to somewhere hot later in the year. It would be their first holiday abroad together and Sophie was excited at the thought of going away together.

'Yes, that's right, Kate normally arranges everything. And Steve has never texted us to meet up before. I wonder what's going on?' Sophie mused. Kate and Steve had been together a couple of years now and they'd all had the occasional night out together, Kate and Steve, Sophie and Glenn, and Maddie with whoever she was going out with at the time – Maddie was a commitment-phobe but attracted men like a magnet with her vivacious personality. Mainly, though, it was the three girls who had met up. Maddie rarely had a partner long enough to arrange regular nights out with, and Glenn and Steve didn't really have a lot in common.

'Can I get you anything?' A young lad appeared at the table, notebook and pen in hand.

'I'll have a caramel bubble tea, please,' Maddie replied.

A smile tugged at the corners of Sophie's mouth. Maddie was always trying something different. Bubble tea was obviously her current favourite, which was probably why she'd suggested meeting at Not Just Coffee, as many cafés didn't serve the popular Taiwanese drink. 'I'll have a mocha, please,' she told him.

'Here comes Steve now,' Maddie said.

Sophie turned to face the entrance as Steve walked in. Tall, fair-haired and clean-shaven, he looked every inch the marketing consultant he was, even in his beige chinos, white collarless shirt and casual brown jacket. He was the perfect match for elegant, level-headed Kate, who worked as a dental assistant.

'Thanks for coming, you two,' Steve said when he reached the table. 'I really appreciate it.' He pulled out a chair and sat down opposite Sophie. 'I'm just waiting for my brother Josh to join us. He'll be here in a minute.'

Sophie caught the surprised glance Maddie shot her. Why had Steve asked his brother to join them? This was getting even more mysterious.

The waiter returned with Sophie's coffee and Maddie's bubble tea, then took Steve's order for two Americanos. He and his brother obviously liked their coffee the same way.

Steve wrinkled his nose as he looked at the clear plastic cup containing Maddie's drink, and the black balls bobbing around inside. 'I don't know how you can drink that stuff; the balls are so chewy. It's like eating jelly. Kate likes it too and she made me one once. I nearly threw up.'

'Chewing the pearls is the best part.' Maddie sucked the caramel drink up through the fat straw provided, then paused to chew the 'boba' as the tapioca balls were called.

'I'm with Steve – give me a smooth, tasty mocha any time,' Sophie said, ripping open a sachet of brown sugar and emptying it into her coffee.

Steve kept glancing over at the door, obviously looking out for Josh's arrival. Maddie caught Sophie's eye over the rim of her cup and raised an eyebrow, questioning why Steve looked so nervous. Sophie was wondering that herself. What was the big surprise? And why was Steve meeting them to tell them about it instead of Kate?

'Ah, here he is!' Steve stood up to wave as a tall, muscular man, with an unruly mop of wavy raven-black hair atop a disarmingly handsome face strode over to them. He was dressed in well-worn jeans tucked into black motorbike boots, and a zipped-up black leather jacket. A black helmet was tucked under his arm.

'Wow! I like,' Maddie whispered to Sophie.

He was a head-turner, Sophie had to admit; the few days' stubble on his chin only added to his sex appeal. Not that she was interested. She much preferred sensitive men like Glenn to macho biker types.

The man placed his hand on Steve's shoulder. 'Sorry I'm late.'

They smiled at each other. She would never have taken them for brothers. Mind, now she was looking more closely at them, Sophie could see a slight similarity with their eyes – although Josh's were a deeper blue. They were actually quite a stunning indigo.

'Sophie, Maddie, this is my kid brother, Josh.' Steve pointed to them both in turn. 'Josh, this is Sophie and Maddie, Kate's two best friends.'

'Pleased to meet you both.' Josh nodded. 'And can I clarify that I'm only two years younger,' he added, his eyes meeting Sophie's for a moment, then moving on to Maddie who blew him a kiss. He grinned and winked at her.

OK, so it looked like those two had hit it off, thought Sophie. Not that many men could resist Maddie; she was vibrant, outrageous and fun. She left a string of broken hearts in her wake, even though she was always sure to stress at the beginning of every relationship that she was a 'no commitment' woman. Men seemed to see that as a challenge. Josh looked a bit of a player too, though; he was a little too self-assured, a little too aware of his sex appeal. They'd probably be a good match for each other.

The waiter returned with the two Americanos. Josh waited until he'd put the cups on the table and had gone off to serve someone else before asking, 'So, why have we all been summonsed here? It's a bit dramatic, isn't it? Surely you could have just phoned us?' He took a swig of his coffee. 'Pleasant as it is to meet you two ladies, of course.'

'It's too important to put in a text. What if Kate looked at my messages? We don't keep secrets from each other,' Steve replied.

'What do you call this, then?' Maddie shot at him.

'This is different.' He paused, then leant forward, resting his elbows on the table and steepling his fingers. 'You know we're going on holiday to Spain in June?'

'Yup, Kate told us last time we met,' Maddie said. 'Lucky you two!'

Steve took a deep breath and swept his eyes around the table to make sure he had everyone's attention. 'Well, we're going to get married when we're over there. The hotel organises weddings.'

'What? Kate hasn't mentioned it. I didn't even know you guys were engaged! How exciting!' The words tumbled out of Sophie's mouth; she was astonished but so happy for her friend. She loved a wedding!

'That's because she doesn't know. I'm planning a surprise wedding. I'm going to propose to Kate the night before.'

Sophie, Maddie and Josh all stared back at him and a stunned silence settled over the table.

Chapter Two

Josh

Josh watched the expressions on the two women's faces. Maddie, like him, was horrified by Steve's plans, whereas Sophie was clearly swept away with the romance of it all. It was hard to believe that they were both Kate's friends; they were total opposites. Maddie looked so vivacious and outgoing, he could imagine her being the life and soul of the party. Whereas Sophie looked sweet and cute, with her blond curly hair cascading on to her shoulders, her conventional jeans and her cream parka – which was still firmly zipped up. She was pretty too, he acknowledged, with those big topaz eyes that glistened in the light, the cute dimples in her cheeks and the tiny mole on her chin. She was clasping her hands in delight now.

'Oh gosh, that's so romantic!' Sophie exclaimed.

'Romantic? I think it's madness.' Josh shook his head in dismay. 'You haven't thought this through, Steve. I presume you know that Kate definitely wants to get married? And surely she'll want a say in the wedding plans?'

'Trust you to put a damper on it,' his older brother retorted, obviously annoyed by Josh's reaction. 'Of course we've talked about it. We've been living together for two years now. We love each other. It's the next logical step.'

'Is it? Maybe Kate's happy to carry on living together. Have you actually discussed marriage? What will you do if she turns you down?' Josh persisted.

'I think Kate will love it. Ignore him, Steve,' Sophie said, throwing Josh an irritated look.

Steve sighed with exasperation. 'Please excuse my brother, he doesn't believe in marriage – the idea of committing himself to someone is completely alien to him.'

'I'm not against marriage – for other people, anyway – but I do think that it should be a joint decision and that you should plan your wedding together,' Josh shot back.

Maddie, who had been silent up to now, tapped her bottom lip with her rainbow-varnished nail for a moment. 'So, let me get this straight,' she said to Steve. 'You haven't proposed to Kate yet, and don't intend to do it until the night before this secret wedding you're planning?'

'That's right,' Steve told her. 'Can you imagine her face when I tell her that the wedding is all planned for the next day? I'm hoping our families and best friends will fly over for the ceremony too – that means you two, and Glenn, Sophie.'

So, Sophie was in a relationship, then, thought Josh. He'd presumed so. No wonder she was so excited about this wedding, she'd probably like to get married herself. Her eyes were wide and shining as she leant forward to talk to Steve. 'Ignore these two doom-mongers. I think it's a wonderful idea.'

'Thank you, Sophie.' Steve glared pointedly at Josh, then Maddie.

'Honestly, Steve, I really think this is a bad idea. Even if you

9

have talked about getting married, you can't presume she will go along with your wedding plans. You need to propose to her then plan the wedding together,' Josh advised. 'What if she is so furious that you've organised it all that she says "no" and finishes with you? Then what will you do?'

'I'm with Josh; you can't just assume that Kate will accept your proposal even if you have talked about getting married and – more to the point – that she will be happy in having no say in her own wedding,' Maddie pointed out. 'Kate is going to hate this; I know she will.'

Steve looked hurt. 'I should have known you wouldn't agree. You're such a commitment-phobe you wouldn't know romance if it hit you in the face.'

'Charming. Maybe this is where I should go?' Maddie started to get up, but Steve immediately looked regretful. 'I'm sorry, Maddie. I didn't mean it. It's just I'm trying to do a nice thing here. Kate is always saying that I take her for granted and always leave everything for her to organise, so I thought this would be a way of showing her how much I care.'

'Well, I think that Kate will love it.' Sophie smiled reassuringly at Steve. 'It's a really lovely romantic gesture, Steve. Don't let these two cynics put you off.'

'Thanks, Sophie.' Josh could see the relief in his brother's eyes. 'It's going to be wonderful. The hotel organises beach weddings so they'll do all the preparation. Imagine Kate in a gorgeous white wedding dress, and me in a white suit, the sun shining down on us, with our family and friends watching . . .'

'A white suit?' Josh leant back in his chair, his eyes wide. 'Steady on, bro, this is beginning to sound like one of those soppy romance movies.'

'Does Kate want to wear a white wedding dress and have a beach ceremony?' Maddie asked. 'Have you discussed the sort of wedding you'd like.'

'Er, no . . .' Steve stammered.

'Well, you need to. Kate might want to get married in a castle, and to arrive there in a horse and cart. Or to have a traditional service in a church,' Josh pointed out.

'I can't discuss it with her, it's a surprise . . .'

Sophie glared at them both. 'Stop being so negative. You can see how much this means to Steve. I'm sure Kate would love a beach wedding.'

Josh sighed. He held a palm up. 'OK, let's assume that Kate will be happy to marry you, and for you to plan your wedding without any input from her,' he said to Steve. 'What about the practicalities?' He lowered his hand and started counting on his fingers. 'Your holiday is in three months' time. How many guests are you thinking of?'

Steve scratched his chin. 'I haven't worked out a list yet. Hopefully both sets of parents can make it.'

'What if everyone you want to come can't get the time off work?' This was from Maddie. 'Some people might have already booked their summer holiday and can't afford another one.'

'Good point. Are you paying for the guests to come over or expecting them to pay for themselves?' Josh asked.

'I can't pay for everyone, it'll cost a fortune!' Steve looked horrified. 'I'll pay for the flights and hotel stay for two nights for the parents on both sides, and for you three.'

'That's really kind of you,' Sophie said. She looked a bit thoughtful. 'It is a lot to plan in only a few months though,' she conceded.

11

At last Sophie was seeing reason too, Josh thought in relief. 'It's not going to be straightforward, Steve. You're expecting people to get time off work at short notice. I don't know if I can manage time off in June,' he said.

'Nor me,' Maddie agreed.

Steve looked disappointed. 'Surely you can all manage a couple of days off work to come to the ceremony?'

'I'm sure me and Glenn can make it, we haven't booked our holidays yet,' Sophie said.

'I hope you can too, Josh,' asked Steve. 'I don't want to get married without my little brother there.'

Talk about emotional blackmail. But there was no way he wouldn't attend his brother's wedding, and Steve knew that. 'I'll be there – of course I will.'

'Thanks, because I'm counting on you. The thing is, I was hoping you'd all help me plan the wedding. And I know that Kate would love you two –' Steve flicked his gaze from Sophie to Maddie – 'to be her bridesmaids.' Then he turned to Josh. 'And I want you to be my best man.'

How could he say no to that? Josh thought, realising in dismay that he had no choice but to help Steve with this secret wedding whether he agreed with it or not. He couldn't let his brother down.

Chapter Three

Maddie

That news took Maddie by surprise. 'Me, bridesmaid? You want me to wear a chiffony dress and put my hair up?' She pushed her purple locks behind her right ear to reveal an array of assorted piercings running down her outer ear and a black cross dangling from her lobe.

Josh's eyes danced with amusement. 'I have to say, I can't imagine you in a bridesmaid's dress.'

Neither could Maddie; she didn't do pretty frocks and had never imagined anyone would ask her to be a bridesmaid at their wedding. It was *so* not her.

Sophie, on the other hand, looked delighted. 'Come on, Maddie, surely you can do this for Kate? It would mean such a lot to her.'

'You two are her best friends,' Steve pointed out. 'Kate will want you both as her bridesmaids. I know she will.'

Maddie was silent for a moment. She fingered the string of black beads that dangled around her neck as she pondered over what to do. Even though she thought this surprise wedding was a mad idea she felt compelled to help if Steve insisted on going ahead. And much as she hated the idea of being a bridesmaid, she knew that he was right and it was what Kate would want; she didn't have any sisters, only a brother, Billy. She couldn't let her friend down. Oh, what the hell, it wasn't going to kill her to wear a traditional bridesmaid's dress for one day, was it?

She shrugged. 'OK. But I'm not dyeing my hair brown or any other boring colour, or taking out my nose-stud or ear-piercings.' Her hazel eyes met Steve's. 'And I'm definitely not covering up the tattoos on my arms.' She'd had her two half-sleeve tattoos done a few years ago: a phoenix rising from the ashes up the top half of her right arm, and a dragon with fire pouring out of its mouth circling the top of her left arm. They were both very large and colourful – and would be very much on display in a summery bridesmaid's dress.

Josh's grin spread wider. 'You have tattoos?'

Maddie folded her arms and gave him a frosty glare. 'Don't you?'

He nodded. 'Yep, I do and I'm not criticising so don't get your dander up. I was just trying to imagine *you* in a brides-maid's dress.'

Sophie jumped to Maddie's defence. 'Don't be so rude, she'll look gorgeous. Her tattoos are amazing. And Kate wouldn't want Maddie to change anything about her appearance, any more than she'd expect you to have your hair cut or shave off your stubble,' she snapped.

Maddie shot Josh a triumphant look. Sophie had a spunky side to her when someone pressed her buttons, as Josh had done. He had gone down in her estimation; he was obviously one of those annoying men who expected women to conform to outdated images of femininity. She was disappointed in him.

'Woah!' Josh held up both hands in mock-surrender. 'No offence meant to anyone. I'm not asking Maddie to change anything. I think she looks great exactly how she is.'

Hmm, cleverly backtracked, Maddie thought. Sophie still looked annoyed with him, though.

Steve met Maddie's gaze and rested his arms on the table, leaning forward as he softened his tone. 'Sophie is right, Kate wouldn't want you to change anything about yourself, Maddie,' he reassured her. 'And I know that she would love you both to be her bridesmaids. Will you? Please.'

How could Maddie refuse? 'OK,' she said.

'Thank you.' Steve turned to Josh. 'And are you on board too? Will you be my best man?'

Josh nodded. 'Of course I will. You're my brother. It'll be an honour.'

Steve looked relieved. 'Great! Thank you, all of you. I was hoping I could rely on you three. I really need your help to pull this off.'

Chapter Four

Josh

Josh finished the last of his coffee whilst he considered how to phrase his words. The last thing he wanted to do was hurt his brother, but he really felt like this was a disaster waiting to happen. Steve, who was usually cautious, hadn't thought this through at all.

'Look, I really don't want to put a downer on this, Steve, but the wedding day is supposed to be the bride's big day. Some women say it's the best day of their lives. Kate's not going to like you taking over and planning it all for her.'

Steve remained unperturbed. 'I'm not taking over, I'm sure Kate will want a beach wedding, and I'm going to make sure it's the best day of her life. That's where you two come in.' He turned his gaze to Sophie and Maddie. 'You can both talk to her and casually bring up the subject of weddings – that way, you can find out what sort of wedding dress she wants, and what colour bridesmaids' dresses and flowers.'

Maddie frowned. 'If we start asking Kate questions like that, she'll suspect something for sure.'

Sophie nodded. 'Maddie's right, we can't ask Kate outright what sort of wedding she wants, Steve.'

Josh nodded, glad that Kate's friends agreed with him. 'I don't think you've quite realised what's involved, Steve. Even if the hotel has an events planner, they will need you to provide all the details for the wedding.' He was trying to conceal his exasperation but he felt like giving his brother a shake. He couldn't believe that Steve had come up with the idea of planning a surprise wedding, as if there was nothing to it. Strange, when in his work as a marketing consultant he was so cool and measured, never making snap decisions. 'And the girls are right, it could give the game away if they start asking Kate questions about what sort of wedding dress she would like.'

Steve's forehead knitted into a frown, then his eyes lit up. 'I know. I've got the perfect solution.' He sat up straight, suddenly energised. 'You can pretend that you and Glenn are planning a summer wedding, Sophie. You can say that you don't want a lot of fuss, so are keeping it quiet and only inviting a few people, but you want Kate and Maddie to help you choose your wedding dress et cetera.' His voice rose in triumph. 'Then it'll be easy to find out what Kate would want.' He leant back in his chair and folded his arms, pleased with his solution.

Chapter Five

Sophie

Sophie was too stunned to speak, but Maddie quickly retorted, 'For goodness' sake, you can't expect Sophie to do that! She can't pretend to everyone that she's getting married when she isn't. And what about Glenn? He's not going to agree to it.'

'Can you think of a better way to find out how Kate would like her wedding to be?' Steve demanded.

'Yes, ask her!' Josh cut in. 'Propose to her and plan the wedding as normal. This isn't fair on Sophie.'

Sophie was only half aware of what they were saying. Her mind was in a whirl as she processed what Steve had said. She wanted to help him, and was sure Kate would be swept away with the romance of it all. Imagine your boyfriend proposing to you then telling you that he had the entire wedding planned and you were going to get married the very next day! She would love Glenn to do that. An image flashed across her mind: Glenn going down on one knee, holding out an open ring box with a glittering diamond ring inside; her hand flying to her mouth, her eyes shining with delight. There would be romantic music playing in the background, champagne chilling in an ice bucket nearby ...

'This is the perfect way to make it work.' Steve's voice pulled her out of her daydream. His eyes were fixed on her face, pleading with her, and his voice was soft as he coaxed her. 'You don't mind, do you, Sophie? You don't have to tell anyone else, just Kate. Emphasise that you're keeping it quiet and you're only telling the people who are invited.'

What harm would it do? And Steve was right, it was the perfect way to find out Kate's wedding preferences without raising her suspicions. Sophie straightened her shoulders as she came to a decision. 'OK, I'll do it.'

'You're mad!' Maddie exclaimed. 'How are you going to pull this off, and what will Glenn say?'

'He won't mind. Once I explain to him, he'll understand.' She was so excited about it all and delighted about finally being a bridesmaid. When she was a little girl, she'd always longed to be one, but it had never happened. And now here she was, being asked to be bridesmaid at the secret wedding of one of her very best friends. Why couldn't Maddie and Josh see how romantic it all was?

Maddie rolled her eyes. 'Mark my words, this is not going to end well. You must be *crazy* to agree to it.'

'It's the perfect solution, as Steve said,' replied Sophie. 'You and Kate can come shopping for a wedding dress with me, you two can choose the ones you like, and then we can secretly get Kate's choice for her.'

Maddie snorted with laughter. 'If I start choosing wedding dresses, Kate will definitely suspect something.'

'Not if you're helping me choose mine. We could start by

looking at some on Pinterest. We can create a secret wedding board, pin the dresses we like to it . . .' *I could make a board for wedding cakes too, and flowers*, Sophie thought, her mind whirring with all the things she had to plan. She glanced over at Josh to see if he had anything to add but he'd taken out his phone and was busy tapping away.

'Is that all sorted, then?' Steve asked briskly, as if he was running a board meeting. 'I'll give you a bank card and pin number, Sophie. I've set up a separate account for the wedding. You can use it to buy the dress and other things.'

'Thanks. Shall I keep the dress at my flat so that Kate doesn't see it?' Sophie offered. 'It's supposed to be bad luck for the groom to see the dress before the wedding. We don't want to risk any of that.'

'Good idea. Thanks, Sophie.' Steve took his wallet out of his jacket pocket and pulled out a bank card. 'Here's the card and I'll text you the pin number now.' He took out his phone and started tapping.

'Thanks.' Sophie slipped it into her purse. Then Steve's text pinged in. 'Now we need to organise a get-together with Kate asap. I'll see if she can meet up one night this week and maybe go wedding-dress shopping next Saturday. Which day is best for you, Mads?'

'I'm free Thursday,' Maddie told her.

'Me too,' replied Sophie. 'Do you know if Kate can do Thursday?' she asked Steve.

'I think so. She hasn't mentioned that she's busy.'

'How about you both come to mine? I'll get some nibbles and we can google some wedding dresses and stuff. See which ones Kate likes best,' Maddie suggested.

'Sounds good to me,' Sophie told her. She turned to Steve. 'We'll soon get this sorted out.'

Josh looked up from his phone. 'I hate to put a spanner in the works but getting married in Spain is not as straightforward as you seem to think, Steve. I've just been doing an Internet search about it and apparently, unless you're a Spanish national, you can only have a symbolic ceremony. You have to do the legal part in the UK or Gibraltar. So your beach wedding won't be legal.'

Steve went pale. 'Are you sure?' he asked. Josh passed him his phone and he read the screen in dismay. 'There must be a way around it.'

'There is. Forget this mad idea. Propose to Kate on holiday – it'll be a nice, romantic gesture – then you can both plan the wedding when you come home.'

'I'm with Josh – forget the surprise, propose to Kate, and then you can fine tune the wedding together,' Maddie cut in.

'Will you two stop being so negative? I want to surprise Kate and there must be a way I can do it.' Steve got out his phone and was quiet for a few minutes while he made a few taps on the screen. Then he looked up triumphantly. 'Here we are, problem solved. Gibraltar is only three quarters of an hour or so drive from Estepona, where we are going on holiday, so we can get married in Gibraltar in the morning and drive to the beach ceremony for the afternoon. Simple.' He put his phone back in his pocket. 'Now, remember, not a word to anyone. I'll tell the family and friends who need to know. And I'm relying on you two –' he looked from Sophie to Maddie – 'to choose Kate's perfect wedding dress, and find out all the other things we need to know.'

21

'No pressure then, girls,' Josh drawled.

'All it takes is organisation,' Sophie said. She whipped out the notebook and pen she always carried in her bag. 'Let's start by making a list of things we need to do, then working out who is going to do what.'

'You and your lists,' Maddie said with a mock groan.

'Actually, she's right. That's exactly what we need to do.' Steve pulled his chair closer to the table and leant forward. 'Go ahead, Sophie, what should we do first?'

'Ask Kate,' Josh said.

Sophie shot him a warning look and he grinned. 'Sorry.'

'What date have you booked for the wedding?' We need to make sure that there's availability at the register office in Gibraltar on that day too, or at least the day before.' Maddie flicked a strand of hair behind her ear. 'I'm presuming you've booked it pretty close to the beginning of your holiday so that the rest of the holiday can be your honeymoon?'

Sophie tapped the notebook with her pen. 'You definitely must. Otherwise it'll be difficult to hide the wedding dress, and your suit, from Kate. You're going the second week in June, aren't you? Is it a couple of days after you arrive?'

Steve looked worried. 'Er, I haven't actually booked the wedding date yet. I wanted to run it past you guys first.'

A loud groan resonated around the table. 'For pity's sake, Steve, that's the first thing you need to do,' Josh told him. 'What if the hotel is fully booked up for weddings the time you're over there? Couples book months – even years – in advance, you know.'

Steve scratched his ear. 'I never thought of that.'

'When do you actually go on holiday?' Maddie asked him.

'Wednesday 8th June,' Steve told her. 'And yes, I was planning on us getting married within the first couple of days. I don't know how long I can keep it all a secret.'

'Well, the first thing you need to do is check if the hotel can fit your wedding in,' Josh told him.

'I will. I'll email them later today,' Steve promised, looking a bit deflated now.

Sophie felt sorry for him. 'If they can't, I'm sure we can find a wedding planner to sort it out for you.'

Steve looked a bit more relaxed.

'We also need to get a wedding planner to find out the requirements for getting married in Gibraltar, that's the biggie, and organise the legal stuff there. I'll do that,' Maddie volunteered.

'We'll have to figure out how we're going to get to Gibraltar – we're all going to have to be there for the official wedding, so are we going to fly directly there or drive over from Spain?' Josh glanced around.

Steve looked uncertain. 'Well, our flights are already booked so me and Kate will drive there from Spain. I guess you three could fly direct to Gibraltar. I'd like you to get there two nights before the ceremony if possible so you can celebrate our engagement with us on the day I ask Kate and then make it to the wedding on time. Obviously, I'll pay for the flights and hotel on Gibraltar for the three of you. I've got a bonus due, so Kate won't know.'

'I'll check out if it's cheaper to get a single to Gibraltar then return from Malaga. Either way we're all going to have to drive back to Estepona for the beach wedding and stop over in Spain that night at the very least. I'll check out flights and rental cars – and how long it will take. And accommodation availability near your hotel, Steve. You'll have to give me the name of it.' Josh picked up his phone as Steve told him the name and pressed a few keys. 'There, it's in my notes now.'

'That's all great.' Sophie scribbled a bit more in her book. 'You need to write out a list of who you want to come to the wedding, Steve, and ask them asap so they can make arrangements. Have you told your parents or Kate's yet?'

'No, I'm going to sort it at the weekend.'

'Then there's the wedding dress, bridesmaids' dresses, your suits –' her eyes flicked to the two men, and she tried to imagine Josh in a suit instead of his motorbike leathers – 'the cake, flowers and food, invites . . . I'm happy to organise all that – apart from your suits, of course – with your help, Maddie.' She moved her gaze to her friend.

'Fine by me,' Maddie agreed.

'So, shall we all meet up again or just message each other with details?' Josh asked. 'There's going to be a lot of toing and froing of messages.'

'We could sort out a lot with a group chat, but we probably should meet up every couple of weeks or so as things can get confusing in a message,' Sophie said.

'I'm all for meeting up regularly.' Maddie smiled at Josh and he grinned back.

Things had got a bit tricky over the tattoo remarks but it seemed like something was budding between these two again, Sophie thought.

'I can't meet up again. Kate will get suspicious,' Steve said. 'You're going to have to be the point of contact over this, Josh. If anyone needs to contact me, use my work email.' He took out his wallet, opened it up, fished out a couple of business cards and passed them around. 'If you message me on my phone, Kate might see it. I don't want anything to ruin the surprise.'

'No problem,' Josh said. 'We'd better swap phone numbers, then.' He handed his phone to Maddie. 'Pop your number in here, then pass it to Sophie. I'll send you both a quick text so you have my number too.'

Maddie keyed her number into Josh's phone, then passed it to Sophie who did the same before passing the phone back to Josh. A couple of minutes later a text pinged into both their phones. Sophie opened hers to see an emoji of a hand wave.

Josh pushed back his chair and stood up. 'Right, I have to go. Keep in touch, you two, and we'll meet up in a couple of weeks to compare notes.'

'I'm going too,' said Steve. 'We can walk out together – there's something I wanted to ask you, Josh.' He got up. 'Thanks so much for your help, both of you,' he said to Maddie and Sophie. 'I really appreciate it, and I know that Kate will too.'

'Or she'll be furious with us for going along with this and fall out with us,' Maddie muttered.

'No, she won't, because we're going to make sure she has the best wedding ever,' Sophie said determinedly.

Chapter Six

Josh

'I'm going to tell the parents on Friday evening,' Steve said as he and Josh left the café. 'I wondered if you could pop in too, give me a bit of backup.'

'Yeah, OK. But why leave it until then? The more notice the better, surely?'

'I want the wedding booked so I have a date and time for them.'

Josh guessed that made sense. 'What about Kate's Mum and Dad? When are you telling them?' he asked. 'And no, I'm not coming with you to back you up on that one; I don't even know them.'

'I'll talk to them over the weekend and let them know.' Steve shivered and buttoned up his coat. 'I've got to go now. I'll catch up with you in the week.'

Before Josh could say anything else, his elder brother turned and strode off down the street towards the train station.

Steve was determined to go ahead with this mad plan, Josh realised. He wondered if Kate's parents would try and talk him out of it. Surely they would think Kate should know. They were divorced but Steve got on well with them both, and their new partners; they'd be pleased to have him as a son-in-law, he was certain. And his and Steve's parents were very fond of Kate. There was no doubt that she brought out the best in Steve, but he was sure that, like him, they would think it was risky to plan a surprise wedding like this. Especially when his brother and Kate weren't even engaged.

It didn't help that Kate's friend Sophie had been so enthusiastic about it. Her eyes had been positively glowing with excitement and she'd agreed to the plan to pretend that she and her boyfriend were getting married far too readily. He wondered what her boyfriend would make of the idea. It was almost as if she was wishing it was her wedding. An image of Sophie dressed in a floaty white wedding gown flashed across his mind and he brushed it away. Sophie was pretty but she was too quiet and sweet for him, plus she was taken and that was a no-no for him. Now Maddie, on the other hand, seemed like a whole lot of fun. He guessed he shouldn't go there either, though – if it all went wrong there would be a bad atmosphere at the wedding. He shrugged. *Shame.* But there were plenty of other women happy to have a 'no-strings' relationship. Like Crystal, his current sort-of-girlfriend. They were going to a gig in the concert hall in town later. He was really looking forward to it; he'd been lucky to get tickets. The Cosmo were a very popular group but luckily – well, luckily for Josh anyway – their van had broken down a couple of days ago just as Josh had been passing in his breakdown truck. He'd towed it to the garage and got it going for them within an hour, so as well as paying the bill they had given him two free tickets to the show. Crystal had been thrilled.

It would be a good night, he was sure. He loved to listen to live music. The support group was an up-and-coming local band too, so there should be a good turnout. He walked back to the car park. He had a few hours before he had to meet Crystal, which was good as he wanted to get a bit more renovation done on his house. He'd bought it for a knock-down price a few months ago, but it needed a lot of work and, what with running the garage, and going out with Crystal – who was proving to be a little bit demanding – it was taking longer than he'd planned. And now it looked like his weekends would be taken up planning this perishing wedding! Honestly, why couldn't Steve do the normal thing and propose, then he and Kate could plan the wedding together. It would be so much easier for everyone.

Chapter Seven

Maddie

After saying goodbye to Steve, Josh and Sophie, Maddie headed straight for the shops. She wanted to get a special outfit for that night, something vibrant and exciting. Ezri, her musician friend, and his group Twilight, were the support act for Cosmo, a popular band who were playing in the concert hall tonight. Ezri had asked her to step in for Suki, their singer, who had fallen ill. Maddie had sung with them a few times before. When she'd dated Ezri last year for a couple of months, he'd asked her to join the band but Maddie had refused; whilst she loved to sing, it wasn't something she wanted to do as a career. And she didn't like the band lifestyle. It was too chaotic for her.

People often thought that because Maddie dressed a bit 'out there' and dyed her hair bright colours that she was completely unconventional and lived a wild life but, actually, nothing was further from the truth. Whilst it was true that Maddie often had a couple of guys on the go, worked in the media and loved to party, she liked peace and order in her home life. No shouting, no coming home drunk, no smashing plates or punching fists into walls. She'd had enough of that growing up, when too much alcohol would turn her funny and charming father into a growling, shouting bully. He had never hit her, or her mother, but his rages had been awful, and she would never forget sitting on the stairs shaking as she listened to him, praying that he would soon fall asleep, knowing that he would wake up hours afterwards with no recollection of how he had been, full of apologies when her mother berated him over what he had done and promises never to drink again. It had been traumatic and scary, and she had wished many times that her mother would leave, but she always made excuses for her father.

Maddie had left home as soon as she could, and her parents had split up not long afterwards. It was almost as if Maddie walking away had made her mother realise that she could walk away too.

Her father had carried on drinking and had died a couple of years ago, while her mother was now happily remarried and lived in Wales. But Maddie's childhood had scarred her. She'd felt different – in the sleepy village where her family lived, her parents were always warring, whilst everyone else seemed to have a 'picture perfect' marriage. She'd heard the gossiping, seen the looks she and her mother got, so in her teens she had started to dress and act differently. Somehow, dressing outrageously and dyeing her hair had given her more confidence, and the bullying she'd endured in the first years of high school had stopped. When she'd left her mother's house, she'd been determined to keep her own home peaceful and made the conscious decision to live alone, refusing to even consider taking in a flatmate, even though she had often struggled to pay the rent in those early days. She didn't want anyone else to rule her life, for their moods to blight her happiness. She liked living on her own, being in control of her own life. A couple of people had suggested she got a pet, but she hadn't wanted to be tied down. Then a couple of years ago she'd gone down to the bins with some rubbish and heard a pitiful miaowing. She'd opened a carrier bag and found a little tortoiseshell kitten with a damaged left ear dumped inside it. She'd taken the kitten home, called it Jax after the name of the store on the bag, and the little cat had become part of her life.

As she pushed open the door of Funky Chic, her favourite boutique, the chimes overhead jangled to announce her entrance.

'Hi, Maddie.' Shara, the assistant, looked around from the display of feather and bead necklaces she was arranging on the jewellery stand. 'I was hoping you'd pop in today. Something came in yesterday that I think you'll love. I've put it in the back so that no one buys it.'

'Really?' replied Maddie. 'That's fantastic. I'm doing a gig with Ezri tonight and need something a bit unusual.' Shara often put an outfit aside if she thought Maddie would like it, so that she could have first option on it.

'Where are you singing?' Shara asked.

'In the concert hall. Ezri is the support group for Cosmo.'

'Wow! How exciting. Then you definitely need this outfit. Wait here a sec.' Shara disappeared, returning a few seconds later holding up a purple satin jumpsuit with a plunging neckline and yellow psychedelic swirls all over it, which flared out just below the knee into pleats over the calves, Maddie's mouth fell open.

'It's perfect.'

Shara grinned. 'Isn't it? Go and try it on. And come out and show me.'

Maddie took the silky jumpsuit over to the corner of the shop and pulled aside the curtain of the solitary cubicle, placed her bag down on the floor, and shrugged off her coat to hang it on the hook on the wall. A few minutes later, she looked approvingly at her reflection in the rectangular mirror in front of her. The jumpsuit fitted her like a glove.

'*Tra la!*' she announced as she pulled back the curtain and stepped out.

'Stunning!' Shara said, a wide grin spreading across her face. 'As soon as I saw it, I knew it would suit you. You're going to wow them all tonight.' She looked down at the boots on Maddie's feet. 'Do you have something to wear with it?'

'I was thinking of my silver platforms?'

Shara clapped her hands. 'Perfect!'

Chapter Eight

Sophie

Glenn looked up when Sophie walked in. 'Hi, how did it go? What's Steve's big secret?' he asked. He was sitting on the sofa, feet up on the pouffe, watching a film.

'It's wonderful news. I can't believe he's planning something so romantic.' Sophie put her bag on the floor beside her and shrugged off her coat.

'What's he doing?' Glenn looked curious. 'I didn't think Steve went in for romantic gestures.'

Sophie put her coat on the back of the sofa, sat down next to him and pulled off her boots. 'He doesn't usually, but this time he's really gone for it. He's planning for him and Kate to get married when they're in Spain in June!'

Glenn frowned. 'I didn't even know they were engaged. Why did he need to talk to you and Maddie about that? I'd have thought Kate would want to tell you herself.'

'They're not engaged. Steve's going to propose when they're on holiday. And Kate doesn't know anything about it. It's a surprise.' Sophie tucked her legs up underneath her and snuggled up to Glenn.

He turned his head towards her, astonishment written all over his face. 'What a crazy thing to do. I'm amazed that you didn't try to talk him out of it. What if Kate says no to his proposal? And even if she says yes, she might not want a surprise wedding! I don't think many people would.'

Sophie bit back her disappointment at his reaction. 'Maddie and Josh – his brother – did try and talk him out of it,' she admitted. 'But Steve's adamant that Kate will love it. And I think it's romantic. Anyway, it's going to be a beach wedding and he's asked me and Maddie to help him so he can make sure he organises it how Kate would want.'

'I don't see how you can help. You don't know how she'd want her wedding, do you? Unless you've all discussed that sort of stuff?' He looked a bit cagey. 'You haven't, have you?'

'No, of course not.' She was puzzled at Glenn's reaction. Maybe now might not be the best time to tell him that Steve had asked her to pretend she and Glenn were getting married as a cover story so she could get Kate's opinion on all things wedding-related. She reached out and touched Glenn's hand. 'We're both invited to the wedding. He wants me and Maddie to be brides-maids. The legal bit is being done in Gibraltar then we're driving over to the beach ceremony in Estepona. Steve is paying for our flights and hotel for a couple of nights, so it means we get to go to Gibraltar, then Spain, which will be fantastic. I thought maybe we could stretch it to a week or even two?' Once the wedding was over, they could have time to relax, to chat, to have long lei-surely mornings, afternoons sightseeing or sunbathing, and evenings walking along the sand in the moonlight, or sitting hav-ing cocktails on the beach. It would be so romantic. 'Isn't it lucky that neither of us has booked our holiday yet?'

'What date is it? I might not be able to get time off. We're really busy right now. And I was waiting for the employees with families to book their holidays first,' Glenn told her.

'We haven't got the exact date yet. Steve said their holiday begins on 8th June – which is after the half-term break and before the long summer holidays, so it shouldn't be a problem – and they're going for two weeks. He's hoping to book the wedding for the beginning of their holiday.' She felt her heart sinking a bit. She was already looking forward to this break; it would be awful if Glenn couldn't get time off. 'Surely you can come. Even if it's only a couple of days to go to the actual wedding.'

He shook his head. 'I don't know, but I'll try. Don't let it stop you, though. You go ahead and see if you can get the time off. I'll come if I can.'

'It won't be the same without you. It would be our first time abroad together,' she said, trying to keep the disappointment out of her voice.

'I've said that I'll do what I can, Soph, but I can't promise. And you'll still enjoy it. Kate and Steve are more your friends than mine, and you'll have Maddie there,' he pointed out. 'Anyway, it would be nice to spend our first holiday abroad together just the two of us, not as part of someone else's wedding party, don't you think?'

It wasn't really the reaction she'd hoped for, but she guessed it wasn't Glenn's fault if he couldn't get away – although, it sounded to her like he didn't really want to. 'I guess so,' she agreed.

Glenn got up. 'I'm going for a cycle ride.' He was a keen cyclist and regularly went out on his bike.

'Fancy bringing a Chinese back with you?' Sophie asked, putting a smile back on her face. 'It'd be nice to have a takeaway and open a bottle of wine.'

'Sure. Sweet and Sour with egg-fried rice?'

'Perfect.' As soon as Glenn had gone out, Sophie scrolled for Kate's number on her phone and gave her a call.

Chapter Nine

Josh

Josh did a double-take as he looked at the woman on the stage, singing with the band. Her purple hair flopped around her face as she turned his way, dancing across the stage. Maddie. She looked gorgeous in a funky purple satin jumpsuit with a yellow swirly pattern all over it and she sang really well. She swirled around and danced back across the stage in gravity-defying silver platform shoes to face the male singer, then they both leant towards each other, singing down the mic. She was amazing.

'Do you want to pop your eyes back into your head?'

He blinked and turned to Crystal. 'What?'

'You're practically drooling at that woman singing.' Crystal was scowling petulantly and he could hear the irritation in her voice.

'Sorry, it's just I met her earlier on. I had no idea she was a singer.'

Crystal frowned. 'Where did you meet her?'

She was acting all possessive and they'd only been going out together for a couple of weeks. Maybe he should end it before she got too serious. 'My brother is planning a surprise for his partner, Kate, and asked me to meet up with him and Kate's two best friends so we could help him plan it.' He thought he'd better not mention that it was a secret wedding; the fewer people who knew about that the better.

The band were playing another song now, and Maddie was once again singing with the man. Was she his girlfriend? Josh wondered. She hadn't mentioned that she was a member of Twilight, but then none of them had talked about anything personal, had they?

He and Crystal headed for the bar when the band took a break. It was heaving. 'A large white, is it?' Josh asked.

'Please.' Crystal went to the ladies while Josh took his place at the bar.

'Hello, fancy seeing you here.' Maddie was walking away from the bar, two shandies in her hands, and had stopped to talk to him. 'Are you enjoying the show?'

'We are. I'm here with a friend,' he added. 'I didn't know you were a singer.'

'I'm not. Not professionally. But Ezri gets me to sing with him now and again.'

'Is Ezri your boyfriend?' he asked.

'More of a friend with benefits, if you know what I mean.' Maddie winked. 'Enjoy the rest of the show.'

She was so carefree, it was attractive, Josh thought as the queue shuffled forwards. He bet she would be like a breath of fresh air to go out with. Not that he'd go there, even if he wasn't temporarily with Crystal. It would make life far too complicated with this secret wedding to plan. *Fun, though*. He smiled at the thought.

Chapter Ten

Maddie

'Miaow.' Jax rubbed himself against Maddie's face on Sunday morning. Maddie opened her eyes. 'Morning.' She reached out to stroke the little cat's head. Jax nestled closer to her, enjoying the fuss for a few minutes before miaowing again, getting to his feet and nudging Maddie's hand with his head, as if urging her to hurry up.

She yawned. Light was streaming in through the curtains, so she knew, even without looking at the digital clock on the little table by her bed, that it was late morning. Not surprising, as it had gone two by the time she had arrived home. They'd all gone out for a curry after the gig had finished, and sat around chatting for a while. Ezri, Guy and Finn were great company and she'd enjoyed catching up with them, even agreeing to sing for them again if Suki hadn't recovered from the flu for the gig the following weekend.

'Are you hungry?' she said softly, throwing back the bedcovers. Jax miaowed again, jumped off the bed and headed for the door. Maddie followed him into the kitchen. She'd never intended to have a pet, but now she couldn't imagine life without Jax. He had such a sweet, playful nature, and looked so quirky with his almost black eye and black paws, which seemed at odds with his tortoiseshell body. Much as she loved living on her own, Maddie had to admit that it was good to have a bit of company, someone to greet her when she came home, and when she got up – without putting any demands on her, apart from for cuddles and food, of course.

She opened the fridge and took out a small tin of tuna cat food – Jax's favourite – and spooned it into the cat dish at the side of the fridge, whilst Jax brushed against her legs, his tail up in the air, miaowing approvingly. While the cat tucked in happily, she poured herself a blueberry smoothie. She was still too full after last night's curry to want to eat, but her throat was dry, which was normal when she'd been singing the night before. She took her smoothie over to the table and sat down, her mind going back to the previous night. She'd been surprised to see Josh there, and wondered idly whether his friend was male or female. Her mind drifted to the meeting with Steve yesterday. Even though she thought it was a crazy idea, she'd agreed to help because Kate was a good friend. It wasn't going to be easy, though. And three months wasn't much time. Thank goodness Josh was doing all the sorting out on the Spain side. And Sophie would be in her element choosing dresses, flowers and shoes.

She guessed that she had better do some research on the legal requirements for getting married in Gibraltar today; she wouldn't have much time in the week when she was working, and the sooner they had the official stuff sorted out the better. Then they could all relax and get on with the fun bits such as choosing their outfits for the holiday that would follow the wedding – hopefully she could get the two weeks off – and planning a bit of sightseeing. She had been to Barcelona and Madrid but not down to the southern end of Spain, so was really looking forward to visiting it. She had an aunt living in Andalucia her father's elder sister, and it would be lovely to catch up. Although she couldn't remember the address and had lost touch with her cousins, maybe she could find them on Facebook. It would be good to see them all again. If it wasn't too far from the hotel. Andalucia was a big region.

She fetched her laptop and logged on, then did an Internet search for getting married in Gibraltar. There were quite a few wedding planners advertising their services so that seemed the best way to go, she thought, as she downloaded the legal pack. As they'd learnt from Steve's quick search at the café yesterday, it was possible to get married in Gibraltar, which was good, and the main legal requirement seemed to be that the couple had to spend at least one night in Gibraltar and had to supply hotel bills to confirm this. People who had never been married before needed their passports and birth certificates. So far, so easy. She checked out a few of the wedding planners, finally selecting the one with the best reviews and filled in the enquiry form for them to contact her. The most important thing was to get the ceremony booked at the register office. Nothing else could happen without that.

She set up a group chat with Sophie and Josh, as Sophie had suggested, saying that she'd approached a wedding planner and would let them know as soon as she had confirmation on any dates that were free during Steve and Kate's holiday so she could arrange the beach ceremony. She also reminded Josh that he had to check the flights and hotel accommodation. It all sounded a bit complicated but hopefully it would all fit together OK.

That done, she had a shower and, after saying goodbye to Jax who was now snoozing on the sofa, she set off for the local market to get some fresh fruit and veg and take a look at the material stall. Her mother had often made their clothes when Maddie was younger and had taught her how to sew too. There was enough time before the wedding for her to make a couple of unusual outfits to wear. After wearing a bridesmaid's dress all day she'd be glad to change into something more unconventional.

Honestly, she hoped Kate appreciated the sacrifice she was making. And approved of the secret wedding idea. She daren't think of the outcome if she didn't.

Chapter Eleven

Sophie

On Sunday morning Sophie decided to start wedding planning while Glenn was playing chess online in the bedroom, so she had something to talk to Kate about when she returned her call. As Kate hadn't answered last night, Sophie guessed she and Steve were out, so Sophie had left a message to tell Kate about 'my and Glenn's surprise wedding' but asking her not to tell anyone. She couldn't wait to see Kate's face when she realised that the surprise wedding was actually for Kate herself and Steve.

In fact, she hadn't got around to telling Glenn about the plan yet. He'd seemed so moody the previous day. I'll tell him today, I just need to find the right words, she told herself. I'm sure he won't mind. It's not a big deal really. What harm did a little lie do if it helped Kate have the perfect wedding? She hoped Glenn could get the time off for the wedding, perhaps even a week. It would be lovely for them both to go, they hardly seemed to have any time together.

She was sure Pat, her manager at Pat's Posies – a bespoke little shop selling flowers and small quirky gifts such as teddies with flowers to celebrate a birth, horseshoes and garters for wedding bouquets, and chocolates, vases and other gifts for birthdays – would try to let her have a week off, although June was a popular month for weddings so they were always busy then. Pat was going away in September, and Janine, the other woman who worked in the shop, wanted two weeks in August so that she could spend some time with her children who would be off school then.

Sophie booted up her laptop, then logged on to Pinterest to look for wedding dresses. Creating a secret board called 'Spanish Wedding', she shared it with Maddie; she'd add Kate to it once she'd had time to talk to her. Then she did a search on weddings and added some pins to the board. She was so engrossed she didn't hear Glenn come in.

'What are you up to?' he asked, walking over and glancing at the screen.

'I'm doing a search on weddings in Spain, just in case the hotel Steve and Kate are staying at can't fit them in,' she told him. She was amazed at the range of venues, from dreamy beach restaurants where the reception could be held, with the ceremony on the beach in front of them, to magnificent castles and stunning villas. Hopefully one of them would have a vacancy for a wedding around the first week of Steve and Kate's holiday.

They all look amazing, Sophie thought, as she scrolled down past pictures of gorgeous venues with beautiful love-struck couples holding hands and gazing out to the sea, or up at the stars. It was all so romantic. Kate would be over the moon. Then she paused and gasped at the stunning photo of a couple getting married in a picturesque cove.

'Glenn, come and take a look at this. It's wonderful.'

'Must I?' Glenn asked reluctantly.

'Glenn, my best friend's partner is planning a secret wedding for them both and has asked me to help. Surely you can show a bit of interest?'

Glenn groaned and got up to walk over to her. 'As long as you remember that it's Kate's secret wedding not ours.'

'Look, you can have the ceremony conducted right on the beach in this beautiful cove and have the reception at the beach restaurant. Isn't that romantic?' she said, ignoring him.

A warm glow spread through her as she looked at the couple standing barefoot on the caramel sand, the crystal-blue sea behind them. They were facing each other, holding hands, gazing into each other's eyes. Guests, also barefoot, stood behind them, and the wedding celebrant in front of them, her back to the sea. It was totally gorgeous. She could almost imagine herself and Glenn standing there, hand in hand, saying their vows, she thought a little wistfully.

Was Kate ready for it? She pushed the thought away. Of course she was. Steve had said that they'd discussed marriage.

Glenn leant over her shoulder and glanced at the screen. 'Yeah, looks pretty good,' he said nonchalantly. 'Not sure it's what Kate would want though. She strikes me as a bit more formal than that. And I can't really see Steve standing barefoot in the sand with his trousers rolled up to his knees, can you?'

He had a point.

'Maybe not. There's lots of fantastic weddings to choose from, though. Obviously we need to find one pretty close to the hotel they're staying at.'

'I'll leave you to it, I'm going to take a shower,' Glenn told her.

'I was hoping you'd take a look at some of them with me and help me draw up a shortlist.' She tried to keep the disappointment out of her voice.

'Sorry; planning someone else's wedding isn't my scene,' Glenn said shortly and headed for the bathroom.

Sophie turned her attention back to the screen, deciding to select about a dozen of the best venues and save the links to share with Maddie and Kate.

When Glenn came back in, he seemed in a better mood. 'Shall I start lunch?' he asked. 'There are some pork chops in the fridge if you fancy them? I could cook them with roast potatoes and broccoli.'

Sophie nodded. 'Perfect. I'll just finish this, then I'll lay the table. How about opening a bottle of wine to go with it?'

'Yep; there's a bottle of Pinot in the fridge.'

She added a few more pins to the board until she was satisfied that she'd got enough for Maddie and Kate – once she'd added her – to think about, then shut down the laptop. Glenn was humming in the kitchen as he prepared the broccoli. The pork chops and roast potatoes were already in the oven, she noticed.

'Be about twenty minutes,' he told her.

Sophie cleared the table, laid the white lacy tablecloth over it, got the tablemats out of the drawer and put them out, then placed knives and forks either side. Then she got out the plates.

Glenn looked over his shoulder and smiled at her. 'Thanks. I'll pop them in the oven to warm up just before I serve.'

Half an hour later they were sitting at the table, eating their meal and chatting easily about their week ahead. Sophie loved times like this, when they actually had time to talk and share things with each other.

'How about we have a lazy afternoon finishing off this wine and watching a film?' Glenn suggested. 'There's a good comedy on.'

Sophie smiled. 'That sounds perfect.'

Just as Sophie put her last roast potato in her mouth, her phone rang. She glanced at the screen. It was Kate.

'I'll phone her back,' she told Glenn.

'It's probably best to talk to her now, then we can watch the film in peace,' he said.

Pleased that Glenn seemed to have changed his attitude a bit about the wedding, Sophie propped up the phone, switching the loudspeaker on as she answered the call without stopping to think.

'OMG, I've just heard your voicemail. I can't believe you guys are getting married. That's crazy. Massive congratulations!' Kate's voice boomed.

There was a loud crash as Glenn's wine glass smashed to the floor.

Chapter Twelve

Josh

'And then Jordan said that he thought that I'd look better in the red dress so I had to get changed again,' Crystal said as they tucked into Sunday lunch in a restaurant in Tewkesbury, where she lived.

Josh nodded, only half-listening to her, his mind on Steve's bombshell yesterday afternoon. When his brother had asked him to meet up Josh hadn't expected him to drop the news on him that he was planning a surprise wedding. He wished he could talk Steve out of it. He had an awful feeling that it was going to be a disaster.

'So, when I was standing there stark naked . . .'

Crystal's words cut through his thoughts. 'What? What do you mean stark naked?'

'That got your attention. I've been talking to you for the past five minutes and you haven't heard a word I've said, have you?' She pouted.

'Sorry, I've got a lot on my mind.' He focused his attention on her. 'I'm listening now. Want to tell me again?'

'No, I don't. Honestly, Josh, you hardly spoke to me last night and couldn't take your eyes off that woman singing, then you invite me out to lunch today and can't be bothered to even talk to me. I know we said no commitment, but that doesn't mean you can treat me like I'm not here.'

She was right, he had only been half-listening to her. He'd got other things on his mind and, to be honest, he'd realised that he didn't have much of a connection with Crystal. They had nothing in common. It had purely been a physical attraction, on his part anyway, and had run its course. It was time to let her down gently. 'The thing is . . .' Josh started to explain, but Crystal pushed her chair back, picked up her bag off the table and stood up, leaving her meal half-finished.

'You are not dumping me, Josh. No one dumps me. Ever. I'm ending this. Bye, Josh.'

He watched her strut out, head held high, wondering if she expected him to call her back, or run after her and apologise. If so, she didn't know him at all. He never ran after a woman. Never begged anyone to stay with him. And never would. Not since River. He'd begged River not to go but she had gone anyway, without even saying goodbye, taking his heart with her. That was fifteen years ago, when he was in his late teens, but he could still remember the devastation he had felt when he realised that she had gone, that he would never see her again. He closed his eyes as an image of River flashed across his mind, her long auburn hair, big green eyes and figure to die for, with flower tattoos on both her upper arms and her calves. Wild, untameable River. He had fallen head over heels for her and thought she had felt the same. They had been inseparable, spending every spare moment with each other, but in the end her freedom had meant more to River than he had. It had taken him a long time to get over her and when he did, he had promised himself that he would never allow anyone to get close enough to break his heart again. So, he kept his relationships casual, always ending them if there was any sign of either of them getting serious.

His phone pinged as a message came in. I can't believe you've let me go like that. You're self-centred and arrogant, Josh. You'll end up a lonely old man.

Josh deleted Crystal's message. Better a lonely old man than being with someone he didn't have any connection to, or having his heart broken by someone he loved and didn't love him back. He didn't need Crystal; he didn't need anyone. He was fine exactly how he was.

Chapter Thirteen

Sophie

*D*amn. *I should have found time to tell Glenn first.* She stared at the pool of white wine on the kitchen floor, trying not to mind that one of their best glasses was now smashed into smithereens. Glenn was staring at her, horrified.

'It's only pretend. I'll explain in a minute,' she whispered, dragging her eyes away from the mess and back to the phone, from which she could hear Kate saying, 'Sophie? Are you there?'

'Yes, sorry. Glenn dropped a glass. I'd forgotten to tell him that I'd mentioned the wedding to you. We're only having a small wedding and don't want to offend anyone so are keeping it quiet. You won't tell anyone, will you?'

'Of course I won't. Tell Glenn not to worry, my lips are sealed. It's amazing news. When did Glenn propose to you? Did he get down on one knee? Have you got a ring?'

Glenn was staring at her so intensely that Sophie felt uncomfortable. 'Er, not yet. He only proposed last night so we haven't had time to choose one yet,' she mumbled. 'I was wondering if you could help me plan the wedding?' She picked up her wine glass, whispered to Glenn that she'd finish the call in the bedroom, then walked out, still talking to Kate. 'I've started a Pinterest board and was hoping you could help me choose a dress and the flowers. Maddie's helping too. I'll send you the link.' She lifted the lid of the laptop which she'd left on the bed and it immediately sprang to life. She keyed in her password and it opened on the Pinterest board she'd been looking at. 'Do you have time to take a look at the board now?'

'Sure. I'll grab my iPad; won't be a sec.'

Sophie added Kate to the board and they spent ten minutes talking as they browsed wedding dresses. 'I think this would really suit you,' Kate said, adding an ivory lacy gown to the board. 'You love sweetheart necklines, don't you, and it's so pretty, nipped in at the waist like that and then spreading out into a full skirt.'

Sophie chewed her nail as she studied the photo. Yes, it was exactly the sort of dress she would wear. It was almost as if it had been designed for her, but it wasn't the sort of dress Kate would wear; she was sure her friend would go for a simpler, more elegant style. Had Maddie been right when she said their planning Kate's secret wedding wouldn't work? Kate was choosing what would suit Sophie, not what she would wear herself.

'It is pretty,' she acknowledged. 'Is that what you would go for?'

'It doesn't matter what I would go for, this is your wedding. You must choose what you want. It's your wedding day. And here's another one.' Kate added a gorgeous strapless white dress with an appliquéd bodice. Another Sophie dress. This was going to be more difficult than she'd realised. How was she going to find out what dress Kate would like?

'I'd really like your input, though. I was thinking of wearing something simpler, more elegant.'

'Really?' Kate was silent for a couple of minutes, then she said, 'How about these?' and added a couple of dresses to the board. They were definitely the style Kate would wear.

'Yes, that's more like it.'

'Are you sure?' Kate sounded doubtful. 'You have to feel comfortable, Sophie. Just because you're not having a big wedding doesn't mean you can't have the dress you want.'

Sophie looked up as the bedroom door opened and Glenn came in. 'The film is starting in ten minutes,' he said, still looking annoyed. He was obviously waiting for an explanation about their 'engagement'.

'Five ticks,' she mouthed then turned her attention back to Kate. 'You're right. That's why I want you and Maddie to help me choose everything. I'd really appreciate advice from you both. Maddie's invited us round to hers on Thursday so we can talk about it all. Can you make it?'

'Of course. I'm so excited for you. I have to go now, though, sorry. Massive congratulations again. I'll see you on Thursday.'

'Bye.' Sophie ended the call then closed her laptop. Well, she'd made a start with the Pinterest board and if, on Thursday, Maddie started talking about how she'd like her wedding as well, maybe Kate would too.

Except that Maddie planning her wedding would sound very strange. And if Maddie did decide to get married in the very far-off future she would probably wear something totally unique like a rainbow wedding gown. Or even a black one to be completely different.

We'll sort it somehow. I'm going to make sure that Kate has the wedding of her dreams, she thought. She went back through the kitchen into the lounge to discover the shattered wine glass had now been cleaned up and Glenn was sitting on the sofa, his eyes fixed on the TV where the film was just starting.

'What's going on, Sophie?' he demanded without even looking at her. 'Why did you tell Kate we were getting married?'

She sat down by him and tried to snuggle up but he stiffened and edged way. *OK, so he was really annoyed then.*

'Sorry about that, it must have been a shock, but it was Steve's idea. He thought that if I pretended that me and you were having a surprise wedding, and asked Kate and Maddie to help me arrange it, I could find out the sort of things Kate likes. So, really, I'm planning her wedding, but Kate doesn't know that.'

Glenn turned to glare at her. 'That sounds nuts. Are you going to be telling everyone about our so-called wedding? And am I supposed to lie about it too??'

'Not everyone, no, only Kate. And you won't be seeing that much of her as we'll be meeting up at Maddie's, so it shouldn't be a problem. I'm going to say that we just want it low-key so are only telling a few people. You don't mind, do you?' she asked, although it was obvious that he did, which surprised her a little. What difference did it make?

'Actually, I do. It's a crazy idea. But you haven't given me much choice, have you?' He was clearly irritated. 'You could have run it by me first.'

'I told you, it was Steve's idea, not mine. And I meant to tell you yesterday but you went for a bike ride, then we got a take-away and I forgot.' She put her hand on his and gave it a squeeze, but he kept his eyes fixed on the TV screen. 'It's only for a little while. Just so we can find out the sort of wedding that Kate wants.'

'Well, I don't like it. I don't like it one bit,' Glenn retorted, stony-faced. 'You're crazy to get involved in this.'

Sophie bit back her irritation, not wanting an argument, but she couldn't understand why he was so upset; all she was doing was helping to plan a nice surprise for her friend. What was wrong with that?

Chapter Fourteen

Sophie

Abba music was playing from the CD player in the back of the shop when Sophie arrived at Pat's Posies on Monday – which meant that Pat was in a good mood. She put her umbrella in the bucket and went through to the back, intending to seize the opportunity to tell Pat about the wedding and ask for the time off. She quickly explained about Steve planning the secret wedding in Spain and wanting her to be one of Kate's bridesmaids.

'Well, June is a busy month for us, you know that, Sophie. We have lots of weddings to cater for,' Pat told her, pushing her gold-framed glasses back up her nose. 'How long were you wanting off?'

'I'd love a week, but a couple of days, just to attend the wedding, would be fine. I don't know the exact date yet, but Kate is going away for two weeks from 8th June, and her boyfriend wants to book the wedding for the first week.' She crossed her fingers behind her back. 'It would mean the world to Kate for me and Maddie to be there.'

Pat nodded. 'I understand. Well, thankfully my daughter Zania finishes university the first week of June and is coming home for a while, so I'll ask her if she'll help out at the shop. If she will then you can have a week, or even two off, but if she can't then it will have to be only a couple of days, I'm afraid.'

Sophie grinned. At least she could definitely go to the wedding. 'Thanks so much, Pat.'

Sophie hummed to herself as she and Pat put out the tubs of flowers at the front of the shop underneath the awning which was protecting them from the drizzle. When the last pot was out, she went into the back of the shop to put the kettle on for their morning cuppa, still humming.

'You sound happy,' Janine said when she arrived twenty minutes later. She worked between nine thirty – when the shop officially opened – and three in the afternoon to coincide with school hours so she could pick up her two children, Oscar and Lizzie.

'She's off to Spain in June for a secret wedding,' Pat told her. 'All right for some, isn't it?'

Janine's eyes widened. 'You and Glenn are getting married? That's wonderful!'

I wish. Sophie shook her head. 'It's my friend Kate.' She explained again about Steve planning a secret wedding for them both and asking her, Maddie and Josh to help arrange it. 'Isn't it romantic?'

'My Ned didn't even propose properly. He just said I suppose we should get married, how does next month suit you?' Janine chuckled. 'Good job I know he adores me.'

'Shame the wedding isn't in the UK, I could have given you a discount on the flowers,' Pat told her.

'Never mind a discount, a beach wedding in the sun sounds perfect,' Janine said. 'I'm dead jealous.'

It will be perfect if Glenn can get time off work to come too, Sophie thought. She really wanted him to be there too and to see her looking all glamorous in her bridesmaid's dress. It would be such a lovely, romantic occasion and it would be nice to enjoy it together. All this talk about weddings was making her feel that she would like to get married too. She loved Glenn and they got on well; maybe they should think about it. They were both in their early thirties, an age when a lot of people thought of settling down.

The door chimes announced that a customer had come in, so Janine hurried out to serve them.

'I need to leave a bit early; I've got a couple of deliveries to make. Could you arrange the bouquet for Wendy Gibbons?' Pat asked Sophie. 'She'll be in for them just before five. And would you mind locking up too?'

'Of course.' Arranging the bouquets was one of Sophie's favourite jobs. It was Wendy Gibbons' mother's birthday and she had ordered a bunch of her favourite flowers to pick up after work. Pat smiled. 'Thank you. And remember that I'm at the suppliers in the morning so you'll have to open up too. You won't be late, will you?'

'I'll be here well before nine to get everything outside,' Sophie promised.

It was a busy day, several customers called in or telephoned to order flowers for Mother's Day, which was the Sunday after next, and there was a constant stream of visitors to the gift shop too. Many of them wanted one of Sophie's special gift boxes, where she combined a small teddy bear – or other soft toy – with a flower or plant relevant to the recipient to make the gift really personal. Cute teddies holding a red rose, with a miniature bottle of fizz or a small box of chocolates were particularly popular, especially for Valentine's Day, Mother's Day and birthdays. It was something that Sophie really enjoyed doing, especially when a customer wanted a bespoke gift box, containing something that was relevant to their dear one. Today she was making a box for Oscar's friend's fifth birthday. Janine had been stressing out about what to give him and asked Sophie if she could come up with a gift box idea. So Sophie had suggested a soft green dinosaur with a huge tub of green slime, packed with a Venus fly trap. Most children, especially boys, enjoyed watching the plant trap flies, and slime was usually a winner with kids too. 'You're a genius,' Janine had told her.

'That looks great,' Pat said when Sophie had finished the gift box. 'You have a talent for this, Sophie. These gift boxes, and your terrariums, really add something to our gift selection.'

Pat wasn't one for dishing out praise too readily, so Sophie flushed with pride. 'Thank you.' She really enjoyed making the more personal gift boxes and terrariums – miniature gardens in a bottle. Living in a one-bedroomed flat, there wasn't much room for plants. She kept a few orchids and had a couple of window boxes of colourful flowers and had even made a terrarium for herself a few months ago, with ferns and dwarf palms. She'd been delighted with the finished result so had made one for Pat's birthday. Pat had been really pleased with it and asked Sophie to make some to sell in the shop, with Pat suppling the plants and taking a small percentage of the sales. Sophie had readily agreed and the terrariums had proved to be very popular.

'It's brilliant. Thank you so much, Sophie,' Janine said now, when Sophie showed her the gift box. 'You are so good at this, and really have a great imagination.'

'Ah, but you're so good at looking after the flowers,' Sophie told her. Which was true, they did seem to thrive in Janine's care, and when she'd popped some shopping in to Janine one day because one of her children was home ill she had been really impressed with the beautiful array of pots and plants in her garden.

Sophie was looking forward to the day – hopefully soon – when she and Glenn could move into a house and have their own little garden. She'd already got the garden planned in her head. She wanted a patio area with a table and chairs, and a lawned area surrounded by flowerbeds: tulips, sweet peas, nasturtiums, roses. Baskets of petunias, fuchsias and begonias would hang above the front and back doors, so when they stepped out into the garden they would be greeted by a variety of colours and aromas, as Sophie was when she walked into Pat's Posies every day.

Janine left for the day, followed soon afterwards by Pat, leaving Sophie alone for a couple of hours. Not that she minded, the florist wasn't usually busy this time of the day and she had the bouquet to prepare. She knew that Wendy's mum loved pink and white flowers so gathered some pink spray roses, white lilies, white chrysanthemums and pink carnations, then slipped in some pistacia too, and arranged them all artistically. She expertly wrapped the flowers in pretty white-flecked cellophane, then selected a wide pink ribbon and tied a bow with it. Satisfied, she washed her hands and glanced at her watch. It was almost five. Then she heard a message ping into her mobile. She usually kept it in her handbag as Pat didn't like her getting messages or calls at work, but with Pat out she had slipped it in her pocket just in case Glenn sent her a message. It wasn't Glenn though, it was Kate.

Hi, sorry I couldn't talk much last night but wow, what fantastic news! Steve couldn't believe it when I told him you and Glenn were getting married. Have you told your parents yet? Who else knows?

Kate sounded really excited about their 'wedding', Sophie thought. Did that mean she would be excited when she knew that it was actually Kate herself and Steve getting married? Maybe she was secretly hoping that Steve would propose to her. Wasn't it everyone's dream to find their true love and want to be with them for the rest of their life? She bet that even cynical Maddie would one day meet someone who would sweep her off her feet. Then she'd change her mind and be happily planning a wedding herself, too.

She messaged back that she was ecstatic but still at work so would call Kate tonight as Glenn was out. She had just sent it when the door opened and Wendy Gibson walked in. Her eyes fell on the bouquet of flowers and her face lit up. 'Are those for Mum? They're heavenly.'

'I'm glad you like them. I know your mum likes lilies and roses,' Sophie said.

'You really have a skill for arranging flowers, Sophie,' Wendy said. 'Have you ever thought of having your own florist shop one day?'

Sophie had dreamt of it sometimes, a small florist's and gift shop, like Pat's Posies, with a café where she could sell coffee and homemade cakes. It was only a dream, though. She would never have the finance to rent her own shop and set herself up. 'Maybe, but it's a big expense,' she said. 'And I'm happy working here.'

She was too. Pat was a good boss, fair and kind, and the wages were quite generous. Even so, when Wendy had left with her bouquet, Sophie couldn't help thinking how wonderful it would be to be her own boss, specialising in the flowers she wanted, making up exquisite, personal bridal displays. She was looking forward to selecting the flowers for Kate's wedding; it would be so awesome to see her friend walk down the aisle carrying flowers that Sophie had personally chosen for her. Part of her wished that Kate knew about the wedding, so that she could discuss it with her. It was one of the biggest events of your life. Were Maddie and Josh right in thinking that Kate would be annoyed she'd not been given the chance to plan it? Then she imagined the delight on her friend's face when Steve proposed to her and she realised that they had all been secretly planning her dream wedding. It was such a romantic thing for Steve to do.

I'll do everything I can to make sure that this is the best day of Kate's life, she vowed.

Chapter Fifteen

Josh

Josh checked his phone when he'd finished work for the day and saw a message from Maddie in their 'wedding chat' group. He read it twice to make sure he had understood it correctly. Apparently she'd contacted a wedding planner in Gibraltar to organise the wedding and the planner had informed her that the full birth certificates and passports had to be scanned and emailed over before the wedding, and the bride and groom had to provide proof that they had spent a night in Gibraltar. And both had to go to the register office together by ten thirty at the latest the day before the wedding to present these documents in person. Then they would be given an affidavit to take to the notary for it to be signed and sworn then picked up and handed back in to the register office by three o'clock that afternoon too. Which was all doable but not as straightforward as Steve had thought. And meant that Steve would have to propose to Kate two nights before the official wedding, rather than the night before, as he'd planned. He thought that was much better than Kate being whisked off to the wedding early in the morning the day after she said yes. *If* she said yes.

Thankfully, the wedding planner would organise it all for a reasonable fee so at least the paperwork would be in order. Apparently, there was a date available on both Friday 10th and Monday 13th June otherwise the wedding would have to be later in the month – after the holiday. Sophie had replied saying she thought that Steve would go for the tenth and Josh had to agree. He was sure that Steve wouldn't want their wedding date to be the thirteenth. If he went for the tenth, though, he and Kate would have to drive over to Gibraltar the same day they arrived in Spain, or very early the next morning, which Josh thought was risky. If they were delayed and missed their appointment the wedding wouldn't be able to go ahead the next day.

And there was also the little matter of whether the hotel in Spain could fit in the wedding, which Steve was still waiting to have confirmed. He couldn't believe that his brother hadn't checked that first. It was such a hare-brained scheme anyway and hopefully their parents would say the same when he and Steve went around on Friday evening. It was their mother's birthday the next day and they were all going out for a meal so Steve wanted to tell their parents on Friday as Kate wouldn't be there, and wanted Josh as backup. Josh couldn't help thinking that rather than Steve organising a secret wedding for Kate and himself, he was expecting Josh and Kate's two best friends to do it. *Typical Steve.*

He quickly replied that he thought the tenth would be best too and would email Steve right away and let them both know what date he wanted. It would be a lot easier if Steve was in the WhatsApp group chat too, Josh thought, as he copied and pasted Maddie's message into Steve's work email, adding, 'Let me know which date you prefer.'

He pressed send and slipped his phone in his pocket. Then he locked up the garage and set off home. He'd promised himself a quiet night in with a couple of cans of beer tonight.

He'd finished the first can and was about to open the second when there was a knock on the door. *Who the hell was that?* He was all settled for a relaxing evening and hated unannounced visitors. He was tempted to ignore it and pretend he wasn't in when a text buzzed in. **It's me. Open the door. Steve.**

'I can't stay long, Kate thinks I'm meeting a client,' Steve announced as he walked in. *That explained the smart suit, shirt and tie then.* 'I just wanted to tell you that the hotel in Estepona have confirmed that they can fit in our wedding on 10th June, apparently they've had a cancellation. Which is perfect as the register office in Gibraltar can do that date too.' He was beaming. 'I knew this was a good idea. It's all slotting together perfectly.'

Josh had to admit that was good news. 'There is the little matter of having to drive over to Gibraltar on the day you arrive, or early the next morning,' he pointed out.

'I know.' Steve ran his hands through his hair. 'Kate will wonder what's going on if we head off straight to Gibraltar as soon as we arrive at the hotel, but leaving it until the next morning is risky.'

'Then propose to her now, tell her your plans, you can get married quietly before you go to Spain and have a beach ceremony while you're over there. It's the obvious answer.'

'No, I've told you. I want us to have a surprise wedding. It's more romantic. I can't wait to see Kate's face when I tell her it's all arranged. She'll be made up.' Steve nodded towards the can of beer that Steve was holding. 'Do you have any more of those?'

'Sure. Take a seat and I'll grab you one.' *There goes my quiet*

65

evening! Josh surpressed a groan and headed for the kitchen. Steve looked like he was here to stay for a while.

'When's Kate expecting you back?' he asked as he handed Steve the cold can.

'I told her I didn't know how long the meeting would take.' He jerked the can pull to open the can and took a long swig. 'It would probably be best for you, Sophie and Maddie to take direct flights to Gibraltar, and return flights from Malaga, don't you think?'

'What about both sets of parents? Do you want them to attend the legal ceremony too?' Josh asked.

Steve shook his head. 'No; as far as I'm concerned the beach wedding is the real deal. The registrar stuff is just a formality. Can we take a look at flights? Are there any available to Gibraltar on 8th June?'

Josh picked up his phone, jabbed a couple of keys and got up the flights from Birmingham to Gibraltar on the screen. He scanned it quickly. 'There are no direct flights available that day. I'll try Heathrow.' He tapped a few more keys and nodded. 'Plenty from Heathrow and they're not a bad price either.'

'OK, so it's doable. I'll tell Kate that I've always wanted to go to Gibraltar so have booked us into a hotel over there. I can make up some story about being interested in the history of the place, or wanting to go and see the dolphins. In fact, I'll book us a trip to see the dolphins while we're over there. Kate will like that.'

'So when do you want us to arrive?' Josh asked.

Steve looked thoughtful for a moment. 'I want to propose properly, have a romantic evening, and a meal at a nice restaurant, so if you three could get there by the evening of the eighth, that would be great. Just make sure that Kate doesn't see you before I propose.' He put the empty beer can down.

'I'll run it by Sophie and Maddie and see if it's doable for them. And what about Sophie's partner? Are you paying for him too?'

Steve stroked his chin. 'Yes, I guess I ought to. I'd really like to get this all booked so I can relax about it. Can you message them both now and check if that's OK?'

Josh glanced at the clock. Just gone eight. It wasn't that late. 'I'll put a message in the group chat but remember they might be busy so don't fret if they don't answer tonight. I should think they'll need a bit of time to think about it. They probably haven't had chance to arrange time off work yet. And they might only be able to get enough time off to come to the wedding itself.'

'I know.' Steve sighed. 'I hope they can at least get there the night before the wedding, so Kate can have a hen night with them.'

Josh put a message in the group chat explaining it all to Sophie and Maddie. This wedding was going to be a pain in the backside. He just hoped that Steve was right and Kate would be delighted with his plans, because if she wasn't it could be the end of her and Steve. And he knew that his brother would be devastated if that happened.

Chapter Sixteen

Maddie

Maddie arrived at work early on Tuesday morning. She'd left Jax with fresh food and water, clean litter in his tray and plenty of toys to play with because she knew that she would probably be home late. The agency had recently signed an advertising deal with a major sportswear company and today was the launch day of their new brand of gym wear. As Maddie was in charge of the account she had to be there. She needed to pick up a few files then she was going straight to the conference centre where the launch was taking place. The company, FiddleFit, had wanted a complete rebrand and had a new logo and a new image which had all been received very well.

It was a hectic day but the launch went well, although, as Maddie had guessed, it was late by the time she arrived home. And there had been no chance to discuss her holiday plans at work, she'd have to sort that out tomorrow. At least they had a date for the wedding now, 10th June, although according to the message Josh put in the chat yesterday, Steve wanted the three of them to arrive in Gibraltar on the eighth if they could. At least he was paying! She quite fancied going to Gibraltar, and it would be great to have a hen night with Kate. She knew Sophie would like that too. From what Sophie had told her Glenn wasn't keen on going, though, and if she went without him, Maddie knew that Sophie would just fret over him and wouldn't enjoy herself. She was glad that she had no guy to consider.

People tended to think that Maddie's dislike of commitment was because she'd had an unhappy love affair, or because her parents were divorced. Neither was true. Her mother was happily remarried now, and Maddie had enough friends who were happily wed for her to realise that not all marriages were the disaster that her parents' had been. It was simply that Maddie had never been in love so had never had her heart broken. She'd had plenty of short-term relationships but after a month or two she always started to feel restless. She wanted to live her life on her terms, not to be tied down to someone. Her mother said she would change when she met the right person. Maddie hoped she'd never meet the right person then; she was happy with her life exactly how it was. She had peace, control, fun. Something she hadn't experienced when she was growing up. She considered that thought as she heated up a carton of carrot and coriander soup, too tired to rustle up anything else. Maybe her desire not to commit was a little bit influenced by her unhappy childhood, after all. Her mother had compromised so much because of her father. Maddie didn't want to compromise for anyone.

She figured it was too late to reply to Josh now. She'd wait until she found out how much time she could get off work, tomorrow, and then reply to him. Soup finished, she yawned and stretched. She would love to go for the whole two weeks. She could do with the break. It had been ages since she'd had a holiday. And two weeks would give her time to look up her aunt and cousins. Jax would be quite happy at the cattery; he'd stayed there a couple of times when she'd had to go away with work.

'Miaow!' As if sensing her thoughts, Jax jumped on the table and nudged her hand, demanding attention. It had been a long day for him alone in the flat. Maddie pushed her now-empty bowl away and patted her lap. 'Come on, then.'

Jax jumped on her lap and cuddled up, purring happily as she stroked him. 'We don't need anyone else in our lives, do we, Jax?' she murmured. 'Relationships complicate things. We're fine just the two of us.'

Chapter Seventeen

Sophie

'Steve is booking both weddings for Friday 10th June and wants us to stop over in Gibraltar with them for a night or two beforehand,' Sophie told Glenn that evening. 'Did you remember to ask if you could get any time off?'

'No, we were that busy it went out of my mind,' he told her.

'Please remember tomorrow. Steve's paying and it would be a lovely romantic break for us. We'll need to book up soon or all the hotel rooms will be gone.'

Glenn looked doubtful. 'I know you're looking forward to it, Soph, but I'm not sure it's going to be much of a romantic break when we're spending it with a bunch of almost strangers. I barely know Steve and Kate; they're your friends. Can't we just go off somewhere ourselves a bit later in the year?'

He was right, it would be nice to have a romantic week to themselves. But she really wanted him to come to the wedding with her. She would miss him. And she had to go, she was one of the bridesmaids. Besides, a wedding was a celebration of love and Glenn should be by her side. 'That would be lovely,' she agreed, 'but it would mean such a lot to Kate for me and Maddie to be at her wedding. If we fly over on the Wednesday or Thursday and fly back on the Sunday we will still have lots of days, holiday left so can have a longer break together later in the year.'

Glenn sighed. 'OK, I'll see what I can do, but if I can't get the time off, you must go without me. I don't mind.'

But *she* minded. A lot. It wouldn't be the same without Glenn. And it would give him a chance to get to know her friends more if he came. Steve was good company, as Glenn would find out if he spent a little time with him, and she was sure that Glenn would get on with Josh too.

Pat was out collecting flowers the following morning so Sophie kept her phone on her in the shop, anxious to hear if Glenn called. He messaged about eleven to say that he couldn't get time off until September and for Sophie to go to the wedding without him. She read the message twice, feeling really disappointed. Part of her felt that he hadn't really tried, because he didn't want to go. He didn't seem to realise how important attending her friend's wedding was to her, and how much she wanted him with her. Perhaps she should try talking to him again tonight. The trouble was Josh needed to know today so he could book the rooms and flights.

A message pinged into the group chat from Josh to say that the wedding was all booked, the legal service in the register office was going to be in the morning and the beach ceremony in the afternoon in Estepona. It was all slotting in nicely.

Maddie phoned Sophie at lunchtime to say that she'd managed to get the two weeks off work. 'Thank goodness! Two weeks in the sun is just what I need right now,' she said. 'Could you get the two weeks off as well? We could have a girly holiday.'

'I don't really want to go away for two weeks without Glenn,' Sophie said.

'Sophie! Can you cover the shop while I deliver these to Elsie, please?' Pat called. 'I'll be about an hour.' Sophie and Janine did most of the deliveries, but Pat had her special customers that she would deliver to, like Elsie. Elsie's son sent her flowers every week and Pat would stay and have a cuppa with her, checking that the old woman, who lived alone, was OK.

'Sure,' Sophie told her. She had some bridal and bridesmaids' posies to make up for a wedding the next day and was looking forward to the task. As she carefully selected the flowers her mind drifted to Kate's wedding. What flowers would she want? Now, if Sophie was getting married she would want delicate pastel colours, shades of pink, white, cream. The bride who was getting married the next day wanted a vibrant bouquet of coral and navy-blue roses mixed with Tweedia.

Sophie glanced over her shoulder as the door chimed then opened and Josh walked in. His face registered surprise then pleasure. 'Hello, Sophie. Do you work here?' Then he grinned. 'Stupid question, of course you do. Why else would you be making up a bouquet? Looks great by the way.'

'Thanks.' She put down the flowers and smoothed her hands on her overall. 'I presume you've come for some flowers?'

'Yep, a bouquet for my mum, it's her birthday on Saturday.' He glanced around. 'And I see that you sell gifts too so perhaps I can find something to go with them. As I'll be giving her a bunch of flowers next week, on Mother's Day, too, it would be good for her birthday ones to be a little different.'

'I could do you a gift box if you like?' Sophie offered. 'Look, I'll show you a couple in our order book, but it won't take long to make one up if you prefer a custom-made one.'

She picked up a folder and flicked through until she came to the 'floral gifts' page. 'Here we are.'

As Josh leant over to look she could feel his warm breath on her neck and a warm tingle spread through her body. Surprised at her reaction, and hoping he hadn't noticed it, she edged away a little.

'Hey, there's some great ideas here,' he said enthusiastically.

'What hobbies does your mum have?' Sophie asked him.

'Yoga, painting, reading . . . I guess nothing that lends itself to one of those bears or flower boxes.' He paused as he came to a bottle garden with a Buddha in the centre on a base of white pebbles, surrounded by a selection of plants. 'Now, that's lovely. Do you have one in stock?'

Sophie smiled, pleased that he liked it; that particular terrarium was one of her favourites, and sold very well. They'd actually sold the last one yesterday and she hadn't had time to make another one up yet. 'No, but I could do one for you if you don't mind coming back on Friday for it,' she told him.

'You make them yourself?'

'Yes; I started making terrariums as a hobby and gave one to Pat for her birthday last year. She loved it and asked me to make some to sell in the shop.'

'They're stunning. Are you sure you'd be able to make one for Friday? I could pop in about five if that's OK?'

'That should be fine. There's a few more Buddha designs actually. Take a look through before you decide.'

Josh scanned through the brochure and pointed to a

wide-necked bottle with a pathway leading up a base of rocks and mossy plants, with a white Buddha figure sitting on top. 'I think Mum would like this one best. Are they difficult to care for?' he asked.

'No, they're pretty easy. The main thing to remember is to keep it out of sunlight and away from direct heat such as on top of a radiator, but not in a dark, cold place either – and not to overwater it,' Sophie told him. 'There's a few plants in this one so it's best to water it twice a week with either a spray gun or special terrarium water bottle – it has a pointy nozzle that helps you guide the water. You also have to remember to prune the plants, remove dead leaves and to clean the glass inside and out so that enough light can reach the plants, but that's basically it. We provide a leaflet on how to keep the terrarium healthy.'

'That sounds perfect. I think Mum will be chuffed with it. Do you want me to leave a deposit?' he offered.

'No, it's fine. If you're not happy with it we can sell it in the shop. They're very popular so we'd easily sell it.'

'Thanks, Sophie. See you on Friday then. Oh, and you're meeting Kate tomorrow for wedding planning, aren't you? You can let me know what you manage to find out about her wedding choices on Friday.'

'Will do. See you then.'

He gave her a warm, friendly smile. 'You will. And thanks again for doing this for me.'

'It's a pleasure.'

Maybe she'd got off on the wrong foot with Josh, she thought, as he left the shop. He seemed nice, and was obviously thoughtful, trying to think of a special present for his mum.

'Have we been busy?' Pat asked when she came back.

Sophie looked up. 'Not too bad. A customer wants a Buddha terrarium for Friday,' she said. 'I have a Buddha and bottle at home so is it OK if I take the plants home with me and make it up? I'll bring it in on Friday.'

'Of course. They really are proving to be popular, aren't they? They could soon provide a nice little second income for you.'

I hope so, Sophie thought. Extra funds would come in handy. She was hoping that her relationship with Glenn would move to the next level soon and that they might move to a house.

To Sophie's surprise the flat was empty when she got home. Glenn usually arrived home before her and had the kettle on. She guessed he must be working late, or maybe had popped to the shops for something. She put the oven on and took a cottage pie out of the freezer. They could have that tonight with some frozen vegetables. It was a quick, tasty meal. There was rarely time to cook from fresh in the week what with them both working. Then she made herself a cup of tea and sat down on the kitchen chair to drink it.

She'd just taken the last sip when Glenn arrived home.

'Hi, dinner's almost done,' she said, getting up and going over to give him a kiss on the cheek. 'It's such a shame you couldn't get any time off to go to the wedding.'

Glenn unzipped his coat. 'I know, sorry, but they can't spare me until September so I've booked two weeks then. You go to the wedding with Maddie. I don't mind, honestly.'

Sophie couldn't hide her disappointment. '*I* do. I don't want to go without you. It won't be the same. We haven't been away together yet.'

Glenn sighed. 'Look, Soph, it's not my scene; besides, Kate and Steve are your friends, not mine. You go. Go for the whole two weeks if you can get the time off; you'll have a good time with Maddie. You could probably do with the break. We can go away together in September.'

Sophie still didn't feel happy with the idea. It was generous of him to tell her to go alone without causing a fuss though, she told herself. She was being silly getting upset about it. And it would be lovely for them both to go away in September. And maybe this year they could spend Christmas with her parents in Portugal, where they lived near to her brother Craig, his partner Lori and their two children.

'OK, I'll talk to Pat tomorrow and see if I can get two weeks off in September too. What dates have you booked?'

She made a note of the dates in her phone. 'Fancy a cuppa, I've just finished one?' she asked.

'Thanks. I'll have a quick shower while you're making it.' Glenn strode off to the bathroom while Sophie went into the kitchen. It was silly to get hung up over Glenn not being able to come to Kate and Steve's wedding. It was far more romantic for them both to go on holiday on their own. She'd go to the wedding and come back on the Sunday. Then she and Glenn could plan a holiday together in September. As she flicked on the kettle her mind wandered to where they could go. Maybe Italy. It was such a romantic place and would still be hot there. She imagined herself and Glenn holding hands as they went sightseeing, stopping in little cafés for lunch, spending time on the beach. She couldn't wait.

Chapter Eighteen

Kate

Kate frowned as a message pinged into Steve's phone and he quickly snatched it up. That was the third message he'd received that evening.

'Work again? Is there a problem?' she asked. She didn't mind Steve receiving messages from work, she often did herself, but it was obvious that he was agitated. Something was bothering him but he didn't seem to want to talk about it. She hoped it wasn't a serious problem.

'No, it's fine, but I do need to check something out,' he told her. 'I'll only be a few minutes.'

Kate watched worriedly as Steve went upstairs into the spare room they both used as an office. He had looked strained just lately, as if he had something on his mind. Well, it was no use questioning him, Steve had never been one for sharing his feelings. If he wanted to confide in her he would in his own good time.

Her thoughts turned to tomorrow night when she was meeting Sophie and Maddie to help Sophie plan her wedding. She'd been surprised when Sophie said that she didn't want anyone apart from their parents and a few close friends to know as they only wanted a low-key wedding and she didn't want all the extended family jumping on board. She'd have thought that Sophie would go for the whole works. Mind, Kate could understand her decision. If ever she got married, she'd only want a low-key wedding too. Just she and Steve jetting off somewhere by themselves. No fuss, no big ceremony, no fancy wedding gown. People put too much importance and spent far too much money on a big wedding. It was pointless. She'd rather spend the money on a deposit for a house. She was sure Steve would too. They had briefly mentioned getting married at some point in the future, but it was something they'd agreed that neither of them was ready for yet. They'd been together three years and lived together for two of those and while she adored Steve and they got on well, marriage was a big step. They were both too level-headed and unsentimental to rush it. Although she had to admit she wished Steve was a little more romantic. His idea of a special night out was dinner for two at the same restaurant they always went to. She'd said the same to him the other week when they'd gone out for a meal. 'I do love it here, but it would be nice to do something different,' she'd said.

'Like where?' he'd asked, puzzled.

'I don't know. Surprise me. Do something spontaneous and romantic,' she'd told him.

He'd looked at her as if she'd gone nuts and shook his head. She'd suppressed a sigh. Expecting Steve to do something spontaneous, or to plan a romantic surprise was pointless, it wasn't in his character. He had never even suggested booking a holiday all the time they'd been together, she had suggested it, then booked it. He was loyal, honest, loving and trustworthy, she reminded herself. Those were some of the many reasons that she loved him.

She was surprised that Sophie and Glenn were getting married so soon, to be honest; they'd only been living together a year, which was nowhere near long enough to make the enormous decision of promising to spend the rest of your life with someone. Not that many marriages lasted the course now. Kate's own parents had divorced when she was ten and it had been a very messy affair. Her childhood was plagued with their arguments. Marriage wasn't something to be taken lightly. Both parents had since remarried, with her dad now living in Yorkshire and her mum half an hour's drive away. They seemed happy with their new partners, thank goodness.

She heard Steve's footsteps coming down the stairs. He walked in, looking less troubled now. 'Fancy a glass of wine before we turn in?'

'Sounds good.' She got up and following him into the kitchen. She reached for two wine glasses from the cupboard as Steve took the Sauvignon out of the fridge and unscrewed the cap.

'You've remembered that I won't be coming straight home from work tomorrow, haven't you? We're all meeting at Maddie's to help Sophie plan her wedding.'

Steve nodded as he poured the wine into the glasses while Kate opened a bag of sea salt flavoured crisps and emptied them into a bowl. 'I'll be out anyway; I'm meeting Josh for a drink. He's a bit worried about the parents, wants me to pop over with him on Friday and try and get Dad to take it easy a bit.'

'Good luck with that, you know what your dad's like,' Kate said, picking up her wine and the bowl of crisps. 'I guess it's not the kind of thing you want to talk about when we go out for your mum's birthday meal on Saturday evening.'

'No, not really. That's why I'm going to pop over on Friday night.'

Kate had to admit she was relieved Steve hadn't asked her to go with him. She liked Steve's parents, but having a meal with them on Saturday was enough. She was looking forward to going to Maddie's tomorrow evening; she hadn't had a catch-up with Sophie and Maddie since the beginning of January, when she'd just booked the holiday. Only three months to go now, then a whole fortnight in sunny Spain. Just her and Steve, no work, no family crisis, nothing to do but sunbathe, go sightseeing and relax. Bliss.

Chapter Nineteen

Sophie

Glenn was out at his chess club that evening so Sophie had a couple of hours to herself to make the terrarium for Josh's mum. There was a tournament in a couple of weeks and Glenn really wanted to win it. When they'd first got together Glenn had tried to teach her how to play chess but Sophie couldn't keep the moves in her head. The game didn't interest her at all, but Glenn was a fanatic. Sophie preferred to spend her time gardening. She loved to care for her collection of orchids, and window boxes, and making these terrariums which brought her in some extra income. The more she thought about it the more she thought it would be a good idea to move into a house with a garden. She had so many ideas for it: a rockery, a small fountain, colourful pots. She'd have to talk to Glenn about it. She was sure he would be glad of the extra space too. They could have a shed in the garden for him to keep his bike in, rather than having to bring it up in the lift and keep it in their hall. She thought he might take a bit of persuading to move though.

Glenn didn't like change. When he came home from work he

liked to relax, only going out for the occasional bike ride or chess meeting – which he usually cycled to. He'd long given up trying to encourage Sophie to get a bike and cycle with him too. Sophie had never been able to master the balance of riding a bike; the last time she'd attempted it in her early teens she'd been cycling downhill and not been able to stop, zooming across a busy road, dodging the traffic and managing to swerve in time to stop herself crashing into a shop window, ending up in a nearby bush instead. She'd never got on a bike since and no amount of Glenn's coaxing would tempt her to. 'It would be nice if we could share a hobby together,' he'd said but she didn't agree. It was healthy to have separate hobbies and allow each other a bit of time alone. Anyway, they did both share a love of the countryside and would sometimes take a drive out to the Cotswolds and surrounding area to enjoy the scenery at weekends.

She covered the table with a sheet of plastic and placed the wide-necked glass bottle on it. She always chose a wide-necked bottle without a stopper as it made caring for the plants easier, although she loved the look of some of the terrariums made in narrower bottles such as wine and liquor bottles. Maybe she'd have a go at one of them at some point. She placed the pebbles and slate on the table, then a pot of compost and the plants. Then she put a layer of small pebbles into the bottle, to absorb the water, covered it with activated charcoal then a layer of moss. She added a couple of inches of soil before adding the plants, using a spoon to make a hole for them and chopsticks to lower them into place before covering their roots with soil. Next she added small rocks and slate for steps, building up a mound inside the bottle and placing the little white Buddha on the top of it. She stepped back to admire her work. This was definitely one of her best creations, she thought, and she hoped that Josh – and his mum – would like it too.

'Hey, that's brilliant,' Glenn said when he returned a few minutes later. 'Is it for a customer in the shop?'

'Yes, Steve's brother has ordered it for his mum. It's her birthday on Saturday.' She tilted her face so his lips met hers as he bent down to kiss her. 'How did it go at chess club?'

'Let's say that I'm quietly confident.'

'You've got a tournament coming up soon, haven't you?'

'Yep, next Saturday. Fancy coming and giving me a bit of support?'

She wrinkled her nose. 'I'm not sure. We're meeting Kate to discuss the wedding tomorrow and I think we might have to go wedding shopping that Saturday. There aren't many weeks to arrange everything. Can I let you know nearer the time?' Although she felt a little guilty for not supporting Glenn, she didn't really fancy sitting and watching a chess match for hours.

Glenn took off his cycle helmet and put it down on the chair. 'No problem, you'd probably be bored anyway. Want a coffee?'

'Please. I'll just clear this away,' she indicated the mess on the table. 'I've been thinking,' she blurted out. 'Wouldn't it be great to get a house? Then maybe I can have a shed in the garden to do all this, and you could keep your bike in it too. Plus, we'd have a spare room to use as an office cum chess room.'

'So you'd be up for moving then?' he asked. 'I thought you loved it here?'

'I do, but we don't have much space, do we?' She placed the remaining pebbles, slates, moss and plants back in the box on the floor and carefully gathered up the plastic so that none of the soil spilt on to the carpet then put it into the bin. 'Think of those long summer evenings when we could sit outside drinking wine and sharing what we've been doing in the day. And at weekends we could do a bit of gardening.' She smiled up at him. 'Maybe we could even save up a deposit and buy a house rather than renting?'

Glenn seemed to be considering this. He nodded. 'Maybe,' he said then went into the kitchen to make coffee.

He returned a few minutes later and put a mug on the table beside Sophie, holding it in both hands as he stood next to her. 'You know you really are good at those bottle gardens,' he said.

She felt a glow of pride. It wasn't often Glenn made any comments about the terrariums and plant gifts she created. 'Thanks.'

'You could strike out on your own, Soph. Sell them online. Then you could have all the profit yourself instead of sharing it with your boss, plus you could work from home. If we rented a house, like you said, you'd have plenty of space to work in. And we could live anywhere, we could move to a different area.'

She tilted her head to one side and looked up at him. He'd never suggested that she work from home before or mentioned moving away. She liked living in Worcester and she didn't really want to work from home either and have to rely on selling her gift boxes and terrariums for an income. Apart from anything, she would miss the interaction with Janine and the customers. And Pat wasn't a bad boss to work for. She'd thought that Glenn was settled at work too, even though he'd been a bit stressed lately as the company was expanding and he'd had extra work to do. 'Are you serious?' she asked.

He looked thoughtful as he took a swig of his coffee, as if he was mulling it over. Then he shrugged. 'I don't know. You mentioned moving to a house and it made me think. We don't have to stay in Worcester, do we? It might be exciting to make a fresh start somewhere else.'

Sophie bit her lip. 'I like my job. And this area. We've got friends here. And lots of facilities.' She was wishing she hadn't mentioned moving to a house now if it was giving Glenn ideas about moving away. She thought he was a homebody, like her, that he didn't like change. What was going on?

He put a hand reassuringly on her shoulder then bent over and kissed her cheek. 'Don't worry about it, it was only an idea.'

She felt herself relax. She'd been daft to get so panicky.

'Will you be much longer?' he asked. 'I'm ready for bed when I've drunk this.'

'Almost finished,' she told him.

It was later, when she was almost falling asleep, that the thought occurred to her that Steve and Kate's wedding, and the talk of moving house, might have made Glenn think about the future, of them getting married. And having a family. That could be why he'd suggested Sophie working from home. And the houses here were expensive. Perhaps that's why Glenn had suggested moving away.

Maybe she shouldn't have dismissed it so quickly. She'd think about it and talk about it with Glenn a bit more.

She turned around and snuggled into Glenn, spooning herself against his back, then fell into a deep sleep.

Chapter Twenty

Maddie

Kate arrived a few minutes after Sophie on Thursday evening. 'Congratulations!' she said, giving Sophie a hug then handing her a card. 'I wasn't sure what to get you for an engagement present so I've put a voucher in the card, that way you can both choose what you want.'

Maddie saw Sophie quickly conceal her dismay and plaster a big smile on her face as she replied. 'Thanks so much, but you shouldn't have.'

Damn. They should have known that Kate would bring a card and present. 'You've beaten me to it, I haven't had time to go shopping yet,' Maddie said easily. 'Now, what do you want to drink? Shall I rustle us up a cocktail to celebrate or are either of you driving? In which case I could make a mocktail.'

'I'm driving. I thought I'd better not have a drink tonight as it's a heavy day at work tomorrow. So a mocktail would be great, thanks,' Kate told her.

'I'm driving too so a mocktail would be perfect, please,' Sophie agreed.

'Coming right up! Make yourselves comfy.' Maddie went off

to make the drinks as Sophie shrugged off her coat and put it over the arm of the chair.

Kate bent down and stroked Jax who was nuzzling against her legs. 'Hello, Jax, how are you?'

Jax purred and allowed Kate to pick him up and stroke him. 'You're so gorgeous,' she said.

Sophie smiled. 'If anyone had asked me if I thought Maddie would have a cat I'd have said "no way", but he's the perfect pet for her.'

'He certainly is,' Maddie called from the kitchen area where she was preparing the drinks. 'Although he's a bit spoiled and thinks that he rules the place.'

'That's cats for you,' Kate replied. 'My cat, Smudge, was the same. He was boss of the house; came and went as he liked. Even our dog wouldn't disturb him when he lay in his basket.'

'It's probably in their blood, been passed down for generations, right from Ancient Egyptian times when they were practically sacred,' Sophie said.

'They still haven't lost their superior air.' Maddie returned with a tray of three rainbow-coloured drinks in tall glasses with glass straws sticking out, and a couple of bowls of nibbles. She put the tray down on the coffee table. 'Help yourselves. I've gone for a mocktail too.'

'They look delicious.' Kate picked a glass up and took a long slurp. 'And it tastes heavenly. What's in it?'

Maddie tapped the side of her nose with her finger. 'It's my very own secret recipe, which will never be divulged.'

'We'll get it out of you one day when you've had a few strawberry gin and tonics,' Sophie said with a grin as she reached for her mocktail and took a big sip. 'Oh, divine!'

Maddie looked chuffed. 'There's plenty more, so drink up. And you have the added bonus that you won't get drunk.'

'Which is good as we need to keep a clear head tonight.' Sophie put her glass down and reached inside the large canvas tote bag she'd put by her feet. 'I've brought my laptop with me. I've done a lot of research and bookmarked some useful websites. Want to take a look?'

'Sure, go ahead. Are you OK to put it on your lap or shall we move to the kitchen table?' Maddie asked.

'Here's fine.' Sophie took out the laptop, balanced it on her lap, opened it up and logged on. A couple of minutes later she was online and looking at the Pinterest board she'd created.

'I took a look at it last night, and added a couple more pins.' Maddie sat the other side of Sophie and leant over to point with her finger. 'See, there they are.'

Sophie enlarged an image of a wedding dress. 'It's gorgeous.'

It really was gorgeous, thought Maddie, sleek, slender and stylish – and a bit too simple for Sophie, but ideal for Kate. Which is exactly why she had chosen it; she wanted to get Kate's reaction.

'That's beautiful, so elegant.' Kate peered closer. 'But it's not very Sophie. You know what Soph is like for frills and lace, she'll want a proper meringue and to be princess for the day.' She moved the cursor along the screen and selected another dress, A-line with a nipped-in waist, off-the-shoulder fitted bodice, and full flowing skirt. 'Something like that.'

Maddie could see by how Sophie's eyes widened and fixed on the dress that it was exactly what she would have chosen. It wouldn't suit Kate, though, with her slender, almost boyish figure.

Sophie obviously thought the same as she shook her head. 'It is totally gorgeous but we're having a low-key wedding so I'd like something simpler? Although maybe this one is too simple. I can see you wearing it more than me, Kate.' She hoped she wasn't being too obvious here, but it was important to know if this was the sort of dress Kate would go for.

'Hmm, perhaps. It's all very personal, isn't it? Now if you were getting married, Maddie, you'd probably wear a red or purple one – or both colours together,' Kate said, grinning at Maddie. 'I could imagine you getting a plain white dress and have it dyed in coloured stripes.'

Maddie grinned back. 'Maybe I would – if I ever lost my senses enough to promise eternal undying love to one person. Frankly, I can't see that happening.'

'You will, you'll see. One day you'll find a guy that will sneak into your heart and then you'll be planning a wedding too,' Sophie told her.

'Or she might decide to simply live together. Not everyone wants to get married, you know,' Kate pointed out, reaching for a few nibbles.

Maddie and Sophie both looked at Kate in panic. Was Kate saying that she didn't want to get married? Maddie wondered. If so, they needed to let Steve know asap.

Sophie pouted. 'Don't say I'm the only one planning on settling down. You and Steve will surely, one day, won't you?'

Clever Sophie for thinking on her feet like that and trying to find out Kate's feelings about marriage, Maddie thought, picking up her mocktail and sipping it whilst she tried to assess Kate's expression.

'Who knows? Maybe,' Kate said casually. 'Now, let's have

another look at those dresses. I think you ought to make a list of half a dozen or so that you like, then whittle it down, Sophie. When did you say you were planning the wedding?'

'July.' Sophie said the first date that came into her head. 'We haven't actually booked it yet, but we will soon.'

'July? That's no time. You'll be lucky if you get a dress for then. Most people order their wedding dresses at least a year in advance. You're really cutting it fine, especially if you need alterations. Why don't we all go wedding dress shopping on Saturday? The sooner you start looking the better,' Kate suggested.

'That would be great,' Sophie agreed. 'And maybe we could get the bridesmaids' dresses the Saturday after. Is that OK with you, Maddie?'

'Sure,' Maddie agreed, not really looking forward to it but wanting to help Kate.

'I should be able to get a wedding dress "off the peg", shouldn't I?' Sophie asked. 'I'm a standard size twelve, the same as you two –' she looked at them both – 'aren't you?'

Clever Sophie again, trying to find out Kate's dress size, Maddie thought.

'I'm a ten,' Kate told her.

'Eight,' said Maddie.

'Oh gosh, I feel a right fatty now,' Sophie said.

'Rubbish, you've got more curves than us, that's all. You're a sexy hourglass, Maddie's like a beanpole and I'm sporty – I've lost a bit of weight since me and Steve took up playing badminton.' Kate looked back at the dresses. 'That one would suit you, it's perfect for an hourglass figure.' She saved it to the *Secret Wedding* board. 'Now what other plans have you made? Have you decided on your venue? Flowers – I bet your boss will give you a discount on those – and the wedding cake? Are you having wedding favours? A disco at the reception? There's loads to do, you know. How many people are actually going?'

Sophie looked lost for words, so Maddie took over. 'You're still sorting that, aren't you, Soph?'

Sophie nodded.

'You're going to have to let us know the date as soon as you can so we can book the day off work too,' Kate told her.

'I will. Glenn's only just proposed so we haven't had chance to organise much. It'll probably be in Malvern Register Office, and then we'll book a hall for the reception.'

Kate nodded. 'Sounds ideal. What about bridesmaids?'

'You two, of course,' Sophie said. 'Shall we have a look at some bridesmaids' dresses now? I was thinking something like grey chiffon, or a pale green. What do you think?'

They spent the next hour or so looking at bridesmaids' dresses, flowers and other wedding-related things, then Kate said she had to go. 'See you both on Saturday, about ten outside Grand Central?' she suggested.

'Perfect. Thanks, Kate,' Sophie replied.

'Do you think we managed to pull it off?' Sophie asked when Kate had left.

Maddie wrinkled her nose. 'Yes, but only because Kate has no reason to think we aren't telling the truth. I'm not sure about the wedding dress and bridesmaids' dresses she selected though. She kept trying to choose wedding ones for you and bridesmaids' ones that would suit her and me – as I thought she would.'

'I know. Let's make sure we don't rush her. She doesn't have to choose a dress on Saturday. We can just look around and

Kate can try a few on. Make it a sort of girly day,' Sophie suggested.

'We can take some photos of the ones Kate likes and think about which one would be best,' Maddie added, knowing that Sophie was worried about making the wrong choice.

'Good idea.' Sophie reached for a few crisps. 'Now how about another mocktail before I go?'

Chapter Twenty-one

Josh

Josh wheeled his motorbike into the garage, unfastened his helmet and took it off, then unzipped his leather jacket. He was glad to be home. It had been so busy at work today he'd ended up working late, and tomorrow would probably be even busier. Fridays always were. When he'd first told his family his intention to set up a motorbike specialist repair centre his father had raised an eyebrow, his mother had wished him luck and Steve had told him he was mad and wouldn't make any money from it and that he was wasting his university education. Josh hadn't cared. It was holding on to his university education that had stopped him going off with River, and he had regretted that for a very long time.

Their parents had drilled into him and Steve the importance of getting a good education, of investing in their future, and they had both taken their parents' advice on board, getting good grades at school, going on to college and then university, where Steve had taken a course in business management and Josh had taken a course in engineering; but it was a job he had never really enjoyed. He'd worked part time at a local garage through university and Ritchie, the owner of the garage, had noticed his interest in bikes and started passing over some of the motorbike repairs to him. Then, when Ritchie had sold up a few years later, Josh had taken out a bank loan and bought the garage off him, specialising in motorbike repairs. He loved his job. His father had long since given up trying to persuade him to go back to engineering. Steve teased him good-humouredly but accepted his decision. He knew how much losing River had hurt Josh, how much he had wished he had gone with her instead of playing safe, although he told Josh he'd made the right decision. And as the years passed Josh realised that he had; he'd loved River but she had loved her freedom more than him. It would never have worked out between them.

He'd kept himself busy and the pain had gone away eventually. He enjoyed being his own boss, and 'tinkering with motorbikes' as his father called it. He didn't want to be like Steve, in a monotonous desk job, even if it did mean his brother could afford a big, detached house and a new car. And actually, Josh's garage was far more lucrative than any of them had expected and he could afford a bigger house and new car himself if he wanted to but he didn't. He was happy renovating the repossessed cottage, with a detached garage, which he'd bought cheaply. Possessions didn't interest him that much, he liked to travel. Every now and again he'd close the garage and take himself off for a couple of weeks. He'd travelled all around Europe on his bike and was thinking of going further afield. And now he did these things because he enjoyed doing them, not because River's departing words in the letter she had put through his door – *You stay in your safe, boring little life, me I'm going to travel the world* – rang in his ears.

Sometimes he wondered what had become of River. Was she still teaching her way around the world, her TEFL certificate opening doors to earn a living wherever she went?

He locked the garage and walked over to the cottage. He was hungry, thirsty and tired. He needed a shower, something to eat and bed, in that order.

Later, as his head touched the pillow, he remembered that Maddie and Sophie were meeting Kate that evening to discuss the wedding. Had they managed to find out what sort of wedding Kate would want? he wondered. If she wanted one at all. He couldn't imagine Maddie getting married any time soon but Sophie, he could see, was caught up in the idea. He wondered if Glenn minded that Sophie was pretending they were getting married. It seemed to Josh that Sophie wished it was her wedding; *could Glenn tell that too?* As his eyes closed and he drifted into sleep an image of Sophie in a white lace wedding gown with a long veil floated across his mind. She'd make a beautiful bride, he acknowledged; this Glenn was a lucky man.

His eyes flicked open again as his mind registered in disbelief what he'd just thought. What the heck? All this wedding stuff was already clouding his mind and they'd only just started planning the wedding. He'd be glad when it was over.

Chapter Twenty-two

Sophie

It was gone half five when Josh finally arrived for his mother's present the next day. Sophie and Pat had already started bringing in the tubs of flowers when he strode through the door in his black motorcycle jacket, oil-stained jeans and black Harley Davidson boots. He's such a contrast to Steve, Sophie thought again. It was hard to believe that they were brothers. 'Sorry, I had a rush job this afternoon. Someone needed their bike repaired for the weekend.'

'No problem, we're open until six,' Sophie said. 'I'll go and get the terrarium for you.'

She went into the back, then came out a few moments later carrying the huge bottle garden carefully with both hands, and placed it down on the counter in front of Josh.

Josh looked at it in awe. 'That's amazing. You're very talented. My mum is going to love this.'

Sophie felt a warm glow of pride. 'I'm so pleased you like it. I can wrap it for you if you want?'

'You can?' Josh surveyed the terrarium thoughtfully. 'I don't think it's going to be easy to wrap.'

'I can put some cellophane around it, and tie it with a bow at the top,' Sophie suggested.

He stroked his chin. 'That sounds great.'

Sophie fetched a large sheet of patterned cellophane from out the back and several rolls of coloured ribbon. She placed them down on the counter. 'Which colour do you prefer?' she asked Josh.

'The yellow one, please. It's her favourite colour.'

'I bet your mum is warm, optimistic and creative,' Sophie said as she smoothed out the patterned cellophane, placed the bottle on it, and proceeded to cover it, gathering the ends up above the top of the bottle, holding them together with one hand as she reached for the ribbons.

'Yes, she is ... Here, let me.' Josh placed his hand around the bunched cellophane, his fingers lightly brushing Sophie's. She removed her hand quickly as a tingle ran up it. What was the matter with her? 'How did you guess?' he asked.

'I'm really interested in colour psychology and those are common traits of people who like yellow,' she told him. 'Add to it that she likes yoga, and plants ...'

He tilted his chin to one side. 'And what would you say her negative traits are?'

Sophie cut off a long strip of ribbon and wrapped it around the cellophane. 'A bit cautious, doesn't like confrontation, can keep things to herself, easily spooked ...'

His eyes widened. 'Spot on. And what's your favourite colour?'

'I like all the pastel shades, but blue is my favourite,' she told him. 'The colour of security, trust and loyalty.'

He nodded. 'That sounds like you. And what are the negatives?'

She grinned. 'Passive, predictable . . . boring.' She didn't look up at him as she tied the ribbon into a bow, sure that he was agreeing with those things. Compared to vibrant Maddie who loved purple, red and orange she guessed that she was boring. Glenn's favourite colour was brown. He dressed in beige and brown a lot; it represented reliability, honesty and security, all of which Glenn epitomised. The negatives were pretty much the same as hers; no wonder they got on. They both liked a quiet life, no upheaval. Except that Glenn was now suggesting moving away, she remembered. That would be a big upheaval. 'And what's your favourite colour?' she asked.

'Guess.' He'd released the now secure cellophane and slipped his hands in his jacket pockets, looking at her with challenge in his eyes.

She tilted her head to one side and tapped her bottom lip with her finger. He wore a lot of black, white and grey but she had an idea that was for convenience rather than because they were his favourite colours.

'Hmm. You tend to wear black and white, symbolising power, strength and openness, but you seem quite laid back, and calm.' She looked into his indigo-blue eyes. 'I'd take a guess at turquoise.'

His jaw dropped as he stared at her in astonishment. 'Spot on!'

She grinned, pleased that she'd made the right guess.

'And dare I ask what the negative qualities are?' He sounded amused.

'You can be a bit up yourself and secretive; you don't like opening up,' she said.

'Up myself, eh? Now Steve might agree with that.' His eyes were dancing. 'As for secretive . . . no need to tell everyone everything, is there?' He took out his wallet and handed her his bank card. 'Thanks so much for this.'

She handed him the receipt. 'Let me know your parents' reaction to the wedding, and if they can definitely come. We should start looking at availability of flights and hotel rooms for them and any other guests asap.'

'I know. We're telling our folks tonight and Steve is telling Kate's parents this weekend. He'll have to phone her dad as he won't have time to go to Yorkshire. Then we can tell other family and friends, swearing them to secrecy of course, and find out who wants to come. Good luck with the wedding dress shopping tomorrow.' He picked up the wrapped terrarium and walked over to the door.

Sophie quickly followed him, opening the door as his hands were full. 'I hope your mum likes it.'

'She will.' He smiled and walked off up the street.

She turned back to see Pat watching her, a quizzical look on her face. 'Well, he seems a nice young man,' Pat said. 'Friend of yours by the sound of it.'

'Remember I told you about my friend Kate's partner planning a secret wedding?'

Pat nodded.

'Josh is his brother.'

'Ah, I see. And is he single?'

'I think so.'

'Well, I doubt if he'll be for long; he seems quite a catch.

100

Nice-looking and thoughtful too. Most men grab the nearest bunch of flowers for their mum, not take their time to choose a gift like he did,' Pat said.

Sophie had been surprised at that too. Perhaps there was more to Josh than met the eye.

Chapter Twenty-three

Sophie

Glenn was already home when Sophie got in. 'Fancy going out for something to eat tonight?' he asked.

Sophie hesitated. She'd been thinking of doing some more wedding planning but maybe she could do that in the morning. It wasn't often Glenn suggested eating out.

'That sounds great. What time were you thinking of going?' she asked.

'About eight,' he suggested.

She had just over an hour to get ready. 'Great. I'll just have a cuppa then get showered and changed.'

'Sit down for a few minutes. I'll make us a coffee.' Glenn flicked the kettle on and spooned instant coffee into two mugs.

'Thanks.' Sophie kicked off her shoes and sank down on to the sofa. It had been a long day. Thank goodness she wasn't working tomorrow.

Glenn brought a mug over to her and held it out. She took it off him, cradling it in her hands. Then he sat down beside her and put his own mug on the coffee table and turned to face her. 'I've been thinking, Soph.'

Suddenly Sophie's mobile rang. She automatically glanced at it on the coffee table in front of her. *Maddie*, it said on the screen. Maddie always texted unless it was important. She'd have to leave it, it looked like Glenn wanted to say something important too. She dragged her eyes from the vibrating screen to Glenn, who was also looking at the phone. 'It's Maddie, probably something to do with the wedding. I can call her back.'

Glenn sighed and picked up his mug of coffee. 'No, answer it. I can wait.'

'Thanks.' Sophie grabbed the phone and swiped the screen. 'Hi, Maddie. What's up?'

'I'm going to have to cancel tomorrow. One of my clients wants to meet me urgently,' Maddie said. 'I can't put them off, Soph, this is a major account. Can we make the shopping trip next week? Or you and Kate go without me? I'm not much use choosing wedding dresses anyway.'

'But I need you there to say what sort of dress you'd like, and to coax Kate to tell us her choice.'

'I would never buy a traditional wedding gown full stop. Kate knows that.'

'And there's the bridesmaids' dresses.'

'We can choose them another week, surely?'

'OK.' She bit back her disappointment. She had really wanted Maddie's support, but she knew her friend was dedicated to her job. Of course this meeting would come first. 'I'll fill you in over the weekend. I hope the meeting goes well.'

She ended the call and turned back to Glenn.

'Problems?' he asked.

'Maddie can't come wedding dress shopping tomorrow and

103

we don't have much time so can't postpone it to another week, which means me and Kate will have to go ahead without her.'

Glenn frowned. 'Steve's expecting a lot of you. This is his idea so he shouldn't be palming everything off on you.'

'He can't really take Kate wedding dress shopping, though, can he? And I don't mind; we're all sharing the workload between us.'

'Well, I don't think it's fair on Kate. It's a ridiculous idea to keep the wedding a secret from the bride. Especially when he hasn't even bothered to propose to her.'

Apparently Sophie – and Steve – were the only ones who thought it was romantic. 'Steve means well, he just wants it all to be a lovely surprise for her.'

Glenn fixed his gaze on her. 'And would you think a surprise wedding was a lovely idea or would you prefer to plan it yourself?'

She considered this, wondering if Glenn was asking because he was thinking of proposing to her. 'I would, because I know it would come from a place of love, but actually I guess I would quite like to plan my wedding. A beach wedding in Spain sounds fantastic and I'm sure will be lovely, but I'd like to get married in the UK, in a castle maybe, and ride there in a horse and carriage.' She could hear her voice rising with excitement. 'That would be marvellous, wouldn't it?' She rested her eyes on Glenn. 'What sort of wedding would you like?'

He was silent for a moment. 'I don't know. Low-key, I think.' He finished his drink and stood up. 'Look, it's almost eight now, let's leave the meal until tomorrow night, shall we? I can whip us up a spag bol then I'll go and sort out my bike, I'm going for a ride tomorrow while you go shopping with Kate.'

She nodded. 'That sounds perfect, thank you. I do have a couple of things to sort out tonight before the shopping trip tomorrow.' She loved how understanding Glenn was, and how he never expected her to do all the chores or cooking. They made such a good team.

After dinner, Glenn went to get his bike ready for tomorrow while Sophie did some research on wedding shops in the town, writing a list of ones she thought might be suitable. It wasn't until they went to bed that night and Sophie was about to fall asleep that she remembered Glenn had been going to talk to her about something when Maddie phoned.

Chapter Twenty-four

Josh

'Oh my goodness, Josh, that's wonderful. What a thoughtful present,' Anita Henderson said in delight when Josh handed her the Buddha terrarium.

Steve looked at the gift in surprise. 'You've excelled yourself there, mate. Where did you get it?'

'The shop where Sophie works. She makes them. It's stunning, isn't it?'

'It certainly is.' Steve handed their mother an envelope. 'Puts my present to shame.'

Anita placed the terrarium, still in its cellophane wrapper, on the table and opened the envelope, smiling as she took out a voucher for a luxury spa day. 'Nonsense, they are both perfect presents. It's so good of you two to pop by on a Friday evening. I know how busy you both are. I wasn't expecting my birthday presents until we all meet for the meal tomorrow.'

'Actually, I have something I wanted to talk to you about ...' Steve ventured.

'Uh-oh,' their father said. 'And you needed your younger brother's support to break it to us? This doesn't sound good.'

Both their parents looked worried but Josh's hopes that they would talk Steve out of his ridiculous 'secret wedding' scheme were soon dashed when, after hearing Steve's plans, Anita's face lit up and she clapped her hands in delight. 'Oh, how wonderful! A wedding is just what we need, isn't it, Clive?'

'It's excellent news. Excellent. We'd be delighted to have Kate as a daughter-in-law,' Clive Henderson said, getting out of his seat and shaking Steve's hand. 'Congratulations, son.'

'He hasn't asked Kate yet. She might turn him down,' Josh pointed out.

'Of course she won't. She'll be over the moon. I bet she's been waiting for our Steve here to pop the question. I have to say you've taken your time, lad. Still, better late than never. Now you must let us help you a bit financially. Pay for the flights and hotel rooms for ourselves and immediate family, or the reception. We'll thrash out the details later. Right now this calls for a toast.'

'We're both driving, Dad,' Josh pointed out.

'So you are. Oh well, we'll have to wait until the wedding then. We'll have a proper toast to you both then.'

'Remember not to mention it to Kate tomorrow when we all meet up for the meal,' Steve said. 'I want it to be a complete surprise until the actual day.'

'Of course we won't. How exciting and romantic of you. I was wondering where to go for our holidays this year. We haven't been to Southern Spain so it will be a nice change. Perhaps we could stay for a week, Clive.' Anita was beaming. 'And it's about time one of you got married. I've been hoping to have some grandchildren before too long. Lots of my friends have two or three already.'

'Hang on, Mum, let's get the wedding over first,' Steve said with a grin.

'If Kate accepts your proposal,' Josh reminded him.

'Of course she will. Don't be so negative, Josh,' Anita scolded. 'I think this is wonderful news. You should take a leaf out of your brother's book and find a nice girl to go out with. It would be good to see you settled down.'

'I don't want to be settled down. Can we concentrate on Steve's love life and leave mine alone? I'm quite happy how I am.'

'That's because you haven't met the right person yet,' their father said, putting his arm around their mother's shoulder. 'When you do, it will be a different story.'

'I'll make a cup of tea,' Josh said, wanting to take himself out of the discussion for a few minutes. He took a few deep breaths to calm himself down as he made his way into the kitchen. His parents were always the same, pushing him to settle down. They hadn't wanted him to stay with River, though, had they? They hadn't cared that she was the love of his life, all they'd cared about was him getting his degree.

'We don't mean any harm. We only want to see you happy.'

Josh turned around at the sound of his mother's voice. 'Yeah, I know. But not all of us think that you have to be married to be happy, Mum.'

'Of course you don't. But don't shut your heart to meeting someone, Josh. You and River weren't the right match for each other, otherwise she would have stayed, or you would have gone with her. Surely you realise that?'

She took a tin of biscuits out of the cupboard then handed Josh a tray to put the mugs of tea on. 'When you really love someone, you can't let them go. You two were kids, not even twenty. First love hits hard but it isn't always true love. Me and your dad, we both loved someone else before we met each other, we both had our hearts broken, but it helps you recognise the real thing when you find it.'

She smiled at him then walked out of the kitchen, taking the tin of biscuits with her.

Josh stared after her, stunned. Although he'd assumed his parents probably dated others before they met each other, he'd never thought they'd actually been in love with anyone else.

Chapter Twenty-five

Kate

'Oh, don't worry about it, Maddie isn't the ideal wedding shopping companion anyway. She'd either try to get you to choose something completely unconventional or try to talk you out of getting married,' Kate said when Sophie met her at the train station on Saturday and told her Maddie couldn't make it. She linked her arm through Sophie's. 'Me and you will manage just fine.'

Kate was actually pleased that just the two of them were going wedding shopping, she thought as they headed for the escalators to the vast shopping centre above the train station. She and Sophie very rarely met up alone now, there was always Maddie or Glenn in tow. Kate liked Maddie but she and Sophie had been best friends since primary school and had been inseparable right until Kate's parents left the area in the final year of high school, so it was nice for them both to have a day out together for once. Especially when it was such a special occasion, shopping for Sophie's wedding dress.

'I thought we'd look at wedding dresses first, then bridesmaids' dresses if we have enough time,' Sophie said. 'And I really want your honest opinion, Kate, as I'm looking for something elegant and stylish and you're so good at that. Please steer me away from the meringues.'

Kate laughed. 'I'll do my best, but I suspect you'll weaken when you see all those gorgeous lacy flouncy dresses. And as I said on Thursday, it's your wedding so you must have the dress you want.'

They went into a couple of bridal shops, and picked out lots of wedding dresses for Sophie to try on.

'I'll take a photo of you in each one, then you can look through them later and decide which one you like best,' Kate said, taking out her phone.

It was fun and Sophie looked gorgeous in so many of the dresses, Kate couldn't decide which one suited her best. Neither could Sophie.

'I really don't know which one I prefer,' she said to Kate when they stopped for lunch.

'Why don't we take a look through the photos?' Kate suggested. 'That might help you decide.'

'That's a great idea,' Sophie agreed. 'And there are a couple more bridal shops to visit yet so I'm sure I'll find a dress I like.'

They went into the nearest café, ordered a coffee and sandwich each and then browsed through the wedding dress photos on the phone.

'Tell me which one you prefer; it doesn't matter if you think it suits me or not. I'd just like your opinion,' Sophie said.

To be honest, none of them was the style Kate would choose. They were too dressy. Personally, she would go for something simpler. She studied the photos and pointed to one with a sweetheart neckline, nipped in at the waist and a full skirt. It made Sophie look like a princess. Kate was surprised that her friend hadn't gone for that one straight away. 'This one looks fantastic on you,' she said, enlarging the photo so they could see the detail better.

The waitress came over with their order. 'What gorgeous wedding dresses. Who's the bride-to-be?' the waitress asked, peering over at the photo.

'She is.' Kate pointed at Sophie. 'We've been looking at wedding dresses all morning, but she can't decide which one she wants.'

The waitress took the cups and plates off the tray and placed them on the table. 'You know, when I was getting married I had trouble choosing, then I walked into a shop and there it was. I knew right away that it was the dress for me. If you can't make up your mind, then you haven't found your dress.'

'I think you're right. They're all lovely but none of them seems the right one for me,' Sophie said. 'Have you seen the wedding dress you'd wear yet, Kate?'

Kate shook her head. 'No.'

'Will you tell me if you do?' Sophie asked.

'Sure, if you want me to. But that doesn't mean it's the right dress for you,' Kate told her. 'We both have completely different styles.'

'I know, but it would be good to know.'

'Have you tried the new shop that's opened at the top of the High Street?' the waitress asked. 'It's called Beautiful Brides. It's only been open a couple of months but it's amazing. I went with my friend last week. It's spread over two floors and there are loads of wedding dresses, bridesmaids' dresses and accessories like tiaras and shoes.'

'That sounds great. Let's give it a try,' Kate suggested. 'It would be good to get everything in the one shop too.' Her feet were starting to ache.

'We'll make that our next stop,' Sophie said, thanking the waitress.

Beautiful Brides was massive, with a huge reception area containing a white leather sofa and gold coffee table with a glass top on which a selection of magazines was laid out. 'Take a seat and one of our staff will be with you in a few minutes,' the elegant-looking woman behind the reception desk told them.

'Now this looks the business,' Kate said as they both sat down and picked up one of the magazines to flick through.

A few minutes later a young woman, dressed in a white tunic and black trousers, came forward to greet them, her face wreathed in a big smile. 'Afternoon, ladies. I'm Selina, your wedding assistant. Which of you is going to be the lucky bride?'

'Sophie is,' Kate pointed at Sophie.

Selina smiled again then took an iPad out of her pocket. 'Congratulations, Sophie. Could I ask you a few questions first, so I can get a feel for what you want?'

'Of course.' Sophie answered the queries, hesitating when Selina asked the date of the wedding. 'We're just about to book it. We're thinking of the end of July.'

'Next year?' the assistant asked.

Sophie shook her head. 'No, this year.'

'Goodness, then it will have to be something from our ready-to-wear collection.' Selina led them over to a section with racks of wedding dresses. Kate had never seen so many in her life and Sophie seemed agog at the choice. Surely Sophie would choose her dream dress here.

'Let me take your measurements and I'll tell you which ones we have in stock in your size,' the assistant said.

'Kate is going to be one of my bridesmaids so perhaps you could take her measurements too as we'll be looking at bridesmaids's dresses afterwards,' Sophie said.

'Of course, it will save time later,' Selina agreed.

Kate guessed it made sense, although Maddie would still have to have her measurements taken next week.

When Selina had taken their measurements and jotted them down in her iPad, she showed them several rails of dresses. 'You can choose anything from these. They are, of course, standard sizes, but we have a seamstress who can alter them to give you the perfect fit for a very reasonable cost.'

They browsed through rails of dresses, so many beautiful ones and in such a variety of designs, some of them elegant silk, others frothy, lacy affairs with lots of decoration and trimmings, fitted dresses of almost sheer lace, puffed-out dresses that looked like crinoline gowns. It was a bride's paradise. But Sophie shook her head.

'They're gorgeous but none of them are jumping out at me. Are they you?' she asked.

'Not really,' Kate told her, 'but you'd look fantastic in any of these.'

'Maybe you'll feel different if you try them on,' Selina suggested.

'Why don't you try some on too,' Sophie said to Kate. 'It'll be fun for both of us to. It'll be like we're models!'

Selina nodded. 'Feel free. Wedding dress shopping should be fun.'

Kate shrugged. 'OK.' She didn't mind if it made Sophie

happy. She wanted this to be a happy day for her. The day you chose your wedding dress should be one to remember.

And it was fun. They both had a giggle trying on the different dresses and parading them in front of each other.

'Actually, if you're looking for something a little more elegant and simple, I may have the perfect dress. It only came in yesterday,' Selina was saying to Sophie when Kate came out of the cubicle wearing another dress.

'Yes, please,' Sophie told her.

Selina came back a few minutes later carrying a garment bag. She unzipped it and held it up. Kate gasped. It was gorgeous, sleek, sophisticated, strapless, figure-hugging ivory satin, with an elegant train that spread out like a fan around her feet.

'That's stunning,' she said. 'You must try it on, Soph.'

Sophie nodded. 'I think that's the one.'

Sophie tried the dress on. She looked amazing.

'It's perfect, don't you think?' Kate asked her, her eyes fixed on the dress. It was exactly the dress she would choose. It shouldn't be her choice though, should it? It should be Sophie's choice. Was she talking her into getting the wrong dress? 'But maybe you'd prefer something a little fancier?'

Sophie shook her head. 'This is definitely the one.'

Kate was pleased that Sophie had finally found the dress she loved. She glanced at her watch. Almost five. 'And perfect timing. It's almost five so I need to get going. It's Steve's mum's birthday today and we're all going out for a meal.'

'That late! Thanks so much for coming with me, Kate. You've made it fun and have been so helpful. Are you still OK to shop for the bridesmaids' dresses next week?'

'Of course,' Kate told her. 'Do you mind if I dash off now

and leave you to put the deposit on the dress? My train goes soon.'

'No problem,' Sophie told her.

Kate gave her a hug and made her way to the train station. She hadn't really been looking forward to today, but it turned out a lot pleasanter than she had thought. And Sophie's dress was gorgeous. Exactly what she would have chosen herself. Well, I'll have to hope there's another one I like as much if Steve and I ever get married, she thought. Not that that would be anytime soon. They had both agreed that they weren't ready for such a big step yet.

Chapter Twenty-six

Sophie

When Kate had been in the cubicle trying on one of the dresses, Sophie had whispered to Selina that it was Kate who was actually the bride, and told her the real date of the wedding, which was why Selina had suggested the more elegant dress that Kate had loved.

'Thanks so much for your help,' Sophie said when Kate had hurried off to catch the train. 'You will remember to order the wedding dress to fit Kate's measurements, won't you?'

'I've made a note of it,' Selina assured her. 'How exciting that her partner is planning a surprise wedding.'

'It's so romantic. We'll be back next week for the bridesmaid's dresses,' Sophie said as she left a deposit on the dress, using the bank card Steve had given her, then set off for the train station too. She hadn't meant to be so long; she knew that Glenn would have been back from his bike ride ages ago and would be waiting for her. Although he had said there was no rush for her to get back.

It was almost six by the time she got home. 'Sorry I'm so late,' she said as she rushed in.

'That's OK. How did it go?' Glenn asked her.

'We've chosen a dress that's perfect for Kate. So just the bridesmaids' dresses to go,' Sophie told him. 'Have you booked the meal?'

'No, the Italian is never full. We'll be fine if we go about eight.'

The Italian. Where they went for their first date. 'Perfect. I'll go and get changed then we can have a drink beforehand,' she said, noting the black chinos and pale blue shirt he was wearing. He'd really made an effort, she thought.

'No rush. Fancy a glass of wine first? I'll book a taxi to drop us off and pick us up.'

'I'd love one,' Sophie said. 'Can you leave it in the bedroom for me while I have a shower?'

After a quick shower, and a spray of her best perfume, she quickly flicked through the clothes in her wardrobe, then selected a sleeveless lemon dress that fell in pleats from the waist, and a white jacket. She took a few sips from the glass of wine Glenn had left on the bedside cabinet as she dressed and refreshed her make up.

Glenn whistled as she came out of the bedroom. 'You look amazing,' he told her.

She felt her cheeks glow with pleasure at his praise. 'Thank you. So do you,' she added.

He held up the half empty bottle of wine. 'Shall we finish it off? We've got almost half-an hour before the taxi arrives.'

She nodded and held out her glass, sitting down on the sofa to share this glass with him. It was good to see Glenn in such an upbeat mood. She was really looking forward to this evening.

As Glenn had predicted, the restaurant wasn't very full yet, most people coming in later in the evening. And their favourite table, in the nook in the corner, was empty, Sophie noticed happily. It was lovely to be out together. It was such a shame Glenn couldn't come to the wedding, she thought again. She could imagine them sitting out on a warm Spanish evening, drinking sangria. Never mind, they would have a holiday together later in the year.

They ordered another bottle of wine then studied the menu.

'How hungry are you? Fancy sharing the starters?' Glenn asked. They often did that, as they found the main course so filling.

Sophie nodded. 'Calamari?'

'That's good for me. Then I'm going for carbonara.'

Sophie chose spinach and ricotta lasagne. The waiter took their order and Sophie slowly sipped her wine.

'This is nice. It's been a while since we went for a meal.'

'Yeah, and as I'm away at the chess tournament next week-end I thought it would be good to go out this weekend.'

Damn, she'd forgotten about the chess tournament. Glenn had asked her if she wanted to go with him. 'I'm sorry I can't come; we're going shopping for the bridesmaids' dresses.'

'It's OK. I wasn't expecting you to, I know you find it a bit boring.'

Was that a dig? Her eyes shot to his face at that remark. 'It's not that . . .'

'It's fine, Soph, honestly. I'm not having a pop.' He smiled at her and she relaxed. She was just edgy because she knew that Glenn was a bit fed up with the time she was spending on the wedding. It had been full-on this past week and there was still a lot to do – but she had to make sure she spent more time with Glenn. More evenings like this. She took another sip of wine, a warm glow of happiness flowing through her.

They chatted away easily. Sophie told Glenn about her week at work, and that Josh had loved the Buddha terrarium she had made for his mother.

'Have you thought any more about setting up on your own, making a business out of doing them, and other floral gifts?' he asked.

She hadn't. The week had been too hectic. 'Not really,' she admitted. 'It's an interesting idea though.'

'The thing is . . .' Glenn finished his carbonara, put his knife and fork down and sat back. 'You know that the company is expanding and opening an office up north?'

Sophie nodded as she finished the last of her meal. That was why Glenn had been so busy just lately.

'Well, I've been offered a promotion. A managerial position.'

'Hey, that's great. Congratulations,' she said. So, is this why he'd organised the meal out. To celebrate?

Glenn's eyes met hers across the table. 'It's in Leeds. They want me to start in two weeks,' he said.

Chapter Twenty-seven

Maddie

Maddie read all the messages in the wedding group chat that had come in last night and this morning. As she'd expected, Sophie's messages were a rundown of the wedding shopping trip yesterday. Josh had replied earlier this morning, given the thumbs up to the photo of the dress, promising not to breathe a word to Steve. Maddie messaged back, *Fab news both of you. We're rocking this, we've only known about the wedding for a week!* There was a non-group message from Sophie saying that she hoped Maddie could make the shopping trip on Saturday for the bridesmaids' dresses. Maddie groaned but replied that she'd definitely be there.

She got out of bed, padded barefoot over to the long mirror on her wall and studied herself: her purple hair messed up, her half-sleeve tattoos clearly visible with the orange vest PJ top she'd thrown on last night, just like they would be in a bridesmaid's dress, not to mention the stud in her nose and array of earrings adorning her ear lobes. She wasn't exactly bridesmaid material, was she? And she didn't want to be. Dressing up in a ridiculous frilly gown was the last thing she wanted to do. How the hell had she let herself be talked into this?

Because Kate is one of your very best friends, that's how.

Jax miaowed and rubbed himself against her bare legs – she always wore PJ shorts to bed no matter what the weather. Maddie bent down and scooped him up, cuddling him to her.

'Do you want cuddles or food?' she asked. Jax cosied up closer to her, resting his head on her shoulder. 'It looks like it's cuddles then,' she said, picking up her phone, walking over to the big armchair and sinking into it. Jax nestled down on her lap, ready to snooze. She'd let him nap while she checked her emails – a couple were work-related so she left them for tomorrow, but one was from the wedding planner in Gibraltar. She opened it up and skim-read it. Apparently she needed to scan over Steve and Kate's passports and full birth certificates. The long one with both parent's names on it, the wedding planner said. Maddie put her phone down and rubbed her forehead. She'd have to email Steve about that. Jax moved into a more comfortable position, obviously preparing to settle for the morning. Maddie stroked his head and he lifted his chin for her to tickle him in his favourite spot. She obliged for a few minutes then lifted him gently off her lap and put him down on the floor.

'Sorry, Jax, I've got places to be.' She had arranged to do another gig with Ezri and the band this afternoon as Suki was still unwell. It was only a couple of hours at a local club but as Ezri said, they couldn't afford to turn down work. And she was happy to help. She would probably always have a soft spot for Ezri. He'd been the closest she'd come to loving someone, but her feelings for him hadn't been enough to commit to a relationship, even if Ezri had asked her to. Which he hadn't.

Jax gave her a look then jumped back on the chair and settled down again. 'OK, I get the message. I have to get off, but you don't.' She grinned as the cat stared at her then slowly closed his eyes. She loved this little cat; he was so cute but undemanding and fitted perfectly into Maddie's hectic life. Someone to come home to and cuddle up with but who never expected her to change who she was or alter her plans for him. Not like a partner would.

The gig had gone on longer than she expected, and then they'd all gone for a pizza so it was evening by the time Maddie returned and there was an email from Steve, with her, Josh and Sophie tagged in, to say that he had been to see Kate's mum today, and spoken to her dad, and they were both delighted about the wedding and would be coming for the weekend. They had also both offered to help out financially and insisted on paying for their own flights and hotel rooms. There was also a message from Sophie, sent hours ago. **Need to talk to you urgently. Please message when you can chat, x.**

Maddie guessed it was more wedding stuff. She looked at the clock, ten past eight, she made herself a cup of caramel bubble tea and curled up in her armchair then messaged Sophie: **Home now. Shall I call?**

Jax, who had been sitting on the windowsill watching the world go by, jumped on to the chair beside her.

Her phone rang immediately. Sophie must have been waiting to hear from her.

Maddie listened in astonishment as Sophie blurted out that Glenn's company was expanding and he'd been offered a managerial job in Leeds. 'He wants us to relocate, the company is paying the bill and helping him find somewhere to live,' she

123

said. 'I don't know what to do. He's gone for a bike ride,' she added.

'What do you want to do?' Maddie asked her, although she was sure she knew the answer. Sophie loved Worcester; she'd lived there most of her life. She couldn't imagine her moving away.

'I want to stay here. I don't want to start again, looking for another job, making friends again.'

'Well, you don't need to decide now, do you? Let Glenn move by himself and come home weekends. Make sure he likes his new job and living in Leeds before you uproot yourself.'

'That makes sense. Thanks, Maddie, I knew you would come up with something.' Sophie sounded much happier now.

They chatted a little more, agreeing arrangements for meeting up on Saturday, then Sophie whispered, 'Glenn's back. I have to go.' She quickly ended the call.

Maddie tapped her chin with her phone, thinking about how upset Sophie had sounded when she had first called. She could understand her hesitating, to move away with Glenn was massive. Sophie and Glenn seemed to get on well but she didn't think Sophie should rush into leaving everything behind just because he'd been offered a new job. It was important that both of them were happy. She was glad that she wasn't in a relationship, there was so much you had to compromise.

Chapter Twenty-eight

Sophie

Maddie's right, I don't have to decide right now, Sophie thought. It was best for Glenn to go on ahead and make sure that he liked the job and living in Leeds before she gave up her job, and they let their flat go. She was so glad that she had phoned Maddie. She'd hardly slept last night after Glenn's bombshell about his job offer, and confession that he was seriously considering taking it.

'It's a great opportunity for me, Soph. And I feel ready for a change. I've lived in Worcester for five years now; it's time to move on,' he'd said.

She'd been so shocked she'd hardly been able to speak at first. She'd just stared at him, her eyes wide, her mouth open, trying to process his words.

'I know it's a bit of a surprise but it's not that terrible, is it?' he'd asked.

Finally she found her voice. 'So is this why you were talking about moving away, and me working from home? You really want to do this?'

'Yes, I do. I'd love to manage my own department. And Leeds is amazing, there'll be so much to do there.'

She'd stared at him, hardly believing what he was saying, wondering if she had every really known him. She had no idea Glenn wanted to live in Leeds, that he wanted to run his own department. He'd seemed happy in his job and had never talked about moving to somewhere busier before. What had happened to steady, reliable Glenn, who liked cycling and playing chess? Once she'd got over her shock, she'd promised him that she'd think about it before she gave him her answer, and had wrestled with the dilemma all night. She didn't want to leave Worcester, but she didn't want to hold Glenn back either. Now she had a solution. She put the kettle on and waited for Glenn, who'd gone straight for a shower after returning from his bike ride. Sophie guessed he'd gone for a cycle so he could think and that he would probably want to talk about the promotion again. His boss might want an answer when he went to work tomorrow.

'Want a coffee?' she asked when Glenn finally came in, rubbing his hair dry with a towel.

'Please.' He walked over to her, his hair standing on end where he'd rubbed it dry. 'Have you thought any more about the move? I know I took you by surprise last night, but now you've had time to think about it, can you see how great it could be? We could get a house, like you wanted …'

She made the coffees and handed a mug to him, walking over to the sofa and sitting down before replying. 'You're right, it was a shock. But I have thought about it and can see that you want to go. And I agree that it would be a good opportunity for you.'

His eyes lit up as he came to sit down beside her, putting his mug of coffee down on the table and facing her. 'So you'll move?'

'No, not yet.' She licked her lips as she tried to find the words. 'But I think you should take the job and move to Leeds. See how you like it.'

His eyes clouded over. 'Without you? Are you finishing with me?'

She shook her head. 'Of course not. But we need to be sensible here. Before I give up my job, and this flat, you should try it out. Make sure it's what you want. You can come home weekends; it's not that far to commute. And I can come to visit you too. If after a few months you're sure it's what you want then I can think about moving there too.'

He looked disappointed. 'I wanted us to both move, to look for a place to live and build up a new life together.'

She took a sip of her coffee before answering. 'It's a big decision. Don't you think it's sensible for you to go by yourself and try it out before I uproot myself?'

'So how long do you think it will take you to decide whether you want to live with me in Leeds?' He sounded hurt.

'I'm not sure. I'll come and visit you, see what I think of Leeds. And when you're sure you're settled, if I like it too I can apply for a job there.'

'What if you don't like it?' His eyes narrowed. 'I don't think you want to move, do you? You'd be happy for us to commute every weekend.'

'For a while, yes. We hardly see each other in the week anyway, we're so busy.'

'You're the busy one, planning this secret wedding for Kate. That's why I haven't had a chance to tell you about this before.

My boss asked me two weeks ago and wants my decision by the end of this week otherwise he's going to offer the position to someone else.'

Sophie felt awful as she recalled that Glenn had tried to talk to her a few times over the past couple of weeks and he was right, she had been distracted with planning Kate's wedding. Even so, this was important, he should have told her. 'I know I've been busy, but you still could have told me. What about when we went out for a meal and talked about moving to a house? You could have told me then.'

He looked awkward. 'I guess so. I wanted to be sure before I mentioned it to you. There was no point in upsetting you if I decided I didn't want the job.'

Anger rose in her. 'So you've had time to think about it, and decided it's what you want to do. But I haven't had time. You only told me last night and you want me to decide by Friday if I'm ready to uproot myself and jack in my job for you to take a position in Leeds that you might not be happy with?'

Glenn fiddled with his ear lobe. 'I guess put like that . . .'

'Exactly.' Sophie softened her tone. She didn't blame Glenn for wanting to take this chance and didn't want to fall out with him over it. She reached out and held his hand. 'So how about you try it out for a while? Come home weekends, then we'll talk about it again in a few months?'

He nodded. 'OK.' Then he stood up. 'I'm going into the bedroom to practise for my tournament on Saturday.'

He took his cup into the kitchen then went into the bedroom, closing the door behind him. Sophie sat on the sofa for a long time wondering if she had made the right decision. Should she say she would go with him?

Chapter Twenty-nine

Josh

The rest of the week passed quickly. Josh had a call from Sophie on Wednesday with the final figures for the members of Kate's family who were attending the wedding, and telling him that they were going shopping for bridesmaids' dresses on Saturday. 'You and Steve need to order your suits too,' she reminded him. 'Will you all be wearing the same?'

That was something Josh hadn't thought about. Not for the first time he wished that Steve and Kate were planning this wedding together. 'I don't know. I'll have to check with Steve,' he said. 'I think we could do with a woman's opinion too. Maybe you could come with us?' He doubted if Maddie would. He thought shopping for the bridesmaids' dresses would be more than enough for her.

'Sure. Let me know what day and I'll be there,' Sophie agreed.

They'd gone through the rest of the things they needed to sort out: wedding cake, flowers, wedding favours. 'Don't worry, Maddie and I are covering that, although we're going to need a bit of input from Steve,' Sophie had assured him. Josh was grateful to have them on board, although he had the feeling it would be Sophie who sorted most of it out, Maddie seemed too busy with her job and singing in the band. And it wasn't her thing, whereas he could see that Sophie was enjoying it.

'You'd make a good wedding planner,' he said. 'Maybe you should think about a change of career.'

She grinned at him. 'You must be kidding. I'm doing this for Kate but I never want to plan another wedding again unless it's my own. And that's not going to be anytime soon,' she added.

Steve popped into the garage with an update just as Josh was finishing up on Friday. 'Right, it's all sorted. The legal service in the register office in Gibraltar is at quarter past eleven, and the ceremony on the hotel beach is at two p.m., so that gives us plenty of time to get from there over to Estepona. The reception is in the hotel restaurant.' He took out his phone and showed Josh a photo of a wedding ceremony taking place on the beach, two lines of guests sitting in covered chairs, decorated with bows, the bride and groom saying their vows facing the sea. 'Kate will love it.'

'It looks great,' Josh told him. 'The girls are going to choose their bridesmaid's dresses tomorrow so we need to go and get our suits. Then there's the cake and flowers. Sophie said she and Maddie will sort it but she needs to know if you have any preferred choices?'

Steve rubbed his forehead with the palm of his hand. 'I didn't realise that there was so much to think about. The events co-ordinator at the hotel keeps asking me questions about the reception. She wants to know if any of the guests have food allergies or special dietary requests. Can you deal with her if I let her know that I've given you permission to make decisions on my behalf? It's a bit tricky for me. Kate and I are hardly seeing anything of each other as it is, I'm so busy with all this wedding stuff. She's started asking a few awkward questions.'

'That's what happens when you decide to plan a secret wedding in less than three months,' Josh told him. 'We're all snowed under with it, Steve. I'm already trying to organise the drive to and from Gibraltar and have reserved us into hotels over there, Maddie is dealing with legalities and the wedding planner there, Sophie is sorting out the dresses, flowers, shoes, etc. When you said you were planning a secret wedding as a surprise for Kate I didn't realise you wanted us to organise it all for you.'

Steve looked hurt. 'I know you're all doing a lot, and I am trying to sort things out too, but I don't see how I can keep it all from Kate. What if she uses my laptop when I'm out and sees the emails from the hotel? I didn't realise how much would be involved in the planning.'

'You and me both,' Josh said. 'OK, I'll try to sort out the wedding reception but I'll need your input. I don't want to be responsible for all the decisions and then get the blame if Kate doesn't like what we've chosen.'

'Of course, but don't text or phone me about it, Kate will get suspicious.'

'So what do you suggest – mind-reading?'

Steve shot him a look that told him he didn't appreciate the sarcasm of that reply. 'We'll use a code. If you message saying you want to talk to me about the parents then I'll know you need to talk about the wedding,' he said.

'Won't Kate wonder why we're talking so much about the folk?'

Steve shot him another look. 'I'll come up with something. I'll say they're thinking of down sizing.'

'This is getting more and more complicated.'

Steve loosened his collar as if he was struggling to breathe. 'I know, I'm stressed about it too, but it's going to be great,' he said.

'I hope so,' Josh said heartfully. He managed to stop himself from adding, 'I just hope Kate likes the idea and doesn't turn you down.' He couldn't go there, not even in his thoughts. It would be a major disaster.

Steve looked a bit guilty. 'I do appreciate all of your help; I'll forward the email from the hotel wedding co-ordinator on to you and let her know that I've asked you and Sophie to deal with it on my behalf.'

Things were getting far too complicated for his liking, Josh thought when Steve had left. The sooner they sorted this wedding out the better, he wanted his life back.

He picked up his phone and opened the email that Steve had forwarded to him before he left, groaning as he read the list of questions. Were there any special dietary requirements, such as any of the guests being vegetarian, celiac or allergic to anything? There was a list of buffet food for him to choose from, with a couple of vegetarian options. What colour scheme did they want for the room, did they want chair covers and bows? Table runners? Did they want the room for an evening reception? He couldn't answer this alone. He sent a text to Sophie asking if she would mind helping him sort out the wedding reception. Perhaps she could find out the food requirements for Kate's family whilst he did the Hendersons. **Perhaps we could**

meet for lunch in the week, he suggested. His garage wasn't far from Pat's Posies.

Half an hour later a text pinged back. **How about Wednesday? One o'clock at Sandwiches and Shakes?**

He knew it. It was in the same precinct as the florist.

He sent back a thumbs up.

Chapter Thirty

Kate

Kate met Sophie and Maddie outside Beautiful Brides on Saturday morning and they were greeted by Selina as soon as they walked in.

'I've cleared a couple of hours to help you choose your bridesmaids' dresses,' she said with a smile. 'I've put aside a selection that you might like.' She led them over to the private area where they'd tried on the wedding dresses the previous weekend. Hanging up there were a selection of bridesmaids' dresses. 'Take your time looking through. If you don't like any of them I can bring you another selection,' Selina told them.

Sophie headed straight for the rail. 'What do you think of this one?'

Kate looked at the dress Sophie was holding up. It was pretty – champagne coloured, floor length, with a V-neck and fitted bodice. She was surprised at Sophie choosing it though, she usually loved pastel colours, pinks, lemon, pale blue. But then her wedding dress had been understated too.

'What, you're not having pink?' she asked in surprise.

'No, I told you, I'm not doing girly and frothy, I'm going for the elegant, sophisticated look.'

'I like it.' Maddie took the dress off Sophie and held it in front of her in the mirror.

It did look sophisticated, thought Kate. And the colour didn't clash with Maddie's hair, which was a bonus. Kate reached out and fingered the material, which was soft and silky. 'I like it too. Let's not make a rush decision though, let's take a look at the others.'

Selina had chosen a varied selection of styles and colours. Kate looked through them and pulled out a beautiful gold dress. 'How about this? Or this?' She seized a floaty peach dress with a fitted bodice and a long flowing skirt.

Both dresses were much more Sophie's style than the champagne one, elegant as it was, Kate thought.

Sophie shook her head. 'They're a bit too fussy.'

'How about this one?' Maddie seized a strappy lavender dress with a fitted bodice and a sexy slit up the side. It was definitely Kate's style, she thought.

'Ohh, it's gorgeous! I do love lavender! Hold it in front of you, Maddie,' Kate urged.

So Maddie did.

Kate nodded. 'It suits you. What do you think, Sophie? And it's a lovely pastel shade of lavender. You know you like pastel shades.'

'I'm not sure.' Sophie frowned as she considered if the lilac would clash with Maddie's purple hair.

'Why don't me and Maddie try them on?' Kate suggested. 'You could have lavender ties for the men. It would look very summery.'

When Kate and Maddie stepped out of the fitting rooms Sophie gasped. They both looked stunning. The dress really worked with Maddie's purple hair, even the tattoos on her arms looked artistic.

'I love them,' she said. 'Do you two?'

'As much as I could ever love a dress,' Maddie said with a grin.

'They're gorgeous – they suit the wedding dress so well, sophisticated, elegant and pretty without lots of lace and flounce,' Kate told her. 'If I was getting married I might even pick them myself.'

Sophie smiled. 'You're right. Let's take them.'

Selina smiled too. 'A perfect choice.' She took the tape measure from around her neck. 'Now, I took your measurements last time, Kate, so let me take Maddie's, then I can order the dresses. We'll let you know when they're in and you can come back and check for final alterations.'

When they'd been measured and the bridesmaids' dresses ordered they stopped for some lunch, then went shopping for shoes. Kate was surprised how much Sophie seemed to value her opinion; almost as if she thought that Kate was more sophisticated than her. It was quite touching.

'When's Glenn going shopping for his suit?' she asked.

'Next week, I think, one of his mates from work is going with him,' Sophie fibbed. It was only a small fib, she thought, as the real groom – Steve – was going to choose his suit next week.

'And how are the rest of the plans coming on? Do you have your venue and do you know how many are coming yet?' Kate asked.

'It's a secret venue,' Sophie said. 'We're just asking everyone to arrive at Maddie's on the day, and we've got cars organised to take everyone there. It's going to be fantastic.'

'Well, I'm really intrigued. I've never been to a mystery wedding before.' Kate shoved her phone into her bag. 'Right, I must go, my train leaves in ten minutes. See you both soon. And message if you need help with anything, Sophie!'

'Thanks. I will,' Sophie replied.

Kate legged it to the platform just in time, and luckily there was an empty seat on the train. She sank into it, feeling weary. Shopping was exhausting. After her big lunch she didn't feel like eating much. She just wanted to go home, collapse on the sofa and watch TV. A message pinged in from Steve saying he was going to be late back as he had to meet a client. She let out a sigh of relief. Now she'd have the flat to herself for a bit and could veg out. Then it flitted across her mind that this was the third time in the last fortnight Steve had been out meeting a client, and he never usually met clients on a Saturday evening. There had been a few emails pinging in too, and he'd been very preoccupied.

An unsettled feeling nested in the pit of her stomach. She pushed it away. She could absolutely trust Steve. She knew she could. He would never ever cheat on her. Would he?

Chapter Thirty-one

Sophie

Maddie phoned early the next morning. 'Are you OK to talk?' she asked.

'Sure,' Sophie told her. Glenn was still asleep. He'd got back late from the chess tournament yesterday so she'd left him to lie in. Things were a little awkward between them at the moment. Glenn had told his boss that he was accepting the position in Leeds and was peeved that Sophie wasn't going with him. Whilst Sophie was upset that it was all happening so quickly but determined not to stand in his way.

'I'm all yours,' Sophie curled up into the big armchair, folding her legs underneath her. 'What's the problem?'

'I've booked myself a twin room at the hotel and was wondering, now that Glenn is going to move to Leeds, couldn't you come to Spain for a bit longer? We can share the room. I've got the two weeks off and it would be great if you could come too. We can have a girlie holiday. And I'm going to look up my aunt Valeria, my dad's sister. She lives in Andalucia. You could come with me, if you want. Give me a bit of support.'

Sophie knew that Maddie's father was Spanish and that her

parents had met when her mother was on holiday over there, and they'd often spent holidays with an aunt in Spain when Maddie was young. They must have been close for Maddie to want to look her up. Sophie would have liked to support her friend, but she didn't want to miss seeing Glenn for two weekends. Maybe she could go for a week, though. It would be good to have a break away and Pat had said her daughter could probably cover for her.

'I'll see if Pat can spare me for a week,' she said. 'It'd be nice for you to see your aunt again.'

'She lives near Estepona. I haven't seen her, or my cousins, since my parents split up but it would be good to look them up again. I'm going to ask Mum for Aunt Valeria's address when I phone her to wish her Happy Mother's Day later.'

'I'm going to phone my mum later too,' Sophie said. She'd already organised a bunch of flowers to be delivered to her in Portugal. 'I'll talk to Pat tomorrow and get back to you,' she said.

'Brilliant. Speak to you tomorrow then.'

Sophie had just finished her call when a message pinged in to the wedding chat group.

It was from Josh. The hotel had been in touch about colours for chair tie-backs and table runners. Could they think about it then he and Sophie could discuss it on Wednesday? He was off for a Mother's Day lunch with his parents now.

She sent a thumbs up. Glenn was still asleep so she made herself a cup of coffee, then switched on her laptop, logged into Pinterest and started looking at chair tie-backs and table runners. There were lots of lovely ones to choose from, in various shades of lilac and purple. She liked the chiffon ones best. She added some to the board so they could discuss them on Wednesday then turned to wedding cakes. Would Kate want a traditional three-tier fruit or a sponge one, or the more modern cupcake? And would she want white icing or coloured? Or even a Spanish theme? She'd have to discuss it with Josh on Wednesday. She added a couple of images to the board.

She looked over her shoulder as she heard Glenn come in. One glance at his sulky face told her that he was still narked. 'Working on that secret wedding stuff again?' he said, resentment heavy in his voice. 'Are you going to be on it all day?'

'No, I'm finished now. I was just going to phone my mum to wish her Happy Mother's Day then I thought we could go out for the day – if you fancy it?' She felt a bit guilty then, mentioning phoning her mum. Glenn didn't have much to do with his family, his mum had died some years ago and his father had remarried. He hadn't seen his father or elder sister for years.

'I'd like that,' Glenn said. 'I'm going for a bike ride; I won't be long.' He grabbed a bottle of water out of the fridge, kissed Sophie on the cheek and went out.

They'd have lunch somewhere, spend a bit of time together. They only had two weeks before Glenn moved away to Leeds. She was going to miss him.

Her mum sounded delighted to hear from her. 'Thank you so much for the flowers, they're beautiful. I've got them in my best vase. We're going over to Craig and Lori's for lunch. The weather is gorgeous today.'

'Have a good time, and say hi to Craig and Lori from me. I'll try to come and visit you all soon,' Sophie promised.

'Oh, that would be lovely if you could,' her mother replied.

They chatted for a while, exchanging news, then her mother

said she had to go. She did miss her family, but it was good to know they were all so happy in Portugal, Sophie thought. Maybe she could persuade Glenn to go and visit them in September, even if it was only for a long weekend, rather than wait until Christmas.

She went upstairs and had a shower then had breakfast. She was ready to go out when Glenn came home.

'Want to go for that drive out now?' she asked. 'We could have lunch at a country pub.'

He nodded. 'Sounds great. I'll have a quick shower; I won't be long.'

'Take your time,' Sophie told him.

They'd just got into the car when a message pinged through to her phone. Glenn looked at her. 'I guess you need to answer that?'

'Nope. It can wait until later,' she told him. It was probably wedding stuff, but she was going to forget about that for today. She wanted to spend some time with Glenn.

Glenn turned the radio on and they both sang away to the music. Sophie felt her spirits lift. It was going to be OK. She and Glenn could sort this out. 'Come on, let's grab a drink and lunch. I'm starving. You have a beer and I'll drive back,' she said when they pulled up in the pub car park.

She was more than happy to have a soft drink and let Glenn enjoy a couple of beers. She wanted to make the most of the next couple of weeks.

'I'll miss you,' she said softly.

'You could always come with me,' he said.

She ran her finger around the rim of her glass. 'We've been through this. I really think it's best if you make sure it's what you want first.' She summoned up a smile. 'Besides, you'll probably be busy at first, settling in. And when you come home for the weekend we can spend real quality time together. Go out for meals like this.'

'If you're not too tied up with the wedding planning.'

'I won't be. It's nearly sorted now.' She leant forward and placed her hand on his. 'We can make it work, Glenn.'

He nodded. 'I hope so.'

After lunch, and another drink, they went for a walk along the riverbank, holding hands and walking along in companionable silence.

I'm so glad we had this afternoon out together, we seem to have cleared the air, Sophie thought happily. She hated it when things were awkward between them. She didn't like any kind of conflict in her life. Maddie told her that she was a pushover because she went out of her way to appease people, but Sophie found arguments stressful. Something had to be really important to her for her to argue over it. She didn't want to argue over Glenn taking this job, but she didn't want to be rushed into packing up and moving with him either. It was a big step. She needed time to think about it.

Chapter Thirty-two

Maddie

Maddie had phoned her mother that morning but there was no reply; she guessed that her mother and stepdad, Dylan, had gone for a walk as they often did on a Sunday morning, and the mobile reception wasn't good in the area of Wales where they lived. Maddie had left a Happy Mother's Day message on the landline answerphone too. She'd arranged earlier in the week for a hamper of her mother's favourite treats to be delivered. Hopefully it had arrived, although she'd had no thank you message yet.

She made herself a smoothie and settled down to drink it, Jax on her lap, her mind drifting back to the last time she had seen her aunt Valeria and uncle Juan. It had been years; she'd probably been about fourteen. They'd spent every summer in Spain when she was young, before her father had started drinking so heavily. Tía Valeria and Tío Juan – she had always called them by the Spanish for uncle and aunt – had lived in a spacious town house in one of the picture-postcard white villages that dotted the Spanish mountains. The house had looked small from the outside but when you went inside you were greeted by huge rooms – well, they had seemed huge to Maddie – furnished with dark, polished furniture. There was a balcony where they had sat to watch the Santa Semana (Holy Week) processions at Easter, and a roof terrace.

Her mobile rang, she glanced at the screen, saw it was her mother and swiped to answer.

'Maddie. How lovely to hear from you.' Her mother did genuinely sound pleased. Maddie felt a pang of regret that they didn't speak so often since her mother had moved to Wales, but it was good to hear that Mum was happier now. 'Thank you so much for the beautiful gift hamper you sent me. It arrived yesterday. I thought you would phone today so waited until then to thank you.'

'You're welcome, Mum. I'm glad you like it. How are you?'

'I'm fine, love. Well. Really well. And you?'

'I'm good.'

'Why don't you come over one weekend? We'd love to see you. I was only saying to Dylan the other day that it's been ages since we saw you. You're always so busy working.'

'I will soon, Mum.' Maddie liked Dylan. He was a well-built man, 'cuddly' her mother called him, kind with a loud laugh. He made her mum happy, which was the most important thing, and always made Maddie welcome when she did find time to visit. 'I was wondering – some friends of mine are getting married in June, over in Estepona, Spain . . . Isn't that near where Aunt Valeria and Uncle Juan live?'

'She lived in a little village just outside Estepona. I've no idea if she still lives there though. We lost touch when your dad and I split up.'

'You don't remember her address, do you?' Maddie asked. 'I

x

144

thought maybe I could visit her when I was over in Spain. It would be nice to see her and my cousins again.'

She could almost hear the cogs in her mother's brain working overtime. 'I don't. I'm sorry. It's been ages since we went there. But the village was just before Casares.'

'It's OK, Luis, Miguel and Eliana might be on Facebook, it shouldn't be difficult to find them,' Maddie said. She didn't use Facebook much, preferring Instagram and Twitter as social media platforms, and WhatsApp to message, but she did have a little-used Facebook page. It had been a bit of a long shot, expecting her mum to remember the address of her dad's older sister. Both her grandparents were dead, they only had the two children, Valeria and Thiago, Maddie's father (who everyone called Theo), and she couldn't think of anyone else to ask.

'I'm trying to think who would know ...'

'It doesn't matter. It's only an idea. I might not even go.'

'No, really, she would love to see you. And it would be nice for you to connect with the Spanish side of the family and see your cousins.'

At the thought of her cousins Maddie was whisked back to hot, Spanish summers when they had all played outside the street cafés while their parents sat drinking vino and *cerveza*.

Only her father always drank too much, always caused a scene.

'I remember that it was a mountain village and that your aunt worked in the bakery.'

'Thanks, Mum. I'll see if I can contact Luis, Miguel or Eliana on Facebook.'

After a bit more general conversation, and promising to visit soon, Maddie said goodbye. Her mum seemed to think it was a good idea if she contacted Aunt Valeria. Should she? Maddie

145

closed her eyes and an image of the familiar white houses scattered over the mountain top appeared in her mind. She remembered how excited she had been when she'd looked up at them. She remembered her father driving through the steep narrow streets and her mother telling him to slow down, warning him of the steep bends.

So many memories flooded her mind. The smell of the thick, dark coffee her uncle loved so much, of the paella her aunt cooked in the huge pan – enough to feed them all – the small, barred windows keeping the house cool against the relentless sun, the trips down the hill to the beach, or up the hill to the castle ruins. The laughter, the sun, the food. They had had some good times. She had got caught up in her parents' divorce and lost contact, and maybe Aunt Valeria and her cousins hadn't looked her up because they were upset about the divorce too. Would they be pleased to see her or should she let sleeping dogs lie?

Chapter Thirty-three

Josh

Josh arrived at Sandwiches and Shakes at quarter to one on Wednesday, claiming an empty table by the window and nursing a black coffee while he waited for Sophie to come in. It felt strangely intimate for just the two of them to be meeting, but Maddie was so busy with work and Steve so hopeless that it seemed to have been left to him and Sophie to sort out the entire wedding. He glanced up as the café door opened and Sophie walked in, her blond curls peeping out of the hood of the familiar cream parka. It was drizzling outside. He saw her glance around then smile and wave when her eyes rested on him. She unzipped her coat to reveal a pale lemon fluffy jumper over black leggings that were tucked into knee-high black boots. She looked gorgeous, he thought.

'Sorry I'm a bit late.' Sophie pulled out the chair next to Josh, wriggled out of her coat, hung it over the back and then sat down. 'It's so busy in the shop this week.'

A waft of perfume drifted over to him — soft, sweet and sensual.

'I bet you could do without having to meet me and help arrange my brother's wedding. I apologise for taking up so much of your time,' Josh told her.

'No worries, we're almost done now.' Sophie looked up as the waiter came over to the table.

'What can I get you?' he asked.

'I'll have a mocha, please.' She glanced at Josh. 'Are you eating?'

'Yep, I'm starving.' He had already scanned the QR code on the table to check the menu while he'd been waiting for Sophie. 'I'll have a ploughman's lunch, please,' he told the waiter.

'Could I have a tuna salad with wheatmeal bread?' Sophie asked. Obviously she'd eaten here before and didn't need to check the menu.

'Sure.' The waiter wrote down their orders and walked off to the next table.

'The Pinterest boards are a great idea. Kate messaged me to say she liked the lilac chiffon bows and table runners. And the three-layered wedding cake with the lilac ribbon – which is what I'd have chosen for her.' Maddie had liked the layers of white and lilac cupcakes best but Sophie was sure Kate would prefer a more traditional one. She was so pleased that she'd thought to create a wedding board and shared it with Kate and Maddie.

'I thought she might go for that one too. I liked your idea of a Spanish theme, so how about we go for this . . .' Josh opened the link on his phone and zoomed in on a three-tier white-iced wedding cake decorated with purple bougainvillea.

'That's gorgeous. Ana, the hotel events co-ordinator, said they can organise the wedding cake to be made if we want so I'll send her that photo.'

'Good idea,' Josh agreed. 'It would be a bit of a nightmare to have one made over here and try and get it over to Spain.'

The waiter came with their lunch now, so they tucked in, whilst looking at images of chair covers, sashes and table runners. Josh had discussed it with Steve and he'd wanted them to keep to the colour scheme of the wedding. 'I think it might be nice to go for the darker purple, like the bougainvillea flowers, rather than the lavender. What do you think?' Sophie asked, leaning over to show him a few images. 'I think Kate would prefer the organza to the taffeta.'

Josh looked at the images on her phone screen. She was right, the organza bows were softer, more delicate. Then she swiped the screen to show him the embroidered table runners in the same shade. He nodded. 'Perfect.'

'Now all that's left are the wedding favours, I think.' A look of alarm suddenly crossed her face. 'What about the rings?'

'Steve's ordered them. A matching pair apparently.'

'Great. So, wedding favours. Do you have any ideas?'

'I'm not actually sure what they are ...'

'Small gifts from the bride and groom to the guests. They don't have to be expensive. A tiny basket of almonds or chocolates, personalised coasters – something to remind guests of the day.'

'How about a Spanish-themed coaster, then, with the date of the wedding?' he suggested.

'Great idea,' she said enthusiastically. 'I'll ask Ana if she can arrange it. She knows lots of local tradesmen.' She put her phone down. 'Has Steve given you any ideas about the reception?'

'Apparently Ana is organising a group to entertain the guests.'

'Then I think we're actually almost there,' Sophie said. 'You two need to get your suits and we need to book our flights to Gibraltar and return flights from Malaga, but that's it.'

'We're going for our suits this Saturday. Do you think you or Maddie could meet us there? It would be good to have your feedback.'

'I'm sorry, but I can't. It's our last weekend before Glenn moves to Leeds.' She briefly told Josh about his company expanding and Glenn being offered a managerial position in the new office. 'Actually, weekends are going to be awkward for a while as that's when Glenn will be coming home. Can you ask Maddie if she can make it?'

'OK. Will do.' Josh looked at her, a little concerned. 'Is it congratulations or commiserations that he's working away?'

Sophie considered this for a moment. 'I'm not sure. Let's see how it pans out.' She stood up and grabbed her coat off the back of the chair. 'I'll have to go now; we really are rushed off our feet.'

'Thanks for all your help with my brother's secret wedding,' Josh told her.

She flashed him a smile that lit up her eyes. 'You're welcome.'

Chapter Thirty-four

Sophie

Sophie spoke to Maddie later and she reluctantly agreed to go suit shopping with Steve and Josh, mumbling that they were grown men and she didn't know why they couldn't choose a suit without her input. 'Did you remember to ask Pat about taking more time off for the wedding?' she asked when they'd finished discussing the suit shopping trip.

Sophie had forgotten, her mind had been occupied with Glenn's forthcoming move to Leeds. 'Not yet. I'll ask her tomorrow,' she promised.

Pat was in and out on Thursday so Sophie didn't get a chance to speak to her until Friday.

'I was wondering if it would be all right for me to take a week off for the wedding in June,' she asked. 'Will your daughter be able to cover?'

'Oh yes, I've been meaning to talk to you,' Pat said. 'Zania is more than happy to work in the shop so you can take the two weeks off if you want.' She narrowed her eyes and looked at Sophie. 'You look tired. It's all this with your chap going away to work, isn't it? Look, take the rest of the day off; you've done two early-morning shifts this week.'

Sophie was tired. She'd hardly slept all week, fretting about Glenn's upcoming move to Leeds. 'Thanks,' she said gratefully.

She stopped off at the supermarket on the way home. She was planning to make a special meal for tonight: they'd open some wine, make some plans for future weekends. Lots of people made long-distance relationships work, she reminded herself.

She was surprised to see Glenn come out of the bedroom looking rather solemn, when she walked in. 'Sophie, I didn't expect you to be home yet.'

'I didn't expect you to be home either,' she said, surprised and a little worried. 'Are you OK? You're not ill, are you?'

'No. I've been given the afternoon off,' he told her. He looked serious. 'There's been a change of plan. There's an emergency at the office in Leeds and they need me there on Monday to sort it out.' His eyes met hers. 'I need to leave tomorrow morning, Sophie. They've booked me into a hotel while they sort out permanent accommodation for me.'

Her heart thudded. This was it. She had thought they had one more week together. Had been planning on making it really special. She took a deep breath to compose herself. It wasn't the end of the world. They had it all sorted. Glenn was coming home weekends. They could make it work.

'That soon?' She wriggled out of her jacket. 'Pat let me leave work early so I've got some shopping to make us a nice meal. We'll make this a special evening,' she said, walking over to him, wrapping her arms around him and giving him a kiss. 'Let me just put this food in the fridge and I'll make us a coffee.'

When she went back into the lounge with the two mugs of

coffee, Glenn was sitting in the armchair. She frowned as she put the mugs on the coffee table. They usually sat on the sofa, next to each other. It was almost as if he was putting distance between them. Was he that upset that she hadn't said she'd move with him? Thank goodness she hadn't agreed to go wedding suit shopping tomorrow with Josh and Steve, she could at least go with Glenn and stay at the hotel with him, see where he was working. She'd come back on the train on Sunday.

She sat down on the sofa and told him her idea but he shook his head. 'I've been thinking about this all week, Sophie, and it's not going to work with me living in Leeds and you living here.'

'Of course it will, lots of people have long-distance relationships.'

'Well, I don't want one. I think we've come to the end of the road, Sophie. Our relationship has run its course.'

She stared at him, uncomprehendingly. Was he dumping her just because she wouldn't drop everything and go to Leeds with him?

He stood up. 'I'm sorry, but I think it's best for us to have a clean break. You can have the flat. I've been to the estate agent and taken my name off the contract.'

'What?' She got to her feet too, the coffee table acting as a barrier between them. 'You mean that you're dumping me?'

Glenn shuffled his feet, dropped his eyes and she knew that this was for real. 'It's for the best, Sophie. We both want different things.'

'Different things?' She couldn't stop repeating his words, she was so shocked. 'What different things? I thought we were happy together. What do I want that you don't?'

'You want to get married, buy a house, have a family. And,

153

well, I don't.' He raised his eyes again, guilt and defiance both mixed up in them. 'I didn't even realise you felt like that until you started doing this perishing wedding planning. Then you went all gooey-eyed over the stupid secret wedding and I can see that you'd like that too. So I think this new job has come at the right time. We both need a fresh start.'

Her legs felt weak underneath her and she sat down, fearing she would collapse. She really hadn't expected this.

His eyes held hers. 'Tell me honestly, Sophie, are you hoping that we'll get married? That I'll ask you to marry me?'

'At some point, yes. I mean, that's not unexpected, is it? We've been living together for a year; it's what couples do.'

'It's not what I want to do. I don't ever want to get married. And I don't want to be tied to a mortgage, or a family. So this is the best way forward for both of us. I'll move to Leeds; you can keep the flat.'

Her eyes welled up and she blinked back tears. 'I thought you loved me. You said you loved me.'

'I do, in a way, but all this talk of weddings has made me realise that we've grown apart and have different long-term dreams. I'm sorry, Sophie, but while you're with me it's robbing you of the chance of meeting someone else who really loves you. You're wonderful, you'll soon get snapped up.'

'Snapped up! I don't want to be snapped up. I'm happy how I am, with you. We don't have to get married. It's not compulsory.'

Glenn shook his head. 'We should have had this conversation before. I'm sorry, really I am, but I'm leaving.' He walked out and returned a few minutes later with a couple of suitcases.

Sophie stared at them. 'You're already packed?'

'I did it earlier. I was going to leave you a note – I wanted to

154

avoid this sort of scene but you came home early. I was going to phone you later and explain,' he added hastily.

She wanted to beg him not to go, to tell him that they would sort it out, but she stopped herself. He was right, it wouldn't work out between them, because if he could leave so callously, even planning on just leaving her a note, then he wasn't the man she thought he was.

She raised her head, swallowed the lump in her throat. 'If that's how you feel then you're right, we are better off ending it. I hope you're happy in Leeds.' She went over to the door and opened it. 'Bye, Glenn.'

'I really am sorry, Sophie, but it's for the best,' he said as he picked up his cases and walked over to the door.

Was that pity in his eyes? She didn't want his bloody pity. She tilted her chin higher. 'You bet it is.'

'Bye, Sophie.' He nodded then walked out of the door.

She waited until she had slammed it shut before she burst into tears.

Chapter Thirty-five

Josh

Sophie looked upset, Josh realised as he sat down at the table to join her and Maddie on Saturday lunchtime, in the same café they'd met up in that first week. And the smile she had plastered on her face didn't distract from the dark shadows under her eyes as much as she probably hoped. Her face was a little pinched too, as if she'd been crying. She'd said that she was spending this weekend with her boyfriend and he was working away from next week. He'd been surprised when he'd seen her message in the wedding chat group that she'd be joining them after all. Had they had a row? Best not to mention it, he decided. If she was trying to put a brave face on things it wasn't fair to draw attention to it or ask her what the matter was. It was none of his business and they didn't know each other well enough for him to pry.

'Hello again.' He looked from one woman to the other. 'How are you both doing?'

'A bit hung-over,' Maddie confessed. 'I had a late one last night.'

He flitted his gaze over her. She was dressed in a bright green jacket today which should have clashed horribly with her purple hair but instead only made her look edgy. The rainbow glasses had gone and instead emerald green eyes stared at him, so bright it was a bit unnerving. Coloured contacts, he realised.

'Singing with the band again?' he asked.

'Yes, the lead singer has had a sore throat and still hasn't recovered enough to sing.' She took a gulp out of the smoothie in front of her. 'Did you enjoy the gig the other week?'

He nodded. 'Yes, it was a great night. You're a good singer.'

'That's what I keep telling her,' Sophie cut in. 'She should join the band. Ezri is always asking her.'

Josh raised an eyebrow. 'Not your scene?'

Maddie shook her head. 'No, too much pressure. I don't mind getting up and joining in now and again, but I don't want to have to do it. That way it stops being fun.'

'I know what you mean,' Josh agreed.

'Ezri and the band are playing again tonight; why don't you come along too, Sophie? Don't stop at home moping over Glenn. Get out and enjoy yourself. You can stop over at mine. It'll be a laugh.'

So his guess was right then, they had had a row.

'Maybe another week. I've got a lot to do this weekend,' Sophie said.

The waiter came over then and they all ordered coffee, apart from Maddie who had her usual bubble tea. Josh ordered an Americano for Steve too. He'd already texted to say he was running late but was on his way.

Maddie turned to face Josh. 'Have you managed to sort out everything on the Gibraltar side?'

'It's all in the hands of the wedding planner. There are forms Steve and Kate need to sign but Steve's dealing with that.'

'Sophie's coming for the two weeks now, so we're booking return flights from Malaga,' Maddie said. 'How about you, Josh?'

'I've got a customer who's moving to Malaga in a couple of months and wants his Range Rover taken over, so I'm going to drive it over, hire a car for the holiday and fly back. I'll take the bridesmaids' dresses and suits with me to make sure they don't get creased. I'll check out the wedding venue, and meet up with the wedding planner in Gibraltar too. I don't want anything going wrong.'

'Are you sure? It's a long drive so it'll mean more time off work for you,' Maddie told him.

'It's no problem. I'm my own boss, I'll close the garage for a couple of weeks. My other customers will wait, and I'm being paid a good fee for me to drive his car over.'

'It's still a lot of money to lose. Can't you get someone in to run it for you?' Sophie asked.

'Not really. I specialise in motorbike repairs and restorations. I can clear the repairs before I go, there's no rush to do the restorations.' He didn't add that the money wasn't really a problem for him, he lived simply, always had, and his bank balance was quite healthy.

Just then Steve came in. He hurried over to the table. 'Sorry, I couldn't get away. Kate was trying to persuade me to go out for the day,' he said, pulling a chair out and sitting next to Josh.

'Thanks for coming today, and for all the help with the wedding,' he said earnestly. 'I do appreciate it.'

'I hope you do. This is the third Saturday Sophie has given up for you,' Josh told him.

'I know – thanks, Sophie. Actually, I'm surprised to see you here, I thought you couldn't make it,' he added.

Sophie was silent, as if she was struggling to speak.

'Is everything all right, Soph?' Steve asked gently.

She shook her head, swallowed, then raised her eyes to meet his. 'Glenn and I have split up. He's taken a new job in Leeds and thinks it's better if we have a clean break. He moved out yesterday.'

Shit! The rat. Josh was angry on Sophie's behalf. She had obviously not been expecting it.

Maddie squeezed Sophie's hand. 'You're better off without him.'

Sophie nodded. 'I know. It was just a bit of a shock. He'd said he was coming home at weekends.' She raised hurt eyes to Steve. 'Please don't tell Kate, we need her to think our wedding is on for a bit longer. There are still things to sort out.'

Steve nodded sympathetically. 'I'm so sorry, though. If you're not up to arranging any more wedding stuff I'll understand. It must be tough for you.'

'I'm OK. It was such a shock, but I want to help. It'll keep me busy if nothing else.'

'If you're sure,' Steve said. 'Now, how are we getting on about sorting the hotel rooms? Can you all stay for the two nights in Gibraltar?'

They all nodded. 'That's great. I've booked me and Kate into the yacht hotel on the marina, but I think it's best if you three don't stay there in case you bump into us before I propose and Kate guesses something is up.'

'Good thinking. I'll book us rooms in a hotel in the town,' Josh said. 'Are you girls OK to share a twin or do you want a room each?'

'How do you feel, Soph?' Maddie asked.

'We're sharing a twin in Estepona so we might as well in Gibraltar,' Sophie said.

'Great. Now, how far have you got with the wedding dress and bridesmaids' dresses?' Steve asked.

'They'll be arriving in another couple of weeks then will be sent off for alterations,' Sophie told him. 'We've chosen the shoes too. And I've been in touch with the hotel in Spain re the flowers, and reception.'

They spent the next hour going through their notes, fuelled by more refreshments, then they all set off to look for wedding suits.

Sophie seemed a bit brighter now, Josh was pleased to notice. It was very good – and brave – of her to continue with this secret wedding planning when her relationship had just fallen apart. He didn't know if he could have done that after River – but then he'd been in his late teens and they say you feel everything more then, especially heartbreak. He certainly had – it had almost destroyed him. Still, it was all in the past now and he could see that it had been for the best.

Chapter Thirty-six

Sophie

She'd known today would be difficult, but she'd wanted to come. And she was glad she had. It had been fun helping Josh and Steve choose their suits. It had taken her mind off her heartbreak too. They'd tried several on but finally decided on a light grey three-piece suit with a lavender tie to match the bridesmaids' dresses.

'Kate loves lavender, so I think we should have purple, white and green as the colour scheme,' Steve said. 'It's the colour of the suffragettes, Kate will appreciate that touch.'

'Sounds lovely,' Sophie agreed. Josh and Maddie nodded too.

'Well, I don't think we'll need to meet up now until we're at the airport in Gibraltar,' Josh said. He'd arranged to meet Sophie and Maddie at the airport and drive them to the hotel.

'I hope not!' Maddie said, then she grinned apologetically as if she'd realised how rude that had sounded. 'It's just I'm busy and all this wedding planning is eating into my time. I'm sure it's the same for you too.'

'You can say that again,' Josh replied.

Sophie was actually glad of the wedding planning now; it took her mind off her break up with Glenn and gave her something to focus on. She'd have been moping in the flat today if she hadn't joined them shopping, she thought. Just then her phone rang. She glanced at the screen. 'It's Kate. I'll talk to her later,' she said, allowing the call to end, but it immediately rang again.

'Best to take the call,' Maddie said. 'It sounds like she really wants to talk to you and it might be something that affects the wedding.' She turned to Steve and Josh. 'Keep quiet, you two, we don't want her to know that you're here.'

'True.' Sophie swiped the screen. 'Hi, Kate …'

'Sophie!' she could hear the sob in Kate's voice. 'I think Steve's having an affair.'

Sophie shot a glance at Steve who was watching her, waiting to hear what Kate wanted. 'I'm sure he isn't, Kate, Steve idolises you …'

Steve and Josh exchanged worried glances.

'Yeah, well, that's what I thought, but there's definitely something going on. I've caught him a few times having whispered phone calls, and he never leaves his phone around, he's always carrying it with him – he's even put a passcode on it, as if he doesn't want me to see something. And …' another sob, 'I came home a bit earlier last week and he was sitting at the kitchen table doing something on the laptop but closed the lid as soon as I came in.'

Sophie's mind was racing. It was obvious that Steve's attempts to plan the wedding were causing him to be secretive and arouse suspicion in Kate. What could she say to reassure her friend? This was really awkward, especially as Steve was listening.

'It's probably all work-related, you know how Steve is about client confidentiality,' Sophie said.

162

'Maybe.' Kate sounded doubtful. 'But there's something different about him just lately, Soph. I don't know how to describe it. It's like he's . . . buzzing inside. If you know what I mean.'

She knew exactly what Kate meant. She'd noticed that about Steve herself. He was so buoyed up about this wedding it was impossible not to notice the spring in his step. No wonder Kate thought he was having an affair, what with all the phone calls and secrecy too.

'I'm going to have it out with him. If he wants someone else, he can have them, but he's not stringing me along.'

God, this sounded serious. 'I'm sure Steve isn't cheating on you. He adores you.'

Steve looked horrified and went pale.

'Men are fickle, Sophie. They can love you one minute and shift their attention to another the next.' She could hear the bitterness in Kate's voice and knew that she was referring to Laurie, her boyfriend of a few years ago whom Kate had discovered had been cheating on her for the last six months. No wonder she was suspicious of Steve. And she was right, men were fickle. Look at Glenn, he upped and left for Leeds without as much as a backward glance, as if the last twelve months of them being together had meant nothing to him. Not that Kate knew about that.

She couldn't keep talking to Kate while Steve was there listening, it felt like a betrayal of Kate's confidence. How could she reassure her? *It's Steve's job to do that.* As the words shot across her mind, she realised they were true. This was up to Steve.

'Look, I'm out at the moment and can't talk, but don't get yourself upset. There will be a perfectly rational explanation.

Wait until Steve comes home, and you can both talk. Phone me back later and let me know everything is OK.'

'I guess you're right. Thanks for listening, Sophie.'

'Well, I think you got the gist of that. Kate thinks you're cheating on her,' Sophie said when she'd ended the phone call. 'She said you're being secretive, keep having "work" meetings and have even put a lock on your phone.'

'Well, I'm not. Of course I'm not!' Steve protested. 'It's all about the wedding, you know it is. I've only put a lock on the phone so that Kate can't see any messages about the wedding arrangements.'

'She doesn't know that, does she?' Maddie said. 'I told you this secret wedding was a bad idea.'

'I'm going to have to go home and talk to her. But what can I say?' Steve looked distraught.

Josh reached out and squeezed his arm. 'We'll discuss it as we walk to our cars. Don't worry, we'll figure out something.'

'I hope they do,' Maddie said as both men walked off. Then she turned to Sophie. 'Now tell me more about you and Glenn. I can't believe you've split up.'

Sophie bit her lip. 'Neither can I.' The tears that she'd been holding back all afternoon finally spilt out of her eyes and down her cheeks. She reached into her pocket for a tissue.

'Oh, Soph.' Maddie reached out and placed her hand on Sophie's. 'I'm so sorry. I can't believe that he's finished with you just because you wouldn't go to Leeds with him. That's so unreasonable.'

'He said that we wanted different things. That he could tell from how I was about Steve and Kate's wedding that I wanted to get married at some point and he didn't. Not ever. He said

164

he was setting me free so I can find someone who wants the same commitment that I want.' She gulped, swallowing back the sobs. She wasn't going to break down here. Not in public. She wasn't.

'This bloody wedding is causing nothing but trouble,' Maddie said. 'Kate is worrying Steve is having an affair and now Glenn has dumped you. I knew it was a bad idea. I knew it.'

Sophie dabbed her eyes with the tissue. 'I'm sure that Steve will be able to talk Kate around,' she said.

'Maybe. But what if Kate is furious when she finds out what he's really been planning? She might dump him and that will be the end of her and Steve too.'

Chapter Thirty-seven

Kate

Kate finished the call to Sophie, her mind in turmoil. Her friend had only been trying to help, she knew that, but she didn't feel as if Sophie had taken her suspicions seriously. She felt as if she had been fobbed off. She knew that Sophie was all loved-up at the moment, planning her wedding with Glenn, but every bone in Kate's body told her that Steve was concealing something from her. She should have phoned Maddie, she wasn't as 'head in the clouds' as Sophie, but then Maddie would just say 'dump him'. Kate loved Steve, and had thought he loved her. She had to make sure her suspicions were correct before she acted hastily. She would have to confront Steve and ask him.

She made herself a cup of strong coffee and sat down to think. She wasn't imagining it. Steve was acting suspiciously. He was secretive when he was using his laptop, hugged his phone to him as if it was the crown jewels, had hushed phone calls with 'clients' but never discussed them with her, fobbing her off with 'it's just business'. And kept going out to 'meetings' in the evenings and even weekends. Like today. Well, much as she loved Steve, and didn't want to break up with him, she had more pride than to allow herself to be cheated on. She wasn't going to be *that* woman who ignored all the warning signs. She was going to face up to this, and if her suspicions were right, she was going to walk out with her head held high even if her heart was breaking.

She swore that she would never be so insecure that she would look through Steve's pockets, or his phone, to find evidence if he was cheating. But now ...

She went into the bedroom and pulled open the top drawer of the bedside cabinet on Steve's side of the bed, not sure what she hoped to find. A row of neatly balled socks greeted her in the top drawer, boxers in the second drawer, and she opened the bottom one to find a pile of neatly folded ties. Not that she'd really expected to find anything in there. Steve wouldn't be that obvious, would he? She went over to the huge double wardrobe and opened the left side where Steve hung his clothes. Shirts and trousers hung from the hangers, T-shirts and jeans folded on the shelves. Not that she thought he would hide anything here either, not where she could find it if she put any of his clothes away as she sometimes did. If he had something to hide he would probably leave it at the office. She turned away, her mind in a whirl. Was she overreacting?

She went back downstairs, then her eyes rested on the coats hanging by the front door. The overcoat Steve usually wore was hanging there, it was warmer today and he'd gone out in a jacket. For a moment she tried to talk herself out of it. *Don't be that woman*.

It was too late. Even as the words were going over and over in her mind she was walking over to the coat. Her hands reached for the pockets, fingers digging deep into the large outside ones, then finding nothing but a pair of gloves. She reached for the inside pocket, and her hand stilled as it rested on a piece of folded paper. She took a deep breath and pulled it out, then slowly opened it.

It was a receipt for a double room in a hotel.

She froze as she heard Steve's key in the lock. The door opened and he stepped inside, his eyes resting on her face, then on the piece of paper in her hand.

'Where have you been?' she asked icily. 'Is it with the woman you're planning a hotel break with?'

Chapter Thirty-eight

Sophie

Sophie couldn't stop thinking about Kate's phone call. She had sounded so distressed. She hoped that Steve and Josh managed to come up with a plausible story between them. She thought back to how excited she had been when Steve had first mentioned the secret wedding he'd been planning, but it was all going wrong. And what if Maddie and Josh were right and Kate refused to marry Steve. Or hated that she'd had no say in planning her own wedding. What if she was angry with Sophie and Maddie for not telling her and fell out with them. Her head was buzzing with scenarios of what could go wrong.

She got up and went into the kitchen to open a bottle of wine; the TV was on in the background but she wasn't watching it, it was on simply to break the silence. The flat seemed strange without Glenn, even though he was often in the bedroom playing online chess or out cycling, his presence was always there. Knowing that someone else lived there, that they would come home at some point, going to bed with them and waking up with them made a difference to your day.

You were happy here before you met Glenn, you can be happy again, she told herself as she poured a glass of white wine and took it into the lounge. Yes, it would hurt for a while but she would get over it. She just had to keep busy. She'd go to the garden centre tomorrow and buy some more plants, make a few more terrariums. She would get through this. And soon she had two weeks in sunny Spain to look forward too.

It was late that evening when Josh called. She swiped to answer the call, hoping that it was good news. *Please don't say Kate and Steve have split up.*

'It's OK. Panic over,' Josh told her. 'But not before things got a whole lot worse. Steve walked in to find Kate looking devastated and clutching the booking for the yacht hotel in Gibraltar, which the stupid idiot had printed out – because he always likes a print copy of everything – stuffed into his pocket to show me and left there. Kate presumed he was taking someone else – she hadn't had time to check the date and location but had seen that it was a double room – so you can imagine the state she was in. Especially as she'd phoned you saying she thought he was having an affair before she even discovered the hotel room booking!'

Sophie sucked in her breath. Poor Kate. 'Did Steve have to come clean about the wedding?' she asked. She was beginning to think it would be a good thing if he did have to.

'No, it was only the hotel booking, not the ceremony details. Steve had to tell her about going to Gibraltar though. He told her he'd booked them both into the hotel as a special treat, to surprise her. He showed her their names on the booking form.'

'So they're both OK now?'

'Well, apparently Kate wasn't too pleased that as soon as they arrived at the hotel in Estepona they were setting off for

170

Gibraltar and staying there for two nights, but yep, all sorted. I swear that I'll be grey before this wedding is over though.'

'Me too. In fact, I'm beginning to think that you and Maddie were right and this is going to be a disaster. Maybe we should persuade Steve to come clean. This could all go terribly wrong on the day and everything will be ruined.'

'What's happened to Miss Romantic?' Josh sounded surprised.

'The idea is romantic. But in practice – this is the most important day of Kate's life, and she should have a say in it. We don't even know if the dress is really the one she would choose, or the colour scheme. She could have been choosing them because she thought I would like them. She hasn't chosen her own flowers, or anything at all. And now this latest develop-ment . . . She'll probably never get that doubt out of her mind. This could ruin the trust in their relationship.'

'That's what I've worried about all along, but there is no talking to Steve. He is adamant that he's keeping it all a surprise,' Josh said. 'All we can do is hope that it goes right on the day.'

Chapter Thirty-nine

Kate

It was no good, she couldn't sleep. For a while Kate lay there, her mind a whirl of thoughts, while Steve lay snoring softly beside her. Finally, she crept out of bed and padded out into the kitchen to make herself a cup of hot milk and honey, her mind still going over the events of that afternoon. Steve had looked horrified when he'd walked in and seen her holding the hotel receipt. He'd stared at her in silence, and she got the impression that he was trying to come up with an excuse. Yet what he'd finally said was the truth, the receipt was for a hotel in Gibraltar and the room was booked in both their names. For two nights. So he had booked it as a surprise for her, as he insisted, saying that he'd always wanted to go to Gibraltar and had booked them a trip to see the dolphins while they were over there, which actually sounded nice. But why travel there on the very day they arrived in Spain? It didn't make sense when they'd have already been travelling from early that morning. Why not go on a day the following week? And why not tell her about it – ask her if she wanted to go? It wasn't like Steve to plan surprises and it wasn't as if it was her birthday, the anniversary of when they first met or anything like that. She'd asked him as much.

'It was a special offer for those dates and I thought it would be a treat. It's less than an hour's drive,' he'd explained earnestly. 'Do you hate the idea? Should I cancel? I can't get my money back but if you really don't want to go we don't have to. I didn't mean to upset you.'

He'd looked so distraught that she felt guilty for snooping and ruining his surprise. 'It's not that I don't want to go. It's just I don't understand why you didn't ask me if I wanted to go. Why you didn't discuss it with me.'

He'd run his hands through his hair. 'You said you wanted me to be more spontaneous and romantic ...'

She recalled the tiff they'd had when she'd told him she was fed up with planning everything and wished just for once he'd be more spontaneous and do something romantic. Well, now he had. He'd walked over to her, put his arms around her and she'd allowed him to hug her, sank into the comfort of his embrace, felt guilty for doubting him, for searching through his pockets. They had always trusted each other. What had got into her?

They'd made love and he'd reassured her over and over again that he loved her and would never cheat on her and Kate had felt even more guilty. Like some sort of deranged bunny-boiler girlfriend who wanted to keep tabs on her boyfriend, wanted to know everywhere he was going, everyone he was talking to.

She inwardly groaned as she recalled how she'd phoned Sophie and told her of her suspicions. How embarrassing was that? Kate prided herself on being balanced, unemotional, yet here she was accusing Steve of having an affair – and that was before she found the hotel receipt. If only she'd had a chance to read it before Steve walked in, she would have seen that the dates were when they were away, guessed it was a surprise and wouldn't have pounced on him like that.

What on earth was the matter with her? She had never doubted Steve before, never questioned him when he said he had a meeting to go to, or was going to see Josh. When had she got so insecure and needy?

The microwave pinged. She opened it up, took out her mug of hot milk, spooned some honey into it and stirred it thoughtfully. Steve has been acting secretively, she reminded herself as she carried the mug over to the sofa and sat down, nursing it. She hadn't been imagining the whispered phone calls, the lock on the phone – but maybe that was all about this mystery hotel stay in Gibraltar he was planning.

Then a thought crept into her head. Had Steve planned this special trip because he was planning on proposing to her?

She examined the thought. Some months ago she and Steve had briefly talked about getting married. They were happy together, comfortable in each other's company, and the chemistry was still there, the passion – last night had proved that. But they had both agreed that there was no rush, they were happy as they were. Had Sophie and Glenn's wedding preparations made Steve realise that he would like to get married too? Is that why he was whisking her off to Gibraltar?

But why Gibraltar? Why not propose to her while they were in Spain? It didn't make sense.

She toyed with the idea of talking to Sophie about it, seeing what she thought, then dismissed it. She'd already made a fool of herself by accusing Steve of having an affair, of taking some other woman away when the hotel reservation clearly showed both their names. If she told Sophie that she thought Steve was going to propose she would feel stupid if he didn't.

Besides, if Steve did propose, what would she say? Was she ready to marry him? She could be wrong about Steve's intentions, but she had to be prepared with her answer just in case. She didn't want to be taken by surprise again. She had to think this through carefully.

She took a sip of her warm milk, feeling the liquid slide soothingly down her throat, her heart thudding a little. Marriage was a major step. Was she ready to take it?

Chapter Forty

Josh

Three weeks later

'It's all going wrong!' Steve blurted down the phone. 'It's a total disaster.'

Josh wrapped the towel around his waist and sat down on the bed. He'd just got out of the shower and was walking into the bedroom drying his hair when he heard his phone ringing. The call had died before he could get to it, but he'd seen it was his brother and had been planning on calling back once he was dressed when Steve rang again. *OK, so he was anxious to talk to him.* Josh had swiped the screen to answer only to be greeted by Steve sounding like he was about to burst a blood vessel.

'Calm down and tell me what's happened,' he said.

'The bloody hotel has just called to say that they've only just discovered that they've double-booked our wedding day. Another wedding is taking place the same afternoon. That means two weddings on the same beach at the same time. Kate will hate it. They said they'd refund our money but how can we find another venue at this short notice?' Steve sounded in a right panic and Josh didn't blame him. There were only six weeks to go until his and Kate's wedding day. This was a massive problem.

'What can I do?' He could hear the tremor in Steve's voice. 'This wedding is doomed. You were right, it was a stupid idea. It's a total bloody disaster.'

Josh guessed this was no time to say 'I told you so'. 'There's got to be a way around this,' he said, trying to sound reassuring. He was Steve's best man; it was his job to calm him down. 'I'll message Maddie and Sophie and see if they have any ideas. They might know of alternative wedding venues.'

'I don't want an alternative venue. I told Ana, the events co-ordinator, that we booked in good faith and have almost paid the full fee, so she should honour our booking and tell the other couple they have to find somewhere else, but it turns out the other couple booked first and they have paid in full. Apparently they had a temporary receptionist in March who had mistakenly written down that they'd cancelled but that was another couple on a different week. It's a right cock-up, and as I told Ana, an apology isn't going to put it right. What the hell am I going to do?'

He was right, it was a cock-up, and Josh had no idea what to do to salvage the situation. He only hoped that Maddie or Sophie could come up with something. 'Try not to panic, Steve. I'll contact the girls, let them know what's happened and we'll see if we can come up with something. I'll get back to you later.'

'Thanks, Josh. I'm relying on you.'

No pressure then. Josh ended the call and phoned Sophie first, thinking she might have more idea than Maddie. Sophie listened in silence as Josh explained what had happened. 'I was wondering if you and Maddie had any ideas for options? Perhaps we could meet up some time over this weekend to discuss it,' he said hopefully. 'Steve's tearing his hair out.'

'Maddie's had to go to Paris for a meeting with a client,' Sophie told him. 'I can meet you though, I have to pop into the florist to take some more terrariums. Shall we make it Sandwiches and Shakes? I can be there in an hour?'

'That's fine, and thank you. I realise it's short notice and you probably have plans.' Dammit, he had plans too but he'd promised to help his brother and he wasn't going to let him down.

'No problem at all.'

As Josh reached the door of the café exactly an hour later, he heard his name called and turned around to see Sophie striding down the street towards him. She looked happier today, he noticed. The bags under her eyes had disappeared and her golden curly hair was bouncing around her shoulders. She was casually dressed in jeans and white shirt, open at the neck and the sleeves rolled up. It suited her. Looks like she was getting over her break up. He was glad. He wanted to ask her how she was, if she'd heard from her ex, if she was coping OK, but he stopped himself. They weren't exactly friends, they were just helping Steve plan his disaster of a secret wedding. And disaster it was turning out to be.

'Steve's in panic mode, it's only six weeks until the wedding,' Josh said as they walked in together. 'I hope we can find an alternative venue.' He glanced around the crowded café. 'There's a table free in the corner if we're quick.'

They both hurried over to the table, pulled out the two chairs and sat down.

'I did a search for venues when Steve first told us about his plans. I found quite a few, I'll see if any of them are free.'

'Can I get you something, madam?' The waiter hovered by, pen and notebook in hand.

'An iced chocolate frappé, please,' Sophie said.

'Caramel frappé for me, please,' Josh said, following Sophie's lead.

'That would be great if you could sort something out,' Josh said when the waiter had left to get their frappés. 'Let me know how you get on and I'll tell Steve. I think he'll be climbing the walls until it's sorted.'

'I can imagine. I'll contact them all this afternoon and let you know if I get lucky.'

'Ana said the hotel can still host the evening reception, so it's the wedding and meal we need to find an alternative for.' Josh rubbed his chin. 'I can't wait for all this to be over.'

'Neither can I.' Sophie wound a strand of hair around her finger. 'I can't believe this has happened.'

'It's a nightmare,' Josh said, pausing as the waiter returned with the frappés and placed the chocolate one in front of Sophie and the caramel in front of Josh, before going off to serve someone else. 'Dad nearly let the cat out of the bag last week,' he continued. 'Steve and Kate came around for Sunday lunch and he was talking about him and Mum booking Tess – their border collie – into kennels for the holiday in June, and Kate said that's when they were going away and wanted to know where our parents were going. Luckily Mum thought quickly and said they were going to stay with Aunt May – that's Mum's sister – in Portugal.'

Sophie looked horrified. 'Thank goodness for that!' She took a slurp of her drink, then said, 'My parents live in Portugal too. They retired there a couple of years ago.'

'Really? Do you go over often to visit them?'

'Not as much as I'd like. We do talk a lot though. I was hoping to go with Glenn this Christmas.'

'It must be tough for you,' Josh said softly. He felt sorry for her, she'd looked heartbroken last time he saw her and he knew what that felt like.

Sophie flashed him a brave smile, her eyes glistening with unshed tears. 'I'll get over it. It was so totally unexpected, that's what's hit me so hard.' She gulped and picked up her glass again, sipping her drink slowly while she composed herself. As he watched her, he was propelled back fifteen years, opening the letter River had pushed under his door. That had been unexpected too. He thought she wouldn't go without him, the shock and pain had been so raw. 'I know it doesn't help right now, but if you're both not on the same page relationship-wise it'll never work,' he said gently.

'True. And don't worry, I'm not heartbroken, although, yes, I'm hurt and betrayed. I thought we were happy together, so it's a shock to realise that Glenn thought so little of me he was prepared to go without saying goodbye.' She told him how she'd come back home early from work to find Glenn already packed. 'He was going to leave me a note, apparently.'

Josh felt furious on her behalf. What a total toe-rag to plan to sneak away rather than talk to Sophie, tell her face to face that he was leaving and why.

Like River. Yes, she'd said she wanted to travel, asked him to go with her, but when it finally came to it, she'd gone in the middle of the night, not even said goodbye.

She did you a favour, he told himself, remembering his mother's words. First love hits you hard but it isn't always true love.

Would he ever know true love?

Chapter Forty-one

Sophie

Sophie read the email in delight. One of the alternative venues, the beautiful cove in front of the beach restaurant, had no weddings booked that afternoon and was happy to fit them in. It was such a romantic venue, Sophie could hardly believe it. She was sure that Kate would love it. It was twenty minutes' drive from the hotel but when she had contacted Ana about having the chair covers, table runners and other things redirected there, Ana had said she would organise that, and the hotel would provide transport for all the guests to the cove and back because the mix-up had been their fault. She was so apologetic about the double-booking and said to let her know if there was anything she could do to help.

Sorted, Sophie thought happily. She immediately phoned Josh to let him know and emailed Steve. She'd tell Maddie all about it when she returned from Paris later that evening. Josh didn't pick up so she left him a message on his answerphone and set off for the garden centre to get some more plants for terrariums – they'd had quite a few orders – only to bump into Josh there.

'Hi. I left you a message. The wedding is sorted,' she told him, telling him what had happened, and what Ana had agreed.

'You're a star. I could hug you,' Josh told her.

Sophie felt her cheeks flush. 'Happy to help. I'll send you a photo of the venue. It's so romantic.'

'Fancy joining me for a drink to celebrate? You can show me there,' Josh suggested. 'There's a lovely little pub, The Malt Shovel, down the road. It'll only mean a soft drink for me, I'm on my motorbike, but it'd be good to sit outside while we chat.'

'I'd love to. And I'm driving as well so I'll settle for a lemonade. Shall I meet you there in about half an hour?' she asked.

He nodded. 'Perfect.'

They sat outside in the beer garden, Sophie with a lemonade and Josh with a coke, and it seemed so natural to be sitting there together, enjoying the sunshine.

'Twice in two days,' Josh said, raising his glass to her. 'I hope Steve realises how much effort we're making to ensure his wedding goes to plan.'

'Yep, it's really hard work sitting here sipping lemonade,' Sophie said with a smile.

'Don't do yourself down, you've worked really hard. I can't believe you managed to sort out the wedding. Steve will be so relieved.'

'I've emailed him with details of the venue.' Sophie took out her phone and got the beach restaurant website up. 'See, the wedding ceremony is on the beach, and the meal in the restaurant. Isn't it romantic? And as I said, it's only twenty minutes from the hotel.'

'It's gorgeous. And great that Ana has offered to take all the wedding stuff over, and arrange transport from the hotel and then back again for the evening reception. I can't believe you've sorted this out. You're amazing.'

Sophie felt her cheeks flush at his praise. 'Ana was so apologetic, I could tell that she felt awful about the mix-up,' Sophie told him. She took her handbag off the back of the chair and reached inside it. 'Anyway, it's all sorted now, thank goodness. And we pick up the dresses at the end of May. How about your suits?'

'Same time. Fingers crossed that nothing else will go wrong. I think I've aged ten years since we've been helping Steve plan this perishing wedding.'

'Me too,' Sophie agreed. She sat back and levelled her gaze at him. 'I can't believe we've pulled it off. Do you still think it's a crazy idea?'

'Yep.' He met her gaze full on. 'I think if you decide to get married you should plan it together. It's important that the day is exactly how you both want it. And that when you propose to a lady, no matter how long you have been with her, or have been living together, you should never ever presume that she will say yes.'

She was silent as if considering his remarks.

'And do you still think that it's a wonderful romantic idea?' he asked.

'I don't know,' she confessed. 'I know Steve means it to be romantic, but I am a bit worried that something will go wrong. And much as we've tried to make sure that we've done exactly what Kate wants, we can't be sure, can we?' She bit her lip. 'I hope it all goes to plan. I really want Kate to have the day of her dreams.'

'I know you do. And you have done your very best to make that happen. We all have.' Their gazes locked and something stirred in the pit of her stomach.

Sophie fixed her gaze on the rim of her glass as she ran a finger around it, trying to steady the butterflies in her stomach. 'I'm so worried that Kate might think Steve is taking her for granted. And that she'll be mad at me and Maddie for not telling her. I keep remembering how upset she was when she thought that Steve was having an affair. I wanted to tell her about the surprise wedding then. She might think that I should have.' She raised anxious eyes to look into his. 'If she turns Steve down, I'll feel awful. They could even split up. I should have listened to you and Maddie. I should have helped you make Steve see reason.'

'Stop beating yourself up, this was not your idea and you couldn't tell Kate because you were sworn to secrecy. If this goes wrong it's Steve's fault and no one else's.' He leant over the table and squeezed her hand. She was surprised at the jolt that shuddered through her as he touched her skin. 'And take it from me, no one can talk Steve out of an idea once he's got it into his head to do something. He'd have gone ahead with it whether we helped him or not.'

She nodded. 'That's what I keep telling myself. And at least this way Kate has had some say in it, but the nearer we get to the wedding the more I realise how drastically it can go wrong.' She took a long swig of her lemonade. 'I just hope everything works out OK.'

'You and me both,' Josh said with feeling. 'I can't wait for this wedding to be over.'

Sophie's eyes met his as she suddenly realised that once the wedding was over she probably wouldn't see Josh again. They would have no reason to phone, message or meet up. She felt a pang of regret. She would miss him.

185

Chapter Forty-two

Sophie

Middle of May

'These gift boxes and your terrariums are selling as quickly as you can make them,' Janine said to Sophie as yet another customer went out clutching a gift box.

Since Glenn had left, Sophie had channelled her energy into making more gift boxes and terrariums, coming up with new ideas every day, and Janine was right, they were proving to be very popular.

'You should start up on your own,' Janine said. 'I bet you could earn a living from this.'

Glenn had suggested that, Sophie remembered, when he'd first mentioned them moving away together. She was glad she hadn't gone with him; she was actually quite happy on her own. Glenn had messaged her a couple of times, asking how she was, apologising for how things had ended. He was happy in his new job, he said, and she could see now that he had done her a favour taking the promotion and moving away. They'd rubbed along together with no big rows or problems and probably would have ticked over for another few months, a year maybe, but then one of them would have met someone else. Someone who made their skin tingle and their heart stir.

Like Josh did. She had to stop thinking about Josh in that way. She was not interested in Josh. Yes, OK, she couldn't help noticing how sexy he was, but she had no intention of acting on her physical attraction to him, even if that attraction was mutual. Which she was certain it wasn't. She wasn't Josh's type and he wasn't hers.

'Earth to Sophie.'

Janine's voice jolted Sophie back to the present. 'Sorry ...'

'I was saying, why don't you talk to Pat about working part time in the shop? Her daughter will be here next month and could cover for you. It would give you a chance to decide if you could make a go of working for yourself – either full or part time. You could still offer to make supplies for the shop. We could be your first customer.'

'I'm not sure. It's a big step,' Sophie said, cautiously.

'What have you got to lose?' Janine asked. But before Sophie could reply, Pat returned from the delivery she'd been making.

Sophie mulled the idea over all day and the more she thought about it the more it appealed to her. She didn't want to give up her job completely but liked the idea of working from home a couple of days a week and slowly building up her own business. Maybe it was time to make some changes to her life. She could move out of the flat, rent a little house instead, like she'd wanted. She didn't need Glenn with her to do that. Yes, it would cost more, and she was already struggling with paying the rent of the flat on her own, but she could get a two-bed and have a lodger. Or maybe she would make a success of her business and be able to afford the rent on her own. It was worth thinking about.

She mentioned it to Maddie when she popped around on Friday evening to discuss the holiday plans. Sophie had decided to go away for the two weeks now, so she and Maddie were planning on doing some sightseeing, as well as visiting Maddie's aunt.

'Go for it, you never know what you can do until you try,' Maddie told her. 'Give it a couple of months and if you're struggling with the rent you'll find a lodger easily. Maybe even a sexy male one.'

'I thought I'd make a decision when I come back from Spain,' Sophie said. 'Pat's daughter will have worked in the shop for a couple of weeks by then so I can see how she liked it and if she will cover for me part time until she gets a job.'

'No harm in looking at available houses though, is there?' Maddie picked up her phone, punched a few keys and looked thoughtfully at the screen. 'I'm guessing you'd want to stay in the Worcester area? There's a couple here that look good.'

She passed the phone over and Sophie looked at the houses on the screen. The first one was a two-bed with a small garden in a close not far from where she lived now. She scrolled through the images, it looked nice, clean and compact. The second one was in a row of terraces, the rooms were bigger but the price was higher. They were both out of her reach financially though unless she found a lodger.

She scrolled on down then paused at the image of a large Victorian house and the words 'bottom floor flat available'. She opened it up and read the spec. The house had been converted to three flats, the bottom floor one had one bedroom, two more large rooms plus a kitchen and the use of a communal garden. The price was within her reach. 'Something like this would be perfect,' she said.

'Why don't you register with an estate agent, tell them what you want and see what they come up with?' Maddie suggested.

'I will.' Sophie nodded. 'I think it's time for a change.' She handed the phone back. 'Thanks, Maddie. Now, have you found out any more about your aunt?'

'Yes, I've contacted one of my cousins, Miguel, on Facebook and he said they'd all love to see me. Sadly, his dad, my uncle Juan died a few years ago,' she replied.

'I'm so sorry,' Sophie said. 'Were you very close to him?'

'Not really. He was out at work a lot, but I remember him as being a jolly, kind man. I'd like to have seen him again.' Maddie's eyes clouded over for a moment then she said, 'At least I can see my aunt and Miguel. He's still living in the same town, my other two cousins have moved away. Miguel sent me the Google Maps location. He said that Aunt Valeria works in the bakery every morning so I'll get there in the afternoon.'

They opened a bottle of wine and chatted all evening; Maddie was staying over on the sofa. It was good to have Maddie's company, Sophie thought, she'd missed 'catching-up' evenings with her friend.

'Want to come and watch the band play tomorrow?' Maddie asked. 'I could get you a ticket.'

'Are you singing again? Hasn't Suki recovered from her throat infection yet?' Sophie asked.

'Yes, she recovered from that weeks ago. I'm just going along to support them.' Maddie took a sip of her wine. 'Me and Ezri, we're sort of back on again.'

'Really? Properly, as in a relationship?'

'No, it's only casual.'

Ezri and Maddie had been 'only casual' on and off for ages now. It was as if they felt comfortable with each other because neither of them wanted to commit, so it was company – and sex – with no strings attached and no heartbreak.

Sophie topped up Maddie's glass, then her own. 'Maybe I should be more like you, keep things casual.'

Maddie took a sip of her wine then shook her head. 'No, Sophie, you should be more like you. Be yourself. Then whatever is meant to come in your life will be.' She looked pensive. 'I keep it casual because I've never met anyone I want to forgo my freedom for. You're different. You like to be in a relationship. You like the security and cosiness of being with one special person.'

'Well, I'm not in any hurry to get into another relationship. I'm enjoying having time to myself, working out what I want to do with my life.' Sophie took a mouthful of wine and swilled it around her mouth, enjoying the fruity flavour before swallowing it. 'This year is racing by. I can't believe that three weeks today Steve and Kate will be married.'

'If Kate says yes, that is.'

Sophie's eyes shot to Maddie's face and could see the worry there that she was feeling herself. What if Kate said no?

Chapter Forty-three

Maddie

Saturday 4th June

'What do you mean you can't find the wedding dress?' Maddie demanded.

'It must be here. You sent me an email to say that the dresses were ready to collect on Tuesday and I messaged back that we would come for them on Saturday,' Sophie added.

Sophie scrolled down her phone for the email, while Maddie turned her attention back to Selina. 'So you're saying that the bridesmaids' dresses are here but not the wedding dress? What's happened to the wedding dress?'

Selina shook her head. 'I don't know. I'm sorry but I've been on holiday for two weeks. I only came back today. The other assistant sent you the email, and she isn't in today.'

'We need that wedding dress urgently. The wedding is next Friday and the best man is driving over to Spain with the wedding dress and bridesmaids' dresses tomorrow.' Maddie tried to keep calm although her heart was pounding. All the while they'd been planning this secret wedding she'd been dreading that something would go wrong at the last minute. Now it had. 'Surely if the bridesmaids' dresses are here then the wedding dress should be,' she pointed out. 'They were all being altered by the same woman, weren't they?' She couldn't believe that this was happening. How could the bridal shop lose the wedding dress?

'They should have been, yes. Unless Mary altered the bridesmaids' dresses first and delivered them. As I said, I've been on holiday for two weeks. Please be assured that I'll do everything I can to resolve this. First, I'll go and check in the store room just in case the wedding dress was delivered and not marked off in the book,' Selina said. She hurried off, leaving Sophie and Maddie exchanging worried looks.

'Honestly, I'm more anxious about this wedding than I would be if it was my own,' Sophie said. 'I don't know what we're going to do if she can't find the wedding dress. Josh is all booked on the ferry, ready to go.'

'Don't panic. If the lady is still altering it then we'll take it over with us. There's still time to book an extra suitcase and we'll fold it very carefully,' Maddie said reassuringly. 'There's a solution to every problem.' She hoped she sounded more confident than she felt.

Selina came back a few minutes later, looking flustered. 'The wedding dress definitely isn't in the stockroom. I'm really sorry about this but there must be a reasonable explanation. Mary is always so reliable. Let me contact her.' She picked up the phone and dialled a number. Maddie listened anxiously to the assistant's half of the conversation. From what she could gather Mary had finished the alterations but there was a delay getting the dress to the shop for some reason.

'Thank you. I'll let the customer know,' Selina said, ending the call.

'The wedding dress is finished but Mary's car has broken down. Someone is repairing it at the moment. The dress will be here later today.'

'We really don't have time to wait. Could we possibly go and collect the dress? Would that be OK? You can give us a letter of authorisation,' Maddie suggested. 'And you can take a photo of us to send to her, so she knows that we're who we say we are.'

Selina looked doubtful. 'That's not our standard procedure. Let me ask the manager.'

The manager telephoned the seamstress who agreed. Selina took a photo of Maddie and Sophie and then sent it to Mary. 'Take your receipt with you too,' the manager said. 'Mary won't hand the dress over without that.'

Sophie shoved the receipt back in her bag. Then Selina gave them the bridesmaids' dresses – each in a protective cover bag – and they carefully carried them back to the car, laying them on the back seat. The seamstress only lived a few miles away but, it being a Saturday, the traffic was busy and it was half an hour before they pulled up outside her house. Maddie could see two men peering over a car that was parked outside, bonnet up. That must be Mary's car.

One of the men raised his head as Sophie and Maddie got out of the car. 'Are you the two ladies come for the wedding dress? I'm Mary's husband.'

'That's us.' Maddie nodded at the car. 'You look like you've got a job on your hands there.'

'Nothing I can't sort with a bit of time. Sorry that it's delayed us getting the wedding dress to you though.' The man took a rag out of his pocket and wiped his forehead. 'Anyway, Mary's waiting for you. Give the door a knock,' he said.

Before they even reached the door a middle aged woman opened it, rubbing her hands nervously. 'You must be Sophie and Maddie. I'm Mary. I'm so sorry that you've had to come out of your way like this. I had the dress all ready to deliver today but the car wouldn't start.'

'It's OK, it wasn't far for us to come,' Sophie told her. She held out the receipt.

'Do come in.' Mary opened the door wider to let them in. 'I really am sorry for the delay. It's the wedding soon, isn't it?' She looked at Sophie. 'Are you the bride?'

'No, it's our friend. Her fiancé is planning a secret wedding,' Maddie told her. Actually, Steve wasn't Kate's fiancé yet, was he? He hadn't even proposed.

'How romantic. Well, it's a gorgeous dress, she'll look beautiful.' Then a shadow crossed her face. 'If it's a surprise wedding she won't have had a fitting. I hope the dress fits her.'

'It will. She thinks she's being a bridesmaid at my wedding so the assistant was able to take her measurements,' Sophie explained.

'Goodness, you've thought of everything, haven't you? What good friends you are.' Mary reached up to a cream, zipped dress-cover bag that was hanging on the door and took it down. 'Here it is. Please unzip the cover and take a good look at the dress before you take it away. I want to make sure you're happy with it.' She picked up a sheet of paper from the coffee table. 'I'll need you to sign this to confirm that you're satisfied. The bridal shop won't pay me otherwise.'

Maddie carefully unzipped the cover and took out the wedding dress. She held it up.

194

'It's beautiful. Kate is going to look stunning in this,' Sophie said.

'Please. Examine it thoroughly, make sure you're completely satisfied,' Mary told her.

Maddie and Sophie did as she asked. The dress was perfect. You couldn't even tell it had been taken in.

'You've done an excellent job,' Sophie said, happily signing the paper Mary handed to her. Then she picked up the wedding dress.

'Thank you. Good luck with the wedding,' Mary said, going to the front door and opening it to let them out. The two men were still tinkering with the car, Mary's husband looked over as Sophie and Maddie walked up the path. 'All OK?'

'Yes, thank you,' Maddie and Sophie said in unison, both waving at the same time.

'Do you want me to come back with you and help carry the dresses back up to your flat?' Maddie asked as she opened the door and Sophie laid the wedding dress carefully across the back seat, with the bridesmaid's dresses.

'That would be great, if you have time. Josh will be here soon; he might have some last-minute things to discuss.'

'Even if he hasn't it'll be nice to see him,' Maddie said with a wink. 'He's easy on the eye is Josh. I think the three of us will have some fun in Spain.' She was glad that Sophie had decided to come for the two weeks. Glenn going off had hit her hard, but she seemed to be getting over it now. A holiday in Spain was just what she needed to get Glenn out of her hair once and for all.

'You know, I think I'm actually looking forward to this holiday. Once the wedding is over,' Sophie said.

Maddie squeezed her shoulders. 'Me too. We're going to have a fantastic time.'

Josh arrived an hour after they got home. He was casually dressed in a white T-shirt and black shorts that fitted tightly around his bottom. Maddie noticed Sophie's eyes drift there too as, after letting him in, she followed him into the lounge. She smiled to herself. It seemed that Sophie wasn't completely immune to Josh's charms.

'I hope you've packed lots of summer clothes, girls. It's scorching over in Spain,' he said. 'You're going to be needing shorts and vest tops.'

'I know. I checked the weather forecast this morning. It looks like it's going to be in the top thirties all week. I can't wait.'

'Me neither,' Sophie agreed. 'I'm looking forward to coming back with a tan that hasn't come out of a bottle.'

Josh grinned. 'Planning on spending the two weeks sunbathing, are you?'

'Some of the time, but I want to get out and about, see some of the country too,' Sophie told him.

'We're going to look up my aunt,' Maddie added. 'I haven't seen her since I was fourteen.'

'Maddie is half Spanish,' Sophie added. 'Her dad is Spanish.'

Josh looked surprised. 'I hadn't realised.'

'No reason why you should,' Maddie said a little abruptly. She hated talking about anything personal. 'Anyway, we had a bit of a hiccup with the wedding dress,' she said, changing the subject and telling him about the events that morning, with Sophie joining in, adding bits too.

'Thank goodness you sorted it out. I'm crossing my fingers

that nothing goes wrong on the actual wedding day. Honestly, I think this secret wedding of my brother's has put years on me.'

'If you're fishing for a compliment that you're still looking young and handsome, we're not buying,' Maddie said with a grin.

Josh grinned back. 'Where are the dresses then? I need to get going. I've got an early start in the morning and there's quite a bit to do before I set off.'

'In the bedroom. I'll go and fetch them.' Sophie went into the bedroom and took the dresses, safely enclosed in their protective bags, from the curtain rail where she'd hung them. 'Here you are. Don't fold them if you can help it.'

'I'm planning on lying them flat on the back seat. I've got our two suits hanging up in the back too,' he told her. 'I'll do my very best to make sure none of them gets crumpled.'

'I know you will.' Sophie handed over the three dresses to him. 'Do you want us to help you carry them downstairs?'

'That might be an idea. I really don't want to trip with them.'

So Sophie took the wedding dress, Maddie and Josh a bridesmaid's dress each and they carried them carefully down the stairs and out to the car park where a white Range Rover was parked. Josh pressed his remote to unlock the car as they walked over to it, opened the door and placed the bridesmaid's dress flat on the back seat, then took the other dress from Maddie and put that on top of it, then finally laid out the wedding dress. 'They should be perfectly safe there.'

Maddie could see the two suit bags hanging on the grab handles at the back, on one side. 'It's going to be a long journey for you,' she said.

'I'm stopping over at a couple of B&B's on the way. I'll be

fine. I like travelling.' He closed the back door. 'Well, this is it. The next time we meet will be in Gibraltar,' he said. 'I'll meet you at the airport. Safe flight.'

'Safe journey,' Maddie said, blowing him a kiss.

'Be careful driving on those Spanish roads,' Sophie told him.

'I'll be fine. I've been around Europe in both a car and on my motorbike,' Josh told her. He got into the driver's seat, buckled up, started the car, gave them both a final wave and was off.

Chapter Forty-four

Kate

Two days before the wedding

The hotel was perfect. Kate looked out over the balcony at the golden beach below, already covered with holiday-makers sunbathing, drinking, paddling and swimming in the turquoise sea. She'd been so looking forward to this holiday and was pleased they'd chosen this hotel. The room was really lux-urious and the view was spectacular. They'd only arrived half an hour ago and all she wanted to do was unpack, then go and spend the rest of the afternoon sunbathing, with a couple of cocktails from the beach bar, followed by a meal at the hotel restaurant and then maybe go down into the lounge and watch the entertainment. She wanted to relax, unwind. Not drive all the way over to perishing Gibraltar then stay in a different hotel for two nights. It seemed crazy to be paying for two hotel rooms on each of the two nights.

She sighed, turned around and went back into the hotel room where their cases were open on the bed, waiting for her to take out what she wanted for their mini-break. If only Steve had mentioned that he wanted to go to Gibraltar before they booked the holiday then they could have flown there first, there was a small airport, or she could have talked him into going in the second week of their holiday. It would have made more sense. And saved a lot of upset. She was still mortified at the scene she'd caused, accusing Steve of having an affair. Things hadn't really been the same between them since. She still sensed that he was hiding something, but how could she ask him after that? She would sound neurotic. Maybe she was, but Steve wasn't his normal self. All she wanted was for them both to have the chance to relax, reconnect. Not go driving off for a couple of days as soon as they'd arrived.

He's just trying to make it a nice holiday, and he said he doesn't mind doing the driving, she reminded herself. *And you did tell him you wanted him to be more spontaneous.* She wondered if she was going to regret saying that.

She glanced around as Steve came back into the room. 'How long before we leave for Gibraltar?' she asked.

'I was hoping we could set off soon. We're going to need our passports to show Border Control so remember to put yours in your bag. I thought we could head straight for the hotel and unpack, then take a walk into town and get a taxi for a tour of the Rock.' He showed her a leaflet detailing all the things they could see. 'Do you fancy it?'

She fought back the retort that all she wanted to do was relax on the beach with a cocktail in her hand and forced a smile on her face as she glanced through the leaflet. There were several things of historical interest but the thing that caught her eye the most was St Michael's Caves. 'I'd love to go there, they look spectacular,' she said. 'And it would be brilliant if we could get a photo with one of the monkeys.'

'I fancy that too. If we set off now we'll have time to fit it in this afternoon. Then tonight we'll go out for a meal. It's so good to have a break from work and be able to spend some time together.' He wrapped his arms around her, his expression tender. 'I love you, you know.'

'I love you too,' she said.

He pulled her into an embrace and kissed her tenderly. 'Thank you for indulging me in this. It means a lot to me.'

She leant back and smiled up at him. 'It's fine. Gibraltar looks interesting and I guess we still have twelve days to enjoy this hotel.'

'Sure.' Steve gazed at her with such love in his eyes that she felt her heart lift. She was so glad that they had booked this holiday. Some much-needed couple time. They were always so busy. And that's how they liked it – they were both workaholics – but it was good to touch base sometimes, to reconnect with each other. And it was lovely of him to spring this last-minute surprise on her, she had to lighten up about it. *Chill and enjoy the holiday*, she told herself.

It was a pleasant drive to Gibraltar and Kate felt a frisson of excitement as she saw the iconic Rock looming in front of them. Now they were here, she was looking forward to spending a couple of days looking around. The queue through first the Spanish then the English Border Control was quite long but thankfully they'd thought to bring water with them. At last they were driving across the runway into Gibraltar itself. Kate expected Steve to head up the hill towards the town so was surprised when he turned and drove to the marina.

'Here we are, our hotel for the next two nights,' he said, pulling up into a parking space alongside a large yacht.

Kate stared at the luxurious floating hotel in front of them, so huge it dwarfed all the other yachts and boats in the marina. 'A yacht?' she asked in surprise.

'A yacht hotel. It's permanently moored here,' Steve told her. 'Do you like it?'

'It looks amazing.' Kate gazed up at the impressive yacht, sitting majestically in the still, blue Mediterranean sea, then back over to the bars and restaurants of the Ocean Village. 'And what a fantastic spot. We could take a walk around the marina later, couldn't we?'

Steve beamed. 'I've booked us dinner at a restaurant overlooking it. I thought you might enjoy that. And tomorrow I've paid for a trip to see the dolphins in the afternoon. How does that sound?'

'Wonderful!' Kate replied. She gazed at the yacht hotel again. Standing here, with the sun on her back, the marina in front of her, about to board the huge floating hotel that would be her home for the next couple of days, she was very glad she'd agreed to this trip to Gibraltar. This was an experience she didn't want to miss!

'Ready?' Steve held out his hand and Kate slipped hers into it. Together they walked up the red-carpeted gangway into the marble-floored reception. Kate felt a frisson of excitement. She had the feeling this was going to be a very special holiday. Had she guessed right and Steve was going to propose to her? She felt a little excited at the thought.

Chapter Forty-five

Sophie

'There he is!' Maddie stood on tiptoe, waving eagerly.

Sophie turned, shaded her eyes from the sun with her hand and watched Josh approach the terminal. He was easy to spot, his head towering above the crowds, and looked casually handsome in his beige shorts and chocolate-brown T-shirt.

'How was the flight?' he asked them.

'Fine, very calm. How was the drive over?' Maddie asked.

'Pleasant. My client was pleased to see his Range Rover, and insisted on paying the cost of my hire car for the two weeks as well as our agreed fee. I transferred the dresses and suits to the back seat; they're hanging up in my hotel room now, all ready for Friday.'

Sophie gazed around, her eyes resting on the huge, majestic Gibraltar Rock rising high in front of them. 'It's lovely weather, isn't it? And according to the forecast it's going to be like this all the time we're here,' she said.

'It gets even hotter in July and August,' Josh told her. 'At least my brother got it right booking the wedding in June.' He nodded to the cases. 'Want me to take those? My car's parked not far away.'

'Nah, they're four-wheelers, no effort at all,' Maddie said with a grin, casually rolling her saffron hardcase alongside her. Sophie had gone for a classy pink vintage case with white straps, just as easy to manoeuvre. When they reached Josh's hire car, a black Toyota, he opened the boot and insisted on lifting the suitcases in, then Sophie and Maddie got into the back and they set off for the hotel.

'Is the hotel that Steve and Kate are staying at very near?' Maddie asked. 'We're not likely to be bumping into them, are we? That would take some explaining!'

'Steve has booked them on to a posh yacht hotel, it's in the marina about ten minutes from our hotel which is in the town. As long as we avoid that area, we shouldn't bump into them.'

'Nice. Kate will love that. Are they eating there tonight?' Sophie asked.

'No. He's booked a table in a restaurant over in Ocean Village to propose tonight. He's even ordered a violin player to serenade them.' He glanced in the mirror, his eyes meeting Sophie's, who was sitting behind him. 'Steve said that they're not driving over to Gibraltar until later, so how about I leave you to unpack, then we could have lunch in the town and go for a tour? There are some interesting sights to see and we might even get close to some of the apes. We can catch a tourist taxi in the centre of the town to take us around the main sights.'

'Sounds good to me. I was looking online the other night and thought I'd like to take a tour,' Maddie said. 'Why don't we have lunch at the hotel? We can take our cases up to our room and unpack later. I'm starving.'

'Sure. Let's go to the restaurant on the roof. I'll meet you up there.'

Ten minutes later they joined Josh in the rooftop restaurant. He was sipping a glass of iced mineral water. 'I need to keep hydrated in this heat,' he said. 'I thought I'd wait for you before I ordered food. There's a good selection of salads and paninis if you only want something light.'

'Salad is perfect, and I'll have a mineral water too,' Sophie said. Maddie had the same. They tucked into their lunch and then left for the town.

There were several taxis offering short tours and longer excursions, ranging from one hour forty-five minutes to six and a half hours. As it was already late afternoon, they decided on the shortest tour. Sophie looked out of the window as the driver headed up the Rock. She really hoped that she got close to one of the famous Gibraltar monkeys.

Their first stop was the Pillars of Hercules, where, their guide informed them, they could see both the Mediterranean and the Atlantic. 'This is where, according to the legend, Hercules had to cross the Atlas mountains to complete one of the twelve tasks he'd been set, but instead of climbing over them he smashed through them and brought both the Mediterranean Sea and the Atlantic Ocean together.' The guide went on to explain that the northern pillar became known as the Rock of Gibraltar and the southern one as Jebel Musa, which was in Ceuta.

They all gazed out to sea in wonder, snapping a few photos. Then they were taken to St Michael's Caves. To Sophie's delight, they passed several of the famous apes on the way, including a mother and baby.

'They're so gorgeous!' she exclaimed, taking a few photos with her phone. As did Maddie and Josh.

The driver handed them their tickets to go into the caves

and told them he would wait for them outside. 'Be back in half an hour, max,' he said.

They went into the cave and followed the crowd down the steps and along the walkway, then stood on the platform gazing around them as the colourful light-show began, illuminating the huge stalagmites and stalactites and other incredible rock formations.

'This is really something!' Maddie said.

'It's magical,' Sophie said softly, gazing down into the enormous cavern below. It was even more spectacular than she had imagined it would be. She'd read a bit about the history and knew that there were several legends about the caves, including that the Barbary apes had passed along a passage under the sea from Africa into the cave, which is how they came to live on Gibraltar. Also, that two Neanderthal skulls had been discovered in the caves so they could have been used around 40,000 BC.

'It's pretty incredible,' Josh agreed, holding his camera up high to try and get a photo of the cave roof. Maddie and Sophie snapped away too, but Sophie knew that no photos would do this spectacular cave justice.

'Apparently the acoustics are so good that concerts are held down here,' Josh said as they walked into the large Cathedral Cave. 'It's the same with the Caves of Drach in Majorca.'

They stood still for a moment, gazing down the steps to the stage in front of them. 'I could imagine Ezri and the guys playing in here,' Maddie said. 'It would be pretty awesome.'

They had started to walk down the steps when Josh suddenly grabbed their arms and pulled them both back. 'Look!' He pointed ahead of them. A man and woman were walking hand in hand down the steps a few metres in front of them. Kate and Steve!

Chapter Forty-six

Josh

What the hell was Steve doing here? Josh thought in dismay. He said they weren't driving over until late this afternoon. They wouldn't even have got to their hotel in Estepona until almost lunchtime and surely they'd both want a rest after such an early start this morning.

'Don't panic, Kate probably won't recognise us, it's pretty dark in here,' Sophie said.

'I think she might recognise Maddie's hair,' Josh pointed out.

'He's right. We'd better go back, if Kate turns around and sees us the whole surprise will be ruined,' Maddie agreed.

'We can't go all the way back, the taxi guy is waiting for us at the exit,' Josh pointed out. 'Let's go back a bit to give Kate and Steve a chance to get ahead.'

At that moment, Steve turned around. Josh wasn't sure if he had seen them, but he turned back again swiftly and ushered Kate through into the next part of the cave.

'We'll have to wait here a bit and make sure they've left the cave before us,' Josh said.

'The problem is, if they're on a tour too then surely we'll bump into them everywhere we go,' Maddie pointed out.

'She's right. We're going to have to ask the taxi driver to take us back. We can't risk Kate seeing us,' Sophie said.

Josh hesitated. They were going to the Sky Walk and the Great Siege Tunnels next, but if Kate and Steve were doing the same tour they were bound to bump into them. 'I guess you're right. Let's keep back until we're sure they're out of the cave, then we'll get out and ask the driver to take us back into town.'

They held back behind Kate and Steve, waiting a good five minutes after they saw them go out of the exit before going out themselves. The taxi driver was pacing around anxiously. 'I thought you'd got lost in there,' he said.

'Sorry . . .' Josh paused as a message pinged into his phone. It was from Steve. **What are you all doing here? You're going to ruin everything.**

'I'm afraid we're going to have to ask you to take us back into town,' he told the taxi driver who looked a bit confused.

'But there's still much to see.'

'Sorry, it's an emergency. We have to go back,' Josh told him.

He couldn't afford another near miss. Steve would never speak to him again.

'Maybe we can come back tomorrow morning. Kate will know we're here then and she and Steve will be busy at the register office,' he suggested as they all climbed back into the taxi. 'Right now, though, I think we had better go back to the hotel and stay there until we hear that Steve's proposed and Kate's accepted.'

'No worries. I quite fancy a swim in the hotel pool anyway. How about you, Sophie?' Maddie asked.

'Sounds good to me,' Sophie agreed.

'Want to join us, Josh?' Maddie asked cheekily.

'I'll pass on the swim, thanks, I'll settle for a cold beer in the bar.' He needed something to calm his nerves. That was a bit too close for comfort.

A couple of hours later they all had dinner in the rooftop restaurant, sticking to Josh's plan not to leave the hotel until they heard from Steve. Then they could all go and celebrate together.

A few more hours and the subterfuge would be over.

Chapter Forty-seven

Kate

After a lovely sightseeing tour of the Rock, Kate and Steve went back to the floating hotel, made love, showered together in the large walk-in shower with its gleaming chrome fittings and half-frosted glass doors, then got dressed up and set off for the short walk to their restaurant. Kate loved Ocean Village; it was so cosmopolitan and buzzing with life, people were mingling around chatting, the bars and restaurants already starting to fill up. She was so pleased that they had come to Gibraltar now. It was a fantastic surprise, and so unlike Steve to plan something so special. Was she right in thinking that Steve was going to propose? As Steve squeezed her hand and smiled at her she felt love flow through her. If he did, she would say yes. She was ready to get married, she decided. And Steve was definitely the only man for her.

'Here we are.' Steve stopped by a quaint restaurant overlooking the marina, the tables laid with delicate white-lace tablecloths. 'I booked us a table inside but we can sit out if you prefer?'

'Inside is perfect,' she told him. 'This looks a really lovely restaurant.'

The waiter led them to a secluded table in an alcove. A red rose stood in a vase on the table which was illuminated in candlelight. As Kate looked at it, she was certain that she was right and that Steve was going to propose to her. Who would have thought he could be so romantic? Her heart swelled with love and her stomach fluttered in anticipation. She was so glad she had booked this holiday to Spain. It seemed so much more romantic for Steve to propose abroad than in the UK. And to go to all this trouble, driving them to Gibraltar, booking them into the gorgeous hotel, bringing her here for a meal. It was such a wonderful thing to do.

She could sense that Steve was nervous as they chatted away whilst they ate their meal, and she tried to give him signs to reassure him, smiling at him, reaching out and placing her hand over his, letting him know that she loved him. When they'd finished and the plates had been cleared away, the waiter brought a bottle of champagne in an ice bucket and two glasses and placed it in the middle of the table, then put a small dish with a silver cover over it in front of Kate. Kate's heart thudded in her chest. Was this it? She looked at Steve questioningly and he smiled, love shining out of his eyes.

Steve smiled. 'This is just for you. I hope you like it.'

She took off the silver cover and there, on the plate in front of her, was a red velvet ring box in the shape of a heart. Tears welled to her eyes as emotion overcame her. So she was right, Steve wanted to marry her. And he really had pulled out all the stops.

Steve got down on one knee, picked up the box and opened it. A single glistening diamond sparkled out at her. She clasped her hands over her mouth as he said, 'I love you, Kate. Will you marry me, please?'

On cue, a violinist appeared and started serenading them.

Chapter Forty-eight

Josh

Josh glanced at the clock. It had just gone nine. Had Steve proposed to Kate yet? He'd told Josh that their meal was booked for eight, so they would have eaten by now. Had Kate accepted? Was she happy about the secret wedding arrangements?

'We should have heard by now, surely?' Sophie said. 'The not-knowing is making me feel sick.'

As soon as the words were out of her mouth, Josh's phone, which had been on the table in front of him for the entire meal, pinged as a message came in.

They all exchanged anxious looks.

Josh touched the screen with his finger and tapped on the message to read it, letting out his breath when he saw the name on the screen. 'It's from Mum.' He swiped it to read it. 'They've just landed in Malaga.' All the guests were arriving at their hotels tonight or tomorrow, ready for the wedding on Friday. Josh closed the message and wrinkled his brow. 'I hope it's all gone OK. I wish Steve would hurry up and phone. I'm dreading him telling us Kate has said no.'

'I would,' Maddie said firmly.

'We know!' Sophie snapped and Maddie's eyes widened in surprise. 'Sorry,' Sophie quickly apologised, 'but this waiting . . .'

Josh knew how they felt. They were all tense. Everything hinged on Kate accepting the proposal. There were thirty guests booked into three different hotels in Estepona, the wedding celebrant on standby there, the reception organised. *It will all be OK*, he told himself. *Kate and Steve love each other, of course she'll say yes.* But Kate was also independent. Would she feel like Steve had railroaded her? Especially when she found out that the wedding was all planned.

'Kate will love it, Steve has gone to so much trouble and it's so romantic,' Sophie said firmly, her fingers crossed as she spoke.

'I hope so, because if she doesn't then she might be furious with us for organising the secret wedding with Steve,' Maddie pointed out.

She was right, Josh thought. It was a big thing they'd kept from her but with the best of intentions. Would Kate see it that way? This could be a disaster not only for Steve, but for Sophie and Maddie too.

Sophie was picking at her meal; he could see that she was nervous. She and Kate had been friends since school, he remembered. She was probably really worried about losing that friendship. Think positive, he told himself. He tried to visualise the scenario. Steve getting down on one knee, Kate clasping her hand over her mouth in delight, the violinist playing, the champagne bottle uncorked.

Then a text came in. Josh grabbed his phone off the table. 'It's from Steve.' He held his breath as he opened the text. Then he smiled and read out: '*Kate said yes! We're engaged! I'll message you when I want you to come and join us.*'

'Oh, that's brilliant!' Sophie clapped her hands in delight.

Even Maddie was smiling. 'Thank goodness Kate wants to marry Steve. Now we've just got to wait and see how she reacts to his wedding plans.'

'We can at least drink to their engagement,' Sophie said. So they ordered a bottle of Cava.

'To Kate and Steve,' Josh said and they all clinked glasses.

Then Josh's phone rang. They all looked at each other as Steve's photo flashed across the screen.

Maddie and Sophie both held up crossed fingers as Josh answered the phone. He turned the speaker on so that Sophie and Maddie could hear.

'Kate's run off!' Steve's voice was shaky but loud and clear.

'What??' Josh gasped.

'It was all going really well. But when I told her that the wedding was planned for Friday and I'd flown family and friends over to Spain and that you three were over in Gibraltar too, ready to be best man and bridesmaids, she was furious. She shouted how dare I plan our bloody wedding without asking her, without letting her make any decisions. Then she stormed out. She's not answering my calls or texts. I don't know what to do.' He sounded desperate.

'Have you had a look around for her?'

'I've looked all around this area but there's no sign of her. I don't know where else to look. I wonder if I should go back to the hotel. She'll go there when she's calmed down, surely?'

'I don't know, Steve. I thought this was all a bit risky.'

'Oh, don't start saying "I told you so" now! I need your help, not a lecture!'

'Look, we've finished our meal, we'll come over to you. With a bit of luck Kate will have returned by then anyway,' Josh told him. He ended the call, his face grim. 'I knew this would happen.'

'Me too,' Maddie agreed.

'No, you didn't, nobody did.' Sophie stood up. 'Look, Kate said yes so she does want to marry Steve. We can salvage this. We just have to make her realise that Steve planned the wedding because he was trying to be romantic, not controlling.' She grabbed her bag. 'I'm going to look for Kate now.'

'Hang on, wait for us.' Maddie finished the last of her Cava and got up too.

'You two go ahead, I'll get the bill,' Josh told them. He just hoped that they could find Kate and put this right. Poor Steve would be devastated. He adored Kate. And there were all the wedding plans and guests either already in Spain or about to fly over. What a mess.

Chapter Forty-nine

Sophie

Sophie and Maddie hurried along the street from the hotel, looking out for Kate.

'She could be anywhere,' Sophie said. 'She might have gone for a walk along the marina, or into a bar to drink away her sorrows. Or even back to the hotel.'

'We'll head for Ocean Village, where the restaurant is,' Maddie said. 'I don't think she'd come into the town by herself.'

'She must be devastated. She probably thinks she can't even turn to us because we deceived her too.' Sophie felt awful as she thought of the distress Kate must be in. And Steve too, because she knew that he really loved Kate.

They hurried over to Ocean Village, looking around all the restaurants and bars for their friend. There was no sign of her.

'Hey!' They turned around to see Josh waving and hurrying towards them. 'Any luck?'

'No. Maybe she's gone back to the hotel,' Sophie said. She was getting out her phone to call Josh when Maddie pointed. 'There she is. Sitting at the table by the window.'

Sophie looked over to the bar Maddie was indicating and

sure enough, there was Kate, sitting at a table in the corner, a glass of wine on the table in front of her. She looked really upset.

Please let me find the right words to say, Sophie silently prayed as she and Maddie walked into the bar and made their way over to their friend. 'Are you OK, Kate?' Sophie asked softly as they both sat down at the table.

Kate glared at them. 'Does it look like I'm all right? Some friends you two are,' she snapped. 'You knew what Steve was planning but neither of you thought to mention it to me!'

'We couldn't, Steve swore us to secrecy. He wanted it all to be a surprise,' Sophie tried to explain. 'I thought it was romantic. I thought you'd love it.'

'I didn't like the idea and was worried you wouldn't,' Maddie admitted, 'but like Sophie said, Steve made us promise not to tell you.'

'Steve loves you. He just wanted to surprise you.' Josh had joined them now. Sophie wondered whether he had held back to give them a chance to talk to Kate or whether he'd given Steve a quick ring to let him know they'd found her. Steve must be going out of his mind. Josh pulled up a chair and sat opposite. 'He's devastated, Kate. He thinks he's lost you.'

'*He's* devastated. How does he think I feel? How dare he not only presume that I would agree to marry him but plan the whole damned wedding without me? He's chosen the dress, the flowers, the venue. Every bloody thing. He hasn't given me any say in my own wedding. Have you any idea how that feels? He's robbed me of all the excitement of planning and wedding shopping . . .' She stopped as if lost for words. Then she groaned and buried her head in her hands, her shoulders heaving as she sobbed.

Sophie swallowed and licked her lips. This was awful. Kate was so upset and so was Steve. 'When you both booked the holiday to Spain and he saw the beach weddings, he thought it would be lovely to do that,' she said softly, wanting to put her arms around Kate's shoulders and comfort her, but not sure if her friend was too mad at her to allow that.

Kate raised her head, her eyes glistening as she fought back tears. 'And it didn't occur to you two, my best friends, that I might want an input in this? That I might want to plan my own bloody wedding?'

'I told you, we were sworn to secrecy,' Maddie told her.

'He was trying to be romantic. To give you a wonderful surprise,' Sophie added.

Kate spun her head around to face her. 'How could anyone think that it's romantic to presume that someone will marry you and plan the wedding for two days after you propose?' she flared.

Sophie felt terrible. She shouldn't have gone along with this. She knew that Kate liked to make her own choices, to be in control. She didn't like decisions being made for her, especially ones as important as this. And now she thought about it, Sophie wondered if she would have liked it herself. Kate was right. They'd deprived her of the chance and the pleasure of planning her own wedding. 'I'm so sorry,' she whispered, tears springing to her eyes too.

Josh, who had been silent up until now, darted a glance at Sophie then placed his arms on the table and leant across to speak to Kate. 'Look, we're all really sorry you're so upset about this. Steve is heartbroken that you're so upset. All he wanted to do, in his stupid, ham-fisted way, was to give you a surprise

218

romantic wedding to show how much he loved you. We all tried to talk him out of it, but he was adamant you would love it. So we thought it best to help him plan it.'

'You can dress it up however you want, but the fact is that you've all been lying to me. Every one of you. I'd never do that to any of you.' Kate wiped the tears off her cheeks with the backs of her hands. 'I honestly don't know where me and Steve go from here. I was so happy when he proposed to me, but now . . . now I just feel angry. And let down.' She pushed back her chair and stood up. 'I'm going back to the hotel. And please don't follow me. I want to be on my own.'

'What are we going to do? If Kate and Steve don't go to the register office tomorrow they won't be able to get married,' Sophie said. This was awful. She couldn't believe it had all gone so drastically wrong. She felt so sorry for Kate, and for Steve, who had thought Kate would be delighted and must now be as distressed as she was.

'Give her time to think it over,' said Maddie. 'It's all been a shock. Hopefully when she's had a chance to calm down she will change her mind. Even if they don't make it to the register office in the morning they can still have the beach ceremony on Friday and maybe legalise the wedding back in the UK when they return home.'

Maddie had a point, Sophie thought. But she was worried that this was the end for Steve and Kate and she didn't know what to do about it. She couldn't help feeling guilty for her part in it.

Josh picked up his phone. 'I'll message Steve and let him know that Kate's coming back to the hotel.'

'Then let's go back to our hotel and wait for Steve to get

back to us and let us know if Kate has thought it over and will go to the registrar with him tomorrow,' Maddie suggested.

They waited all evening. Finally, at eleven p.m. Josh got a message from Steve. 'The wedding's definitely off.'

Sophie and Maddie exchanged dismayed looks. The day had started off so well and now it had gone horribly wrong.

Chapter Fifty

Kate

Kate sat on the deck of the yacht hotel, her head in turmoil. She had been so happy when Steve proposed and now she didn't even know if they had a future together. She closed her eyes, fighting back the tears as she recalled how Steve had begged her to come to the register office with him tomorrow. Saying that if she didn't then they couldn't get married on Friday. He'd pleaded with her to trust him. 'It's going to be a wonderful wedding, Kate, I promise you. Our parents will be there. And friends.'

She felt like he was ambushing her, giving her no time to think. Before she knew it they'd be man and wife. He'd robbed her of all the months of planning and going wedding shopping as Sophie had done. She felt cheated. Yes, she loved Steve but that didn't give him the right to go ahead and do this. She'd told him firmly that she needed some space, and had asked him to go and stay at Josh's hotel. She couldn't bear to share the same hotel suite with him tonight, let alone the same bed. She looked down at her finger where the engagement ring had rested so briefly, the same ring that was now lying on the dressing table in the room. Steve had left and she had come up here, wanting to sit in the stillness and try to sort out her mind.

A message pinged in. She hoped it wasn't from Steve again. She looked at her phone and saw that it was from Sophie.

Please talk to us, Kate. We're very sorry that we upset you but Steve really has planned a wonderful wedding for you. And gone to a lot of trouble to make sure it's your dream wedding. Can we come over to the hotel and explain. Please?

She read it over again. She was so tired and weary all she wanted to do was go to bed but she knew she wouldn't sleep. Sophie and Kate were good friends, she was sure that they wouldn't deliberately do anything to upset her. Neither would Steve. He loved her. But none of them seemed to understand how betrayed she felt. Maybe she should give them a chance to explain. This could be the end of her and Steve's relationship. The thought of a future without him made her feel bereft even if right now she couldn't bear to see him.

She typed back. OK. I'll wait outside the yacht for you.

She had only been waiting a few minutes when she saw Sophie and Maddie walking towards her. She burst into tears when they reached her.

Sophie held out her arms and Kate walked into them. 'I'm so sorry, Kate. But please let us explain and maybe you won't be so upset then.'

Kate sniffed and nodded. 'Come up to our room. Steve's with Josh. I'm so angry and hurt I don't want to see him right now. All I want to do is go home.'

222

She led the way to the lift up into their spacious double room with its huge picture window overlooking the marina.

'Wow! This is amazing!' Maddie gasped. 'Steve has really pulled out the stops here, Kate.'

Kate sank down on to the cream leather sofa. 'Yes, he's gone to a lot of trouble. Shame he didn't go to the trouble of telling me his plans. Or that either of you didn't see fit to tell me!' she said, tearfully. 'This is supposed to be the biggest day of my life and I've had no say in it. I haven't even chosen my own dress.'

'You have though. You've chosen your dress, the wedding theme, the flowers, everything,' Sophie told her.

'What do you mean?' Kate asked, puzzled. She looked from one to the other. 'What's going on?'

'Look, Steve will be mad at me for telling you this, but after the register office service you're driving back to Estepona for a wonderful beach ceremony,' Sophie replied. 'With thirty family and friends. Steve asked us to help him plan it when you both booked your holiday. And it's not been easy, I can tell you.'

Kate looked stunned. 'What?'

Sophie switched on her tablet. 'Let me show you.' She selected the folder 'Secret Wedding' and showed Kate the picture of her wedding dress. 'Do you remember choosing this?'

Kate nodded slowly. 'That's the dress you're going to wear when you get married to Glenn.'

'No, it isn't. I pretended that me and Glenn were getting married so that I could talk about wedding planning to you and try to find out what sort of wedding you would like,' she confessed. 'It was Steve's idea.'

'And me and Sophie are going to be bridesmaids, wearing the dresses you chose,' Maddie added. 'Josh is best man, he drove over to Spain with your wedding dress, the bridesmaids' dresses and suits so they wouldn't get creased up. They're hanging in his room.'

Kate looked taken aback. 'So this . . .' she pointed to the wedding dress on the screen. 'This is my dress?'

'Yes.'

'And when I was getting fitted for a bridesmaid's dress for your wedding – or so I thought – I was actually being fitted for my own wedding dress?'

Sophie nodded, chewing her lip. 'Yes. I'm sorry, but we had to make sure we got the right size dress.'

Maddie leant over and swiped the screen to the next image, showing a couple getting married on a beach. 'This is the actual beach where you're getting married. It's a little cove with a beach restaurant.'

Kate gasped, her eyes wide. 'Oh God, it's gorgeous.'

'Do you want me to show you more or to leave the rest as a surprise?' Sophie asked her, relieved at her friend's reaction.

Kate lifted her eyes from the screen and looked first at Maddie then Sophie. 'All those questions you've been asking me. What sort of cake I'd like, pretending that it was you and Glenn getting married? I can't believe it. You've all been stringing me along.'

'For a good cause,' Sophie reminded her. 'Steve was determined to have a surprise wedding but he wanted it to be the wedding you wanted, so he asked us to help him. Wouldn't you do that for us?'

Kate ran her hand through her hair and stood up, folding her arms as she paced around the room. 'I can see that you've all meant well. And I appreciate it. But what really hurts it that I haven't had the chance to get excited about my own wedding.'

Sophie blinked rapidly and her face crumpled. 'None of us thought of that. I'm so sorry, Kate.' She buried her head in her hands.

Maddie put her arms around Sophie. 'We've all worked hard these last three months to plan you the wedding of your dreams, Kate. Even when Glenn walked out on Sophie, she carried on planning your wedding, and that was really hard for her.'

Kate was horrified to hear this. 'You and Glenn have split up? Oh Sophie, I'm so sorry.' She hurried over and squeezed Sophie's hand.

'It's fine. Yes, I was gutted at first, but I can see now that it was for the best. We didn't really love each other. Not like you and Steve.'

Kate was starting to wonder if she had overreacted. It seemed that Steve had really put a lot of thought into his surprise wedding plans. She pushed a strand of hair behind her ears as she tried to take it all in. 'I just don't understand why he did it. It's not like him at all.'

'Because you'd told him he hadn't got a romantic bone in his body and he wanted to show you that he had,' Maddie replied.

Kate groaned. She had said that, hadn't she? They'd had a tiff about Steve leaving everything to Kate to organise and she'd said he hadn't got a romantic bone in his body and she wished he'd be more spontaneous.

So this was his way of proving her wrong.

'Steve said he's arranged for both sets of parents to fly over for the wedding?'

'Yes, to the beach wedding in Spain. And close family and friends too. There will only be the five of us at the register office service. This is just the legal bit,' Maddie told her.

'Do you want to know more about the plans or do you want to leave them as a surprise?' Sophie asked her again. 'I promise you that you'll be delighted. It will be a wonderful day for you.'

'But he presumed I would say yes. What if I'd said no?'

'Kate, you love each other. Everyone can see that. And Steve said that you'd both discussed marriage,' Sophie pointed out. 'Plus you did accept his proposal so you must want to marry him.'

Kate was silent for a moment as she thought over everything Sophie and Maddie had told her. She did love Steve. And she knew he loved her. And she wanted to marry him. She let out a long breath. 'Yes, I do love him. And yes, I do want to marry him.'

'Great. Then please phone him and tell him that. And turn up at the register office tomorrow to do the legal paperwork,' Sophie urged her.

Suddenly there was a knock on the door. 'It's Josh. Please let me in. I need to talk to Kate.'

Sophie and Maddie both turned to Kate, questioningly. She walked over to the door and opened it. 'Where's Steve?' she asked.

'Down in the reception. He's beside himself, Kate. Could you please at least talk to him? I've never seen him so distraught.'

Kate swallowed then nodded. 'Ask him to come up.'

Josh went to get his brother and Sophie and Maddie got up to leave.

'We'll make ourselves scarce. We'll be down in the bar if you want us,' Sophie told her.

Steve came in, looking pale and distressed, his hair standing on end as if he'd run his hands repeatedly through it. Which he probably had.

'Kate, I'm so sorry. Please forgive me. We'll cancel the wedding. Tell everyone I made a stupid mistake. We'll have a holiday, like we were going to do. And our family and friends can have a holiday too. We don't have to get married ever. Just please don't dump me. I couldn't bear it if you finished with me.'

Kate clasped her hands as she looked at him, her mind in turmoil, only dimly aware of Sophie and Maddie silently leaving the room, closing the door behind them.

Chapter Fifty-one

Sophie

Josh was waiting down in the bar, drumming his fingers on the table. 'How's it looking?' he asked.

Sophie held up crossed fingers. 'Kate has admitted that she loves Steve and wants to marry him, but she's upset about how he went about it. We had to show her some of the wedding stuff so that she knew that Steve had tried hard to find out what wedding she would like and I think she's coming around now.'

'I need a strong drink,' Maddie said, collapsing into the seat next to Josh. 'It was pretty fraught in there.'

'Me too,' said Sophie. 'I'll go and get them. Strawberry gin and tonic?' she asked.

'Perfect. Thanks.'

Sophie glanced at Josh's half-empty glass. 'How about you?'

'I'm OK, thanks.'

When she returned with the drinks, Josh and Maddie were both talking, heads bent towards each other, practically touching. Sophie stood still for a moment, watching them. She guessed it was only to be expected, they were both similar in nature, both not wanting commitment. Maddie had told her that it was back off with Ezri again, so she guessed a fling with Josh was on the cards.

Josh threw back his head and laughed, his gaze meeting Sophie's, his indigo-blue eyes staring straight at her, and something inside her did a little flip. But once again she was surprised at her reaction to him when she had just broken up with Glenn. Well, Josh was an attractive guy and she was only human. It didn't mean anything, just a natural bodily reaction.

They were all on their third drink when Steve and Kate walked into the bar, their hands entwined and both looking loved up, although Kate was still a little red-eyed and pale.

They had obviously not split up, but was the wedding on? Sophie wondered.

As they approached the table she saw the ring glistening on Kate's engagement finger. Did that mean . . .?

Josh stood up. 'I hope this is good news.'

'It is. The wedding's on,' Steve told them and he and Kate both smiled at each other.

'Well, thank goodness for that!' Maddie exclaimed. 'Now let's order a bottle of champagne and celebrate.'

'This is on me.' Josh stepped forward and wrapped his arm around Kate, kissing her on the cheek. 'Welcome to the family, sis.'

Kate smiled and Sophie swallowed a lump in her throat. She had been so worried that Kate and Steve would break up and was so pleased that they'd made it up.

After sharing a bottle of champagne with them, Kate and Steve said that they were going back to their room. 'It's late and we have to be at the register office for ten,' Kate told them. She looked exhausted.

'Do you want to meet us in the square for something to eat

afterwards or do you want to spend some time alone?' Josh asked.

'Actually . . .' Steve looked awkward before continuing, 'I've booked us all a trip to see the dolphins later. My treat to you guys for helping me sort out the wedding.' He turned to Kate. 'I've booked the trip for four p.m., but I can cancel if you prefer to spend the afternoon just the two of us.'

She kissed him on the cheek. 'I'd love for us all to go on the dolphin trip.' She turned back to Sophie and Maddie. 'That is if you all want to?'

'Definitely!' Sophie replied. She loved dolphins.

'And it would be nice to meet for lunch too?' Kate added.

'It would.' Steve looked at her lovingly then turned back to the others. 'We should be finished by midday; if so we'll join you for something to eat then and meet you later at the marina for the boat trip.'

'Great. And we need to plan your hen night. Don't think you're getting away with not having one.' This was from Maddie.

Kate smiled. 'Thank you, both of you. But can we girls just go out for a meal? I'd like a quiet evening with my two best friends. If that's OK?'

'Sure. That sounds perfect,' Maddie told her and Sophie nodded her agreement.

'I guess we'll go out for a meal too, bro,' Josh said to Steve.

'Sounds good. We'll sort out the details later, Kate and I need to go now.' With a wave they both set off into the town.

'Well, thank goodness it all worked out.' Josh let out a sigh of relief as Kate and Steve left. 'Now, do you two fancy going on to a bar for a bit or do you want to turn in?'

Sophie looked at her watch. It was gone midnight and she was exhausted. 'I'm going to turn in, it's been a long day,' she said.

'I'll join you for a pub crawl,' Maddie told him. 'I'm sure there's some brilliant night-life here.' She grinned at Sophie. 'I promise I'll creep in and not wake you up.'

'Oh, don't worry about me, I'll be out like a light as soon as my head touches the pillow,' Sophie told them. 'Enjoy yourselves.'

But when she climbed into bed half an hour later it took a while for her to fall asleep. Images of Maddie and Josh dancing closely together and kissing kept flitting across her mind. For some confusing reason that bothered her. *What does it matter if they get together?* she told herself. *You're not interested in him anyway. He's much more Maddie's type.*

When she awoke the next morning she glanced over at Maddie's bed, her heart lifting at the sight of Maddie sleeping there. So she hadn't spent the night with Josh then. Not that it mattered. At least it shouldn't. Her feelings for Josh were unsettling her.

She threw back the thin sheet covering the bed and headed for a shower before Maddie woke and took over the bathroom. She was showered, dressed and boiling the kettle ready for a drink before Maddie stirred. 'What time is it?' she asked, sitting up and rubbing her eyes, still managing to look sexy even with bed-hair. *No wonder men are so attracted to her*, Sophie thought.

'Just gone ten. I thought I'd leave you to wake naturally.' Sophie popped a teabag in one of the white mugs left on the tray. 'Do you want breakfast tea, coffee or fruit tea — there's chamomile, mint and red berry.'

231

'I'll have black coffee, please. I need something to wake me up, my head feels thick and heavy.'

Sophie kept her back to her friend as she asked, 'Did you have a good night?'

'Brilliant. Josh is such good company. You should have come with us.'

'I was too tired. Anyway, I'm sure you wouldn't want me to play gooseberry.' She felt annoyed as she heard the edge to her voice. She sounded jealous. She took a breath and forced a smile on her face as she turned around and took the coffee to her friend. 'Here you are.'

'We're just having a bit of fun together, it's nothing serious.' Maddie squinted her eyes as she tried to focus on Sophie. 'You're not interested in Josh, are you? Because if you are I'll back off. I'm not serious about him. He's a nice guy, but not my type.'

'I thought you were both just right for each other. Both extrovert, not wanting commitment.' Sophie picked up Maddie's glasses from the bedside table and handed them to her.

'Thanks.' Maddie slipped them on then took the mug of coffee. 'Well, do you fancy Josh?' she demanded, seeming determined not to let the subject drop.

'Of course I don't,' Sophie denied hastily.

Maddie blew on her coffee and took a sip. 'That's a shame because he's fun and very easy on the eye and . . .' she took another sip of her coffee. 'Anyone can see that it's you he's interested in.'

'Don't be daft!' Sophie was genuinely shocked.

Maddie raised a smudged eyebrow. 'Soph, he can't keep his eyes off you. And when he sees you in your bridesmaid's dress tomorrow, he'll be even more smitten.'

Sophie gaped at her. Was Maddie serious? Did Josh really share the growing attraction she was feeling for him? She shrugged. Well, if he did, nothing would come of it. He wasn't her type and she had no intention of getting hurt again. She'd only just got over Glenn. She was going to be a man-free zone for the foreseeable.

Chapter Fifty-two

Josh

Josh woke with a thick head. He massaged his forehead, his mind going back to last night. He and Maddie had taken a walk over to Ocean Village and had a few drinks, not rolling in until gone three this morning. Maddie was good company, and heads certainly turned whenever they walked in anywhere – probably more because of her purple hair and the harlequin patterned jumpsuit she'd worn, although she was striking with her high cheekbones, pouty lips and slender figure.

Not as striking as Sophie though.

He'd hoped that Sophie would join them. He'd have liked a chance to get to know her better. She didn't give any impression of wanting to spend any time with him though. He wasn't sure whether that was because she still wasn't over Glenn, or because he wasn't her type. Which was a shame. She was gorgeous, sweet and caring – the sort of woman you could rely on. Who would never betray you, who wanted a steady, serious relationship leading to marriage, he reminded himself. Which was definitely something he didn't want. It would be best not to get involved with her, even if she was attracted to him. He didn't want to hurt her. Stay away, Josh, he warned himself.

He got out of bed and headed for the shower. He needed to liven himself up and eat something, then he'd feel better. He glanced at his watch lying on the bedside cabinet. Half past ten, and they were meeting Steve and Kate at midday. He hoped everything would go well this morning, that Kate wouldn't have another change of heart.

After showering and pulling on denim shorts and a grey vest he made himself a strong coffee then went to meet Sophie and Maddie in the foyer. They walked in a few minutes later, Sophie wearing a gorgeous floaty floral dress and Maddie dressed in a T-shirt and cropped psychedelic trousers.

'Have you heard anything from Steve this morning?' Sophie asked as they walked into town.

'Nope, and I thought it best not to message him. Let them have a bit of time to themselves. I reckon I would have heard from the wedding planner if Kate had backed out, so hopefully all's well.'

'My head's pounding. How's yours?' Maddie asked.

'Someone's playing football inside it.'

Sophie grinned. 'I'm glad I didn't come with you.'

'You should have, it was a great night even if we are suffering for it now,' Josh told her.

'Yeah, but I wanted to feel fresh for today. I'm really looking forward to it,' Sophie said. 'I hope we get to see some dolphins.'

'I swam with dolphins once in Mexico,' Maddie informed them. 'It was fantastic.'

'I did too in New Zealand,' Josh told her.

Sophie looked from one to the other. 'You two are so alike it's unbelievable.'

'Too alike, we egg each other on,' Josh told her.

'You didn't need much egging on from what I can remember,' Maddie told him.

Josh grinned. 'We should have had Sophie with us, she'd have kept us in check.'

'Don't you believe it!' Maddie scoffed. 'Underneath that sweet exterior Sophie can be quite wild.'

Josh turned to Sophie, the smile on his face reaching his eyes. 'Now that I would like to see.'

They were at the restaurant now, so they sat down at an empty table outside.

Maddie picked up the menu. 'I'm starving. I think I'll go for a full English.'

'Me too,' Josh agreed.

Before Sophie could reply, Maddie started waving. 'Here they are. And they're holding hands too. They must have signed the papers.'

'Thank goodness for that!' Josh exclaimed.

'Well, that's it, all the legal paperwork done and delivered to the notary to sign off. The wedding planner said she'd pick it up from him and take it back to the registry office later,' Steve said as they joined them. He smiled at Kate. 'We're officially getting married in the morning.'

Thank goodness for that, Josh thought as Kate smiled happily back.

'Brilliant news. We've just ordered a late breakfast. Do you two fancy it?' Sophie asked them.

'Toast will do for me,' Kate said, and Steve nodded in

agreement as he pulled out a chair for her, then waited for her to sit down before sitting down himself.

'I'm really looking forward to the dolphin trip,' Kate said enthusiastically. 'And to our meal tonight. I'm going to enjoy my last day of being single.'

'Are you going to change your name?' Maddie asked her.

Kate shook her head. 'No chance. I'm happy being Kate Preston. Steve's changing his name instead.'

'What?' Josh's mouth dropped open and Kate and Steve laughed.

'She got you there, mate,' Steve told him. 'We're both keeping our own names.' He smiled at Kate and reached for her hand. 'I don't mind what Kate calls herself as long as she marries me.'

Chapter Fifty-three

Sophie

Sophie breathed in the sea air and looked around her in wonder. The sea was so blue and calm, like a painting. Puffy white clouds flitted across the summer sky, a slight breeze taking the edge off the sun's heat. It was idyllic. A really gorgeous day. She felt like she could stay on this boat for ever, sailing across the sea. It was like being in another world.

On her right, Steve had his arm around Kate's shoulders as they both gazed at the sparkling ocean. On her left, Maddie and Josh were chatting and laughing, and behind her a couple of families were pointing out to sea, with their children. Everyone was looking out for the dolphins. Sophie would be so disappointed if they didn't see any of the beautiful creatures and knew that the others would be too. There was no guarantee, the captain had told them, but it was very rare that they didn't see any. Especially on a beautiful day like today.

Sophie turned around, her eyes seeking out the far-away shore. They had covered quite a distance in the short time since they'd left.

'Fantastic, isn't it?' Maddie said to her.

Sophie nodded, trying to drink it all in. She was determined to enjoy this holiday, to savour every moment of it, and when she went back home she was going to make a few changes to her life. To try new things, live a little more. She'd played on the safe side for years; now it was time to let go. She was definitely going to move, and she decided that she was going to talk to Pat about working three days a week in the shop and two days on her gift boxes and terrariums, as Janine suggested. It was time she stepped out of her comfort zone.

She heard a chuckle and glanced around to see Kate laughing as Steve talked animatedly to her; they had definitely made up, thank goodness.

'Smile!' Josh said, clicking his phone camera as soon as Sophie turned. 'Now stand by Maddie, I'll take one of you both with the sea behind you.'

She did, and they pouted, giggled as he snapped some more shots. 'I'll send them to you later,' he promised.

'Where are the dolphins? I want to see the dolphins!' a little girl said loudly.

'I'm sorry we haven't spotted any dolphins yet, but don't worry, we're going to change direction and head out a bit further,' the man at the helm of the boat shouted. 'I'm sure we'll see some.'

He turned the boat around and headed off towards choppier waters. They could see another boat in the distance too. After a few minutes Josh placed his hand on the top of Sophie's arm and shouted. 'Dolphins!'

Her eyes followed his finger pointing out to sea. There, leaping out of the water were two – no, three – sleek grey-blue and white dolphins. They leapt high into the air then plunged back into the water again. Gasps and shouts rang through the boat as more people spotted them. The dolphins followed them through the water, alongside the boat. Dozens of phones zoomed in on them, taking photos and videos.

'I think they're giving us an escort!' Maddie exclaimed.

'There's some at the front of the boat now!' a cry rang out and Sophie turned to see dolphins springing out of the water ahead of them. It was as if they were putting on a spectacular display especially for them. She counted nine dolphins, but more were jumping about a little way from the boat.

'They like to swim at the bow because the force of the water pushes them forward too,' the boatman said. 'They're really friendly creatures, and have been known to save the lives of sailors lost out at sea by swimming alongside them and guiding them to land.'

'Oh my God, they're beautiful,' Sophie said in delight.

'They certainly are.' Josh's gaze met hers for a moment then he turned away and she stood there shell-shocked at the electrifying tingle that ran down her spine as his eyes had held hers.

Was Maddie right and he had feelings for her?

Did she have feeling for Josh?

Chapter Fifty-four

Kate

I'm getting married tomorrow. Kate repeated the words over and over in her mind. She could hardly believe it. And yes, she had been upset when she discovered that Steve had planned the wedding in secret and had assumed that she would accept his proposal. She felt as if he had taken her for granted, was being controlling. But then she had seen how devastated he was, and they'd talked, really talked, and she realised that he hadn't taken her for granted, he'd just been confident in their love for each other. And rather than being controlling he'd just wanted to give her a wonderful surprise. And had gone to a lot of trouble to ensure that he planned the wedding Kate would have wanted.

And now. Now she was really looking forward to tomorrow. The dolphin trip this afternoon had been magical, and this yacht hotel was wonderful. *I'm lucky to be marrying someone so thoughtful.*

As if he could sense her thoughts, Steve came up behind her, wrapping his arms around her waist, his eyes meeting hers in the mirror. 'I can't believe that you're going to be my wife. I'm so lucky,' he said softly.

She turned around, wrapping her arms around him too. 'We're both lucky,' she said.

Later that evening Kate went out for a meal with Sophie and Maddie, while Josh and Steve dined together at Josh's hotel then went to a local bar in the town – with Josh promising that he wouldn't allow Steve to get drunk. Steve was spending the night in Josh's room so that he didn't see the bride before the wedding. Sophie and Maddie had brought the wedding dress over as soon as Steve was out the way, and Kate had hung it proudly in the massive wardrobe. She couldn't wait to wear it!

'How are you feeling about the wedding now?' Sophie asked Kate as they started on their desserts.

Kate smiled at her. 'I'm actually really excited about it. Today has been perfect and I'm sure tomorrow will be too. And if it isn't . . .'

Sophie and Maddie both paused, forks halfway towards their mouths, as they waited for Kate to finish.

She shrugged. 'Well, it doesn't matter. I'm marrying Steve, that's all the matters.'

'So we're forgiven, then, for keeping it all a secret?' Maddie asked.

Kate nodded. 'I know you were only trying to help. Thank you both for all your hard work helping Steve plan the wedding. I know it must have taken up a lot of your time,' she said sincerely.

'You're welcome. We're just glad it's all worked out OK,' Sophie told her.

'You bet!' Maddie agreed.

'You're both the best friends anyone could have,' Kate told them. 'Now, how about we have a drink in our room when we've had this meal? I don't want a late night, though. I want to feel fresh and relaxed in the morning.' It would be her wedding day and she wanted to make sure she enjoyed every minute of it.

'Suits me. I haven't recovered from last night yet,' Maddie told her.

Kate looked at her in amusement. 'Yes, Josh said that you both had a late night. You know what they say about the bridesmaid and the best man . . .'

'Yeah, but which bridesmaid?' Maddie winked and put the last morsel of cake in her mouth.

Kate glanced at Sophie who shook her head vehemently. 'Don't look at me. Josh isn't my type at all. And I'm off men.'

I hope Sophie is over her heartbreak now, Kate thought. She had never thought that Glenn was the right one for Sophie though. He was too . . . boring. Sophie was sweet, and fairly reserved until you got to know her, but she was fun and very kindhearted. And she loved to have a laugh. She and Maddie were a right pair sometimes. Sophie should be with someone who appreciated her and made her laugh. Still, it was only natural she'd want time to get over Glenn. Well, hopefully this holiday would help her heal a bit. Two weeks of fun in the sun would do her the world of good.

'This hotel is really something,' Maddie said as they sat on the sofa in Kate and Steve's room sharing a bottle of wine. 'Steve certainly went overboard here.'

'It is gorgeous, isn't it? I almost wish we were staying here another night; it would be quite nice to spend our wedding night here.' Kate picked up the stem of her glass. 'Mind you, the hotel in Estepona is lovely too. And I can't wait for the beach ceremony. The photos will be stunning.'

243

She was really looking forward to the wedding now. Her dress was gorgeous and Steve said her dad had flown over to give her away. Her mum was coming too. She hadn't seen her parents together since their rather bitter divorce, but hopefully the years that had passed would have improved relations between them and they could manage a few hours of not sniping at each other for her wedding. They could ignore each other for the rest of the weekend. Steve had said that there was a reception at the hotel for the guests in the evening too. It seemed like he really had thought of everything, with the help of Sophie, Maddie and Josh. She was feeling very loved.

'Right, we're going back to our room before we open another bottle of wine,' Sophie said when their glasses were empty. 'We don't want you having a hangover for your wedding. Do you want us to come up and help you get ready in the morning?'

Kate nodded. 'Yes, please. Bring your bridesmaids' dresses with you and we can all get ready together. It'll be fun. Can you be here about nine? The wedding is at eleven fifteen and I want to give us plenty of time to get ready.'

'Definitely. We've booked a hair stylist and make-up artist for nine thirty and a the photographer will come just before we leave,' Sophie said with a smile. Kate's face lit up.

'Now get some beauty sleep – not that you need it,' Maddie added hastily as she picked up her bag.

Kate went to the door with them, waving as she watched them walk along the corridor to the lift. It seemed strange to be in the room by herself.

Tomorrow is my wedding day, she thought as she climbed into bed not long afterwards, make up removed and teeth brushed.

Her mind drifted to Steve, sleeping in the twin single bed in

Josh's room. Was he as excited as she was? He must be; he had planned all this.

I hope he's thought of everything. I couldn't bear it if something went wrong. The thought flashed across her mind as she closed her eyes. She dismissed it. It didn't matter if something went wrong. She and Steve were getting married, that's all that mattered, she thought happily.

Chapter Fifty-five

Sophie

The Wedding Day

'I hope Kate appreciates the sacrifice I've made for her,' Maddie said as she smoothed down the front of her bridesmaid's dress.

'Shhh!' Sophie put her finger to her lips. They were in Kate and Steve's suite getting ready. Maddie and Sophie were using the lounge while Kate was in the bedroom.

Maddie wrinkled her nose. 'I don't recognise myself.'

Sophie barely recognised her either. The hair stylist and make-up artist had arrived earlier and worked their magic on them all. Maddie looked beautiful – but very un-Maddie. In a strange way, the colour of the bridesmaid's dress – lavender – worked with Maddie's purple hair. Today she wore purple contact lenses too, which were very striking, and the sleeveless dress artistically revealed her dragon and phoenix tattoos. She looked stunning. Maddie didn't wear dresses often, and when she did they were usually bohemian rather than elegant like this one. Sophie thought she had never seen Maddie look so lovely and was sure Josh wouldn't be able to keep his eyes off her. 'You look amazing,' she said. Maybe she should be more like Maddie. She didn't want purple hair or tattoos, but she could wear brighter clothes, stop playing safe, have more fun.

Maddie grimaced at her. 'I feel stupid, like I'm wearing someone else's clothes. But I'll do it for our Kate. Whereas you look gorgeous and as if that dress was made just for you.'

'Thanks.' Sophie was pleased with the dress actually. It was simple, elegant and cool – although the plunging neckline and slit up the side was a bit racier than she normally wore. It was already feeling hot and it was still morning. She dreaded to think how hot it would be this afternoon. They were driving straight to the beach wedding after the register office service, and hopefully the dresses wouldn't get crumpled in the car.

They both turned to face the bedroom door as Kate shouted, 'Are you two ready? I'm coming out.'

'We're ready!' Maddie and Sophie shouted in unison.

The door opened and Kate glided out. She looked sensational. Her dark hair was swept up in a chignon, with tendrils framing her face, and the ivory gown fitted her perfectly, clinging to her slender hips and fanning out into a fish tail. She did a twirl to reveal the row of narrow buttons down the back of the dress. 'Ta da!' Then she lifted up the skirt of the dress and showed them the ivory satin shoes Sophie had chosen. 'They fit perfectly.'

'You look stunning!' Sophie told her.

'A total knock-out,' Maddie agreed.

'I love it. Thank you for tricking me into choosing it and having my measurements taken. It fits like a dream.' She smiled at them both as she smoothed down the front of her dress. 'You both look so beautiful. I still can't get over seeing you wearing such a girly dress, Maddie,' Kate said. 'I can't wait to see Steve in his suit. And Josh, of course.'

Kate looked so gorgeous, ready to go and marry the love of her life, Sophie thought happily. Thank goodness it had all worked out.

'The bouquets haven't arrived yet,' Maddie whispered.

Sophie checked her watch, they should have been here almost an hour ago. 'I'd better phone the florist,' she said, but just as she picked up her phone there was a knock on the door.

Sophie opened it to see the manager standing there holding a big narrow box containing the carefully laid out bouquets. 'I'm so sorry, these arrived a little while ago but the receptionist got waylaid and forgot to have them sent up to you.'

'That's OK, thank you.' Sophie took the box off him, closed the door and carried the box of flowers inside. 'Here we are, the flowers have arrived.' She took out a glorious cascading bridal bouquet of ivory roses and lilac Cala lilies with deep green foliage. There were two smaller posies of white roses for Sophie and Maddie.

'They're gorgeous – and I love the colour scheme, purple, white and green – it's the colour of the suffragettes, you know. I don't know if Steve chose it deliberately but it's very feminist.'

'He did. He thought you'd appreciate it – those were his exact words,' Sophie told her.

'A good choice and definitely brownie points for Steve,' Maddie said with a grin.

Then the photographer arrived and took several photos of them, and of the flowers.

'I'll head over to the register office now and take some of you arriving,' she said.

It was only a short walk to the register office but Steve had booked a taxi for them. When they arrived, Josh and Steve were already there, both looking incredibly handsome in their light grey suits, a lilac buttonhole in their jackets. Sophie saw the look of relief and adoration on Steve's face as his eyes rested on Kate. 'You look beautiful,' he whispered and Kate positively glowed.

Josh stared at Maddie. 'Wow! I almost didn't recognise you! You look stunning,' he told her, the admiration evident in his voice. Maddie grinned. Then Josh's eyes flitted to Sophie, quickly looking her up and down. 'And so do you, Sophie.'

Sophie flushed, wondering if he had said that so that she didn't feel awkward. It was Maddie he had looked at first – but then Maddie did look really different today, it was only natural he would comment on that.

'You all look amazing,' Steve said, his hand now holding Kate's, their fingers interlaced.

Then a door to a side room opened and a man stepped out. 'We're ready for you now.'

Kate and Steve exchanged a smile and walked in together.

'Well, it looks like I'm the lucky one, two beautiful ladies on my arm,' Josh said. He looped both his arms. 'Allow me.'

Sophie slipped her arm through his right, and Maddie through his left then they joined Kate and Steve for the wedding ceremony. There were two registrars, the man who was conducting the ceremony and a lady who was dealing with the paperwork.

It was a beautiful ceremony. Kate and Steve had both written

249

their own vows – Kate writing hers last night when she'd returned from the hen night with Sophie and Maddie. When the registrar conducting the service had announced them as man and wife, Steve asked if they could dance to their song. The registrars looked at each other in surprise, then grinned. 'Go ahead,' the male registrar said.

Steve propped his phone up on his desk, tapped the screen a few times and then the words of 'Always and Forever' poured out. Sophie swallowed the lump in her throat as Steve took Kate in his arms and started dancing. The photographer snapped a couple of shots and Josh quickly picked up his phone and started to video them dancing together. That final touch had made the ceremony so romantic.

Even the registrars wiped away a tear from their eyes as they watched. When the song had finished, Steve drew Kate in for a final, lingering kiss and everyone in that little room clapped.

'That's the first time anyone has ever done that,' one of the registrars said.

Kate nestled her head into Steve's shoulder.

'Well, that's it, we pulled it off,' Josh said.

Sophie looked up at him and smiled. 'Thank goodness for that. Now there's just the beach wedding to get through.'

The photographer took some photos in the gardens opposite the register office, then they all went back to the hotel to get into the cars to set off for the drive to Estepona.

'Do you ladies want to get changed so that your dresses don't crease?' Josh asked.

'No way, I'm not taking this dress off at all today,' Kate told him. 'If it gets creased, it gets creased.'

'In that case, we'll keep our dresses on too,' Sophie said.

'Besides, if we let Maddie take hers off I don't think she'll put it on again.'

They all laughed as Maddie screwed up her nose and muttered something about the sacrifices she made for her friends. Then they set off for the second part of the wedding.

Chapter Fifty-six

Josh

Josh had found it difficult to keep his eyes off Sophie from the moment she'd walked into the register office with Kate and Maddie, her blond curls swept up in a soft chignon, a sexy tendril each side of her face, and that gorgeous dress that fitted her stunning figure to perfection. She was so pretty, feminine and curvy. When Steve had scooped Kate into his arms to dance, Josh had wanted to scoop Sophie into his arms too. He'd videoed the dance partly as a distraction, to stop himself from gazing at Sophie, and now she was sitting behind him in the car and every time he looked in the mirror he could see her stunning topaz eyes, cute nose and rosebud mouth. He wished Maddie had sat behind him instead, he was finding it difficult to concentrate.

Steve was driving the car in front, Kate sitting on the back seat, the train of her dress now hooked up, and the skirt of her dress spread out so that it didn't crease. Their wedding was at two, so they should have had plenty of time to get there, but Josh soon realised they were cutting it fine. They'd forgotten to take into account the inevitable queues at both border controls for passport checks when leaving Gibraltar. Then there was an accident on the road to Estepona which caused a long traffic build-up. 'We're going to be late,' Sophie said anxiously, as they came to a standstill.

Josh glanced over his shoulder. 'They can't start without the bride.'

'What if the celebrant has another wedding to do? I'll have to let her know we might be delayed.' Sophie fished in her bag for her phone and dialled the celebrant's number. 'Answerphone. Maybe she's been delayed too.' She left a short message to explain what had happened, saying they might be twenty minutes or so late. 'Kate and Steve must be panicking too,' she said.

'It can't be helped,' Josh tried to reassure her. 'It's not that long a drive to the venue, we can make up time once we can get moving properly again.'

'It'll be OK, don't fret,' Maddie said. 'We won't be that late.'

Sophie bit her lip. 'What if the celebrant can't wait though? Kate will be so disappointed if she doesn't have the beach ceremony. It's the main part of the wedding.'

The ring of Sophie's phone made them all jump. 'It's Kate,' Sophie said, answering it.

'Steve's panicking that we're going to be late and I can't phone anyone because I'm not supposed to know about the beach wedding,' Kate said.

'I've tried to phone the celebrant but no answer, so I've left a message,' Sophie told her. 'Should I call your parents? Or how about Peta?' She'd been in contact with Kate's sister-in-law a couple of times over the wedding arrangements. 'She can tell the celebrant what's happened and ask her to hang on.'

'Peta would be best. Thanks, Sophie. I'm presuming you have her number?'

'Yep. And Kate, don't panic, it will all be OK. I'm sure the celebrant can wait a little.'

'I hope so,' Kate said as she ended the call.

Sophie nodded. 'Good idea.' She dialled Peta's number, then frowned. 'That's gone to answerphone too. I wonder if they're all on the beach waiting for us.'

Thankfully the cars in the queue started to move. 'We're on our way,' Josh said.

Steve pulled away, racing ahead, and Josh followed. He guessed that like him his brother was anxious to make up for lost time. Luckily the road was clear for the rest of the journey and they pulled up at the car park at the back of the beach restaurant only ten minutes late.

Kate and Steve had already disappeared into the restaurant to freshen up in the washroom when Peta came hurrying over, looking agitated.

'What's up?' Sophie asked anxiously.

'George fell over and broke his arm this morning. Billy's taken him and June, his wife, to hospital but we haven't heard a word from them since. I've phoned and left countless messages but no reply.'

Josh listened in dismay. Kate wouldn't want to get married without her dad there to give her away.

'George said to tell Kate to go ahead with the wedding if he isn't back in time, but I haven't told her yet because I don't want to worry her.' Peta looked really concerned. 'I can't keep it from her for much longer. If the parents aren't back within the next few minutes, I'm going to have to tell her.'

Sophie nodded. 'How long have they been gone?' she asked.

'Almost three hours. We expected them back ages ago.'

254

'Has everyone else arrived? Is the celebrant here?' Maddie asked.

'Yes, she's already down on the beach. Everything's laid out. All the guests are waiting. It looks beautiful ... and so do you two,' she added as if she'd only just noticed the bridesmaids' dresses.

'Maybe Kate's mum can give her away if her dad doesn't get back in time,' Josh suggested.

'She will, but hopefully George will be here soon. He'll be gutted to miss Kate getting married,' Peta said.

'I'd better pop to the loo.' Josh went into the restaurant – and came out a few minutes later with three bottles of water. 'I thought you might need these.' He handed one to Maddie and one to Sophie then unscrewed the top of the other one and took a long swig.

'Thanks!' Sophie and Maddie both opened theirs and downed the cool drink gratefully.

'Do you need the loo, or a quick freshen up?' Josh asked.

Maddie nodded. 'I do.'

'Me too,' Sophie added.

They'd just disappeared into the restaurant when Peta's phone pinged. She opened the text. 'It's from Billy. They're on their way but they'll be another fifteen minutes,' she said. 'I hope the celebrant can hang on.'

'I'll go and let her know. And I think you should tell Kate about her dad, otherwise it will give her a shock when he turns up with his arm in a sling,' Josh said. He hoped the celebrant could wait. It would be awful if the ceremony couldn't go ahead.

Chapter Fifty-seven

Kate

When Kate and Steve came out of the restaurant a few minutes later, Kate noticed Peta, Sophie and Maddie were huddled up talking. She immediately sensed something was wrong and went over to them.

'What's up?' she asked.

'It's nothing for you to worry about, but your dad had a little accident this morning, he tripped over and fell down a few steps at the hotel and broke his arm.' Peta explained about Billy taking George and June to hospital. 'They're on their way back but are still about fifteen minutes away, so Josh has gone to ask the celebrant if she can delay the wedding ceremony a bit longer so that your dad can give you away.'

Kate looked pale. 'Are you sure he's OK?'

Peta nodded. 'Positive. Apart from the broken arm, that is. I don't know if you want to wait here for them or carry on down to the wedding area on the beach.'

'Is Mum here?' Kate asked anxiously.

'Yes, Tina's here. And Sean.' Sean was Kate's stepfather.

'I'll wait here for Dad. I want to walk down on his arm – the unbroken one.' Kate turned to Steve. 'Can you please go and give everyone an update?' she asked. 'I'll be along as soon as Dad and Billy get back.'

'Are you sure you don't want me to wait with you?' Steve asked.

Kate shook her head. 'You go on ahead and help Josh keep everyone calm. Sophie and Maddie will wait with me, won't you?'

'Sure,' Sophie agreed and Maddie nodded.

'I'll come down with you, Steve.' Peta offered.

'I can't believe this has happened on my wedding day of all days,' Kate exclaimed as Steve and Peta headed down to the beach. 'Poor Dad must have really been in pain.'

'At least it's sorted and he's on his way back,' Maddie told her reassuringly.

To Kate's relief a silver Mercedes ML pulled up a few minutes later and Billy, June and her dad, his right arm in a sling, got out.

'Thank goodness!' She hurried over to them, giving her father a hug. 'I've been so worried, Dad. Are you OK?' She grinned ruefully. 'Silly question seeing as your arm's in a sling.'

'I'm fine. You look beautiful, darling,' her father said, placing his left arm around her to give her a hug. 'I'm so sorry about this, love.' He indicated his arm. 'It's going to ruin the photos.'

'Don't be daft. You're here, that's all that matters,' Kate told him. 'And at least you can still walk me down the aisle. Or should I say down to the beach! It's just amazing that you have managed to make it at all. I can't believe that you got to the hospital and back like that.' She kissed him on the cheek.

'I keep warning him about racing down steps; it's a wonder

257

he hasn't crippled himself,' June said. She gave Kate a hug. 'You look wonderful, darling.'

'Thank you.' Kate smiled. She turned to Billy and hugged him. 'Hello, Billy.'

'Hello, sis. You look incredible,' Billy said, stepping back to admire her. 'Steve's a lucky man. Come on, June, we'd better go on ahead, Kate doesn't want us walking down the aisle with her!' He and June both hurried off to join the wedding party.

'Time to go, honey.' George smiled at Kate.

'I'm ready!' She took a deep breath and slipped her arm through his.

'Hang on a mo!' Sophie unhooked the long train from the back of Kate's wedding dress, then she and Maddie held it up and followed as Kate and her dad made their way to the beach. *It's like a scene from a wedding brochure*, Kate thought as they headed across the golden sand to the area set aside for the wedding. She looked around, trying to take in everything as she walked towards the floral arch. Either side of the arch were rows of chairs draped in white covers with lavender bows, where the guests were seated, and there was a white carpet on the sand between the rows. It was perfect. Her mother, Sean, June, Billy and Peta were all sitting in the front row on the left, whilst Steve's parents and family were sitting in the front row on the right. Her mother turned to smile at Kate as she went past and Peta blew a kiss. Kate swallowed the lump in her throat. Steve, and her friends, had really put in a lot of effort to give her a special wedding day.

She walked under the arch, her arm proudly through her father's, and down the white carpet to the table at the front where Steve, Josh and the celebrant were waiting for her. Steve turned towards her when she joined him at the table, the love evident on his face, and Kate knew that she'd done the right thing in agreeing to the wedding. This is exactly how she would have wanted it to be.

Chapter Fifty-eight

Sophie

'We've actually pulled it off. I can't believe that all the months of stress are over and we can finally all relax,' Sophie whispered as the celebrant put Kate's hand on top of Steve's and said a blessing over them.

Maddie sighed in relief. 'Never, ever ask me to plan a wedding again!'

The ceremony over, it was time for more photos. The bride and groom, with the sea as the backdrop, the groom and best man, the bride and bridesmaids, bride and groom with parents, family, guests: the photographer snapped away. Then Steve and Kate both kicked off their shoes, Kate scooped up her dress in one hand, Steve grasped the other, and they ran along the beach to the sea, running into the turquoise water, throwing back their heads laughing. It was a lovely scene. The photographer and dozens of other cameras captured it.

'Fancy joining them?'

Sophie turned to see Josh standing beside her, his trouser legs rolled up to just below his knees, minus his jacket, his waistcoat unbuttoned and his shirt sleeves rolled up. Suddenly she felt that yes, she did want to run into the sea. She nodded and scooped up her dress, as Kate had done. Josh held out his hand and without thinking, she slipped hers into it and they raced across the sand. Other guests followed until most of the wedding party was paddling in the sea. Except for Maddie, Sophie noticed, surprised. Her eyes searched the beach for her friend.

'If you're looking for Maddie, she's chatting to my cousin, Art.' Josh sounded amused. 'There, over by the main table.'

Sophie followed his gaze and saw Maddie and a strikingly handsome guy with long blond hair tied back in a ponytail laughing together. Trust Maddie.

Then she realised that this meant Maddie had told the truth, she really wasn't interested in Josh. She glanced at Josh to try and ascertain if this bothered him.

'What's up?' he asked.

'I thought you and Maddie . . .'

He threw back his head and laughed. 'God no! She's great but, well, we don't click in that way.'

'Probably too alike, you're both a bit wild and carefree,' Sophie told him.

'Is that how you see me?' Josh sounded bemused but before Sophie could answer, the photographer shouted, 'Smile!' and they both turned to face him, still holding hands, just as he snapped away. Then Josh reached for her, wrapping his arm around her shoulder and the photographer snapped that too.

Kate and Steve were running out of the sea now and everyone followed. The photographer clicked away, shouting orders such as 'Smile!', 'Turn around!' and 'Hold that pose!' Restaurant staff handed out towels and everyone dried their feet then went into the restaurant. A huge table at the back of the room was laden with paella, cooked ham, tapas and salads, seafood, and a variety of breads and cheeses. It looked and smelt heavenly. And it was all served with a selection of wines. When everyone had eaten their fill, the table was cleared, a fresh cloth laid on it and out came the desserts – churros and chocolate, mouth-watering cakes and pastries, bagels, custards and rice puddings. It was a scrumptious spread.

Later, they were all ferried back to the hotel to freshen up for the evening reception.

'It's gone well, hasn't it?' Maddie asked. 'I have to admit, I thought it was going to be a total disaster when Kate called off the wedding the other night.'

'I know. Then we got caught up in all that traffic, and her dad broke his arm – he's a truly amazing guy, to have coped with all that without complaining, isn't he? But in the end they're just minor blips really. I think everyone's enjoyed the day. Now we have a brilliant evening to look forward to and our role is done. The wedding is over, we can let our hair down and enjoy ourselves.'

'Let's go and party then,' Maddie said. 'I'm looking forward to this band. Apparently they play in the clubs in Marbella a lot and are really good.'

There were already quite a few of the guests in the reception area, sitting around drinking and chatting. Sophie looked for Kate's parents. She was relieved to see both of them and their new partners, sitting next to each other, with Billy and Peta, and they seemed to be talking pleasantly. Thank goodness for that. She really wanted this evening to go smoothly, with no dramas.

They both got a drink and sat down. Josh and his cousin, Art, came over to join them. 'It's been a great day, hasn't it?' Art remarked. 'And I hear you two helped Josh arrange it. Well done.'

'There were a few dicey moments,' Sophie told him.

They all filled Art in on some of the pre-wedding dramas.

'I have to admit, I would hate a surprise wedding,' he said.

'Me too,' Maddie nodded. 'I can't believe I got talked into helping plan it!'

They were chatting away when the manager came hurrying over. 'Mr Henderson, there is a problem,' he said.

Josh looked over his shoulder. 'What is it?'

'I'm sorry, but the van, it has broken down. The singers, they have phoned to say that they will be late,' the hotel manager said.

'How late?' Josh asked.

'I'm afraid that at this moment we do not know.'

Great. So now they had no entertainment, Sophie thought. 'Do Kate and Steve – the bride and groom – know?' she asked.

The manager shook his head. 'I do not want to upset them. I tell you first.'

'Could you arrange for some music to be played until the band arrives?' Maddie asked. 'At least it will give the guests a chance to dance.'

'Of course,' the manager nodded.

'I'll go and break it to Steve and Kate. Hopefully they won't take the news too badly.' Josh got to his feet.

Sophie sighed. Just when she thought she could finally let her hair down and relax.

Chapter Fifty-nine

Josh

Kate and Steve, who were having a quiet moment upstairs in their room, weren't too happy to hear the news, but as Kate said, at least the manager was going to organise some music to keep the guests entertained. 'We'll be down in about ten minutes,' Steve said.

When Josh went back down to the reception room he was amazed to see that karaoke was in full swing. Maddie was on the stage with one of the guests, singing 'Don't Mess Me Around' at the top of her voice with the other guests joining in the chorus. Art and some of the others were dancing around the stage, and a group were clapping them on. Trust Maddie to get the party going.

'Come on, Sophie. Let's do a duet!' Maddie called, waving her over.

'Sophie! Sophie!' the rest of the group chanted.

Sophie grinned good-naturedly and to Josh's surprise went to join Maddie on the stage and they both started singing 'Girls Just Want to Have Fun'. And she could sing. OK, not as professionally as Maddie, but she had a sweet, strong voice and sang with gusto. Everyone was clapping and cheering. Josh thrust his hands in his pockets and grinned as he watched them.

When Kate and Steve walked back in a few minutes later, Maddie put on 'Always and Forever' and everyone cheered as Kate and Steve wrapped their arms around each other and started doing a smoochy dance.

When the band finally arrived fifty minutes later, the reception was in full swing and everyone was in good spirits.

Josh watched as Sophie danced with his cousin Art – Maddie was now flirting with the hotel manager. Sophie's eyes were sparkling, the slit up the side of the bridesmaid's dress showing an alluring expanse of tanned leg as she danced. Tonight he was seeing a Sophie he had never seen before.

He didn't really know her though, did he? He'd only met her a few times and they had mainly talked about plans for the wedding. Which would have gone disastrously wrong if it hadn't been for Sophie and Maddie. He hadn't realised Sophie could be so outgoing, so vivacious. And now here she was dancing with Art, both of them centre stage, with everyone clapping around them. Sophie's eyes were shining, her face animated. He could see that she was having a good time. So was Art.

Why did that bother him? She was a free agent and after the way that selfish boyfriend of hers had treated her, she deserved to let her hair down and have a good time. He just hoped that Art didn't take advantage of her. His cousin was a bit of a player. Maddie was more his type, not Sophie.

You're a bit of a player too, he reminded himself. But he never pretended his relationships were anything other than casual. Whereas Art strung people along, broke their hearts and then dumped them.

'Looks like Sophie is having fun. It's great to see her relaxing, isn't it?' Maddie was standing beside him now.

He pulled his gaze away from Sophie and turned to Maddie. 'I was surprised to see her singing and dancing on stage with you. I always got the impression she was shy.'

'We often sing together at parties. Sophie can be a bit reserved until she gets to know people, but get a couple of glasses of wine inside her and she loosens up.' She nodded towards Art. 'Your cousin seems taken with her anyway.'

Josh swallowed the surge of envy that unexpectedly roared up inside him. 'I thought you and Art . . .'

'Oh, he's amusing enough, but I'm happy to step aside for Sophie. She could do with a bit of happiness. A holiday thing is just what she needs to get over the way Glenn treated her.'

Out of the corner of his eye, Josh saw Sophie wrap her arms around Art's neck as they moved in for a smoochy dance. 'I reckon she's well on the way to forgetting him. Fancy a dance?'

Maddie nodded. 'Sure.'

As she slid into his arms and they moved slowly to the music, Josh refused to let his gaze wander to where Sophie was dancing with Art. It didn't bother him one little bit if they ended up spending the night together. Sophie was a free agent.

Chapter Sixty

Sophie

'Morning, sleepy head!' Maddie said cheerily, pulling open the curtains to let the sunlight stream into the bedroom she and Sophie were sharing. 'It's a beautiful day! Fancy going for a swim in the pool?'

Sophie groaned and opened one eye gingerly. 'What time is it?'

'Eleven. We've missed breakfast. I overslept too.'

Sophie edged up on to her elbow. 'I'm not surprised, we didn't get to bed until the early hours of the morning. How come you're so fresh and lively?' Maddie had had just as much to drink – if not more – than Sophie and here she was looking as if she'd had a mug of cocoa and an early night.

'I guess I'm more used to late nights,' Maddie said with a grin. 'You were really knocking the wine back last night.'

Sophie held her head. 'I know. It was just such a relief that the wedding had actually worked out OK. I hadn't realised how stressed I'd been feeling about it all.'

'Me too,' Maddie agreed. 'Kate was happy though, wasn't she? And it was a lovely wedding. I really enjoyed it.'

Sophie raised surprised eyes. 'You enjoying a wedding? Is there a romantic heart in there somewhere?'

Maddie threw her a grin. 'I'm not against romance, it's just not for me.'

'Nor me. From now on I'm going to enjoy my single life. I'll be ten mins.' Sophie opened the door and stepped into the bathroom.

'I'll be down by the pool,' Maddie called.

Sophie turned the shower to cool and stepped under it, allowing the refreshing lukewarm water to cascade over her skin. She really had drunk too much last night. It was simply relief that the wedding went off OK, she told herself, and nothing to do with Josh and Maddie dancing seductively together.

Showered and dried, she pulled on the electric-blue swimsuit she'd bought on Gibraltar when she and Maddie had been shopping after the dolphin tour and with Maddie's encouragement Sophie had also bought some brighter, more daring clothes. The colour did suit her, she acknowledged. Maddie was right, she should go for stronger colours. Maybe she should colour her hair too. An auburn tint might look nice. She knew how colours affected your personality and she'd always gone for pastel shades, boring, stay-in-the-background shades. Now she wanted something more vibrant, something to encourage her to be more outgoing. Well, this swimsuit would do for a start. She pulled on a pair of white shorts over it, shoved a towel, sunglasses, sun lotion and a bottle of water from the fridge into her beach bag and set off for the pool.

It was already crowded, with all the sunbeds taken, but she could see Maddie, her back to her, chatting to Josh and Art. They must have got up early to get a sunbed, she thought. Art raised his hand and waved when he saw her, then Josh looked over and smiled. She saw his eyes rest on her swimsuit for a fleeting moment, then move back to Maddie who was talking.

'Morning. How did you two manage to get sunbeds? Have you bribed someone?' she asked as she sat down beside Maddie, who was now sipping a smoothie.

'I've made friends with one of the staff,' Art said with a grin. 'She reserved two sunbeds for us. Happy to share with you girls.'

'That's very kind of you,' Maddie told them.

'Always a gentleman,' Art replied with a twinkle in his eye and Josh snorted.

Art grinned and stood up. 'Anyone want a drink? I'm going over to the pool bar.'

'Thanks. Orange juice with ice, please,' Sophie said.

'Have you seen Kate or Steve this morning?' Josh asked as Art went off to get the.drinks.

'Not yet – but then they are on their honeymoon,' Sophie reminded him. 'I still can't believe that we pulled it off. Kate and Steve looked really happy and everyone had a great time.'

'Maybe we should have a new career as wedding planners,' Maddie suggested.

Josh shot her a look of horror. 'No chance. I couldn't go through this again. It's a wonder I'm not grey.'

'Nor me,' Sophie agreed heartily. 'I'm glad it's all over and we can relax and enjoy the holiday.'

'Only kidding!' Maddie replied, a smile on her lips. 'What do you fancy doing today, Soph? Sunbathing or a bit of sightseeing?'

'I'm too exhausted to go traipsing anywhere, I need a chill day. But I'm up for going out sightseeing another day,' Sophie replied.

'I'm taking a trip to Marbella and Puerto Banus on Monday, if you fancy joining me?' Josh offered. 'I've got the hire car, so we can all get out and about a bit if you fancy it.'

'I'm up for that,' Maddie said quickly.

'Me too.' It sounded fun, Sophie thought.

'Can I come too?' Art had returned with two large glasses of orange juice and caught the end of the conversation. He handed one of the glasses to Sophie and sat back down by Josh.

'Sure,' Josh told him. 'Shall we leave after breakfast? We can meet in reception about eleven?'

Everyone agreed.

They sat chatting for a while until they'd finished their drinks, then Sophie and Maddie headed for the beach.

'That swimsuit looks really good on you,' Maddie told her as they laid out their towels on the sand and stretched out. 'I told you it would suit you.'

'Thanks.' Sophie took out her bottle of tanning lotion and started smoothing it over her legs. It would be nice to have a natural tan instead of one out of a bottle. She wasn't like Maddie, she didn't go golden brown the minute the sun's rays hit her, she turned lobster red; so she'd bought a bottle of suncream with a tanning agent. When she'd applied the cream all over her body she put the bottle away, slipped her sunglasses on and lay down to enjoy the feeling of the sun on her body. She was looking forward to the rest of the holiday now that the wedding was over. She was going to relax, enjoy herself and return home renewed and invigorated.

Chapter Sixty-one

Josh

It was good how they all got on, Josh thought as he, Art, Maddie and Sophie went jet-skiing on Tuesday. He'd been ridiculously delighted when Maddie had jumped on the water ski and told Art to get on behind her if he was man enough – a challenge Art couldn't resist, thus leaving Josh and Sophie to partner each other. He was enjoying Sophie's company. There was something different about her the last few days. She dressed more colourfully for a start. It had started with that bright blue swim suit that had clung seductively to her sensationally curvy figure on Saturday; then, when they'd gone shopping yesterday in Marbella and Puerto Banus, Sophie had bought a beautiful bright yellow patterned jumpsuit that hugged her body then flared out from her hips, and brightly patterned tops and shorts. Every night she and Maddie were on the dance floor and they always took a turn on the karaoke. He'd always liked Sophie, she was pretty, sweet and kind, but he had never really considered her as 'fun'. She was, though – fun, outgoing, game for a laugh, gorgeous – and she definitely seemed to have got over the heartbreak of splitting up with her boyfriend.

A spray of water engulfed them as Maddie sped past on the other jet ski with Art's arms wrapped around her waist. Josh waved cheerily. They both looked like they were having a great time. As he was. He was so aware of Sophie pressed close against his back, as close as their lifejackets would allow, her arms around his waist. He imagined her head thrown back, laughter lighting up her face, her eyes sparkling, blond wavy hair flying behind her. The more he got to know Sophie the more drawn he was to her. He found himself thinking about her a lot. And was sure that the fact that she was dressing more colourfully and seemed more outgoing was a reflection that she was happier in herself, and enjoying her freedom.

Art and Maddie were still racing ahead, the beach in sight. Time to pick up speed, Josh thought.

'Hold tight!' he shouted and Sophie's arms gripped him tighter. Josh upped his speed, caught up with Maddie and Art, then zoomed past, waving triumphantly as he reached the shore first.

'That was fun,' Sophie said when they'd returned the jet skis and were having lunch at the beach restaurant. 'Anyone fancy doing a bit of sightseeing this afternoon?'

'I'm up for it. Where do you fancy going?' Josh asked.

'How about seeing some flamenco dancing?' Sophie suggested. 'I've always wanted to see that.'

'Me too, maybe we can find a show to go to tonight,' Maddie suggested.

'Great idea. Let's check if there's any nearby.' Art tapped away at his phone. 'There's a flamenco show at a restaurant about ten minutes away that starts at eight. Shall I reserve a table?' He looked at Josh. 'We can get a taxi to save you driving, then you can have a drink too.'

'I don't mind driving. I'll have a drink at the hotel when we get back. Where's the restaurant?' He peered over at the screen and nodded. 'Yep, that's not far. Want to book a table, you two?'

'Sure,' Maddie nodded. 'I remember seeing some flamenco dancers when I came to see my aunt when I was a kid.'

'Of course, I forgot Sophie said that your aunt was Spanish. You're going to look her up while you're over here, aren't you?' Josh asked.

'Yep, next week.'

'So you're half Spanish?' Art asked curiously.

Maddie nodded. 'On my dad's side. He moved to England when he was in his early twenties though. I was born there. We used to come over and visit my aunt before my parents got divorced.'

Art booked the table for eight o'clock and they went back to the hotel for a snack and to sunbathe a bit before they set off for the restaurant.

'It's smaller than I expected, and pretty full already. There are only a couple of tables spare,' Sophie said when they walked in.

'At least that means it's popular.' Maddie pointed to the stage area at the front. 'I guess that's where the flamenco dancers will perform.'

As the manager showed them to their table, a waitress was clearing the table behind them. She turned as Josh pulled out his seat, bumping him with her shoulder. '*Lo siento, señor*,' she said.

'No worries . . .' Josh started to say, then stopped, his eyes transfixed on the woman's auburn hair, her green eyes, a face he still recognised, as he did the flower tattoos on the top of her arms. 'River,' he whispered.

273

Chapter Sixty-two

Sophie

Sophie knew by the way the beautiful red-haired waitress and Josh looked at each other that they had been lovers. It was in their eyes as they searched each other's faces, in the guarded way they held their bodies, in the tone of their voice as they said each other's names. This woman had meant something to Josh once, and he to her.

'How are you? It's been a long time,' the woman – River, Josh had called her – said.

'Fifteen years,' he replied as if he had counted every day of those years. Sophie felt a lump form in her throat.

She turned away, feeling almost like a voyeur, and sat down. Maddie and Art were already seated.

'I can't talk now, Josh, I'm working. Come and see me here tomorrow, before midday. If you want to,' the woman murmured huskily. 'I guess I owe you an explanation.' She gave him a brief nod then stacked up the used crockery and walked past to the kitchen.

'So that's her then, the woman you almost gave everything

up for?' Art said as Josh sat down, looking a bit shaky, Sophie noticed.

'It was a long time ago, we were just kids,' Josh replied. Sophie could see that he was making an effort to compose himself. 'Now, what's everyone drinking?'

No one mentioned River for the rest of the evening, and when she occasionally came by to clean a table or show someone to their table she never looked at Josh nor he at her.

I wonder if he will see her tomorrow? Sophie thought. Well, it was none of her business if he did. She was on holiday and she was going to enjoy every moment of it, not spend it bothering about what Josh was doing, and who he spent his time with.

They had finished their meal when the flamenco dancers came on stage. A dark-haired man, with an earring through his right ear and wearing flared high-waisted black trousers, a white shirt and black bolero-style jacket revealing a red cummerbund, and a slim woman, elegant and striking in a black dress with a red-trimmed ruffled skirt and black patent shoes. The man played the guitar and sang while the woman danced, tapping her feet, clicking a small pair of castanets, swirling the skirt of her dress and doing intricate body movements in time to the music. It was a wonderful, emotional and entertaining dance. Everyone in the restaurant clapped enthusiastically when it had finished.

'I wouldn't mind having a go at that,' Sophie said.

Although Josh seemed to enjoy the dance, he had a faraway look in his eyes and Sophie wondered if he was thinking about River. It seemed that they had really loved each other once.

'What are you guys up to tomorrow?' Art asked as they all set off home, Josh driving, still seeming distracted and barely joining in the conversation.

'I thought I might go and see my aunt,' said Maddie. 'Kate's brother has hired a car and he said I could borrow it, apparently it's not a problem as it's the car that's insured over here not the driver. Do you fancy coming, Soph?'

'Yes, and don't worry, I can have a walk around while you catch up with your aunt. I don't mind, honestly.' Then a thought occurred to her. 'Are you OK driving on the "wrong" side of the road?'

Maddie chuckled. 'Sure. I hired a car when I went to France and Germany. You soon get used to it, as a driver you're still near the centre of the road, especially with a left-hand-drive car.'

'Well, if you girls are busy I'll have a catch-up with my folks as they're going home on Thursday, they only came for the week,' Art said. A lot of the guests had only flown over for the wedding and had already returned home.

No one asked Josh what he was doing, Sophie noticed, and he didn't volunteer the information. She guessed they all presumed he was meeting River.

An image of the woman, with her vibrant green eyes, high cheekbones and bright red hair flashed across Sophie's mind. River really was stunning. And Josh had been so distracted since he saw her that she was clearly on his mind. She got the impression he had loved her so much, and judging by the soft way River had looked at him, suggesting he meet her tomorrow so they could talk, it seemed she had loved him too. They clearly had unfinished business. Had any of them really moved on, she wondered.

Chapter Sixty-three

Maddie

'Take it easy, we're right near the edge here!' Sophie cried.

Maddie groaned. Sophie had been nervous ever since they got into the car.

'It's fine. I have driven on the right before, you know,' Maddie told her for the umpteenth time.

'Sorry. I can't help it. It feels strange you driving on this side of the road. I keep thinking that you're going to go over into the ditch. I wish there was a kerb like in England.'

'Honestly, you're completely safe. I'm being really careful,' Maddie assured her.

'Take the next right,' Google Maps informed her, so Maddie turned right, on to a dirt track that seemed to lead to nowhere.

'I'm not liking the look of this.' Sophie's voice sounded very shaky.

Maddie didn't like the look of it either but she'd put the location Miguel had sent her in Google Maps, and the app was insistent this was the way she had to go. 'It'll be fine,' she said and started driving slowly along the very uneven track.

Sophie peered out of the window silently as they drove along the muddy track. Then suddenly she gasped. 'There's a big drop off this side, Maddie, make sure you keep to the middle of the road.'

'I'm supposed to keep to the right,' Maddie told her, glancing over to the right and wincing when she saw that there was indeed a big drop. Maybe this wasn't such a good idea after all. Neither she nor Sophie was very good with heights and if she swerved too suddenly she would go right over into that ditch.

Pull yourself together and concentrate on the road ahead. It's wide enough, there's no way you're going over the side, she told herself. She couldn't remember coming along a track like this when she visited her aunt with her parents, but then it was a long time ago and she'd been young. Maybe she'd fallen asleep or they'd come a different way.

Finally, a little white village came into view, scattered about on the mountain in front of them. 'That's gorgeous,' Sophie said. 'Do you remember it?'

Maddie shook her head. 'The thing is, a lot of the white villages look the same. And I was so young, I don't think I took much notice.'

Following Google Maps' instructions, she drove cautiously up the narrow road leading in to the village. *You've got this*, she told herself, her hands gripping the steering wheel. The streets were so narrow, with cars parked either side, that she could barely squeeze through and was glad she wasn't driving a bigger car, even though she definitely needed a four-by-four for this drive rather than the small city car Billy had hired.

'Do you mind if I park the car and we walk?' she asked Sophie. 'My aunt's house isn't far away but I really don't want to drive along these narrow streets.'

'I don't want you to either!' Sophie replied. 'There's a sign there saying Parking.' She pointed to a blue square with a P in it a little further up the hill, to the right.

Maddie cautiously drove up and turned right into the car park. Thank goodness there were some spaces. She steered into one, turned off the engine and took a deep breath. Sophie did the same.

'That was quite an experience,' Sophie exclaimed. 'I wouldn't want to drive here in the dark.'

'Nor me!' Maddie opened the door, got out and went over to the ticket machine. Seeing that the parking was free from two p.m. until four thirty and it was now twelve thirty she put in enough money to cover them until five p.m.

Sophie was standing by the car, waiting for her. 'Which way?' she asked.

Maddie switched Google Maps from driving to walking. 'Up the hill,' she said.

'What a beautiful village,' Sophie said as they walked uphill, past quaint houses with colourful pots of flowers outside. 'And look at that fountain!'

Maddie turned her head, squinting as she saw the fountain against the wall that Sophie was pointing at. There was a tiled picture of a lady that she knew was Mary, or La Virgen as they called her in Spain, at the back of the fountain. She remembered this. She remembered gathering around with her cousins to drink water from the fountain on hot, sunny afternoons, before they went to play in the park on the left. Her aunt's house was a bit further up the hill, also on the left, she was sure it was.

'I remember that and I think I remember where my aunt's

house is,' she told Sophie. She switched off Google Maps and headed uphill, her mind going back to when she was a child and racing her cousins back to the house. She paused as she came to the street on the left, looking down it, recognising the house tucked up in the corner of a little square, with another fountain in the middle of it. They would have a drink from this fountain before they went down the hill to the park, and then from the other fountain before they went back to Aunt Valeria's. Casa de Flores, her house was called. House of Flowers.

'We're nearly there,' she said, leading the way past a row of town houses with dark wooden doors lining the street, many with cars parked outside making it very narrow to walk. She was glad she'd left the car in the car park.

Maddie paused at the house in the corner. Pots of flowers were arranged at the front and there were baskets of flowers hanging from the balcony. There was a nameplate on the wall, with tiny flowers painted around the edge. 'Casa de Flores' it said. Suddenly she felt nervous. She hadn't seen Aunt Valeria since she was about twelve. But Miguel said that her aunt was eager to see her.

'I'll wait here while you go and see her,' Sophie said.

'No, please come with me. It won't feel so awkward with you there.' Maddie took a deep breath then pressed the bell on the door.

Then the door opened and a good-looking Spanish man, probably in his late thirties, dressed in shorts and a black vest, smiled at her.

'Madelina! You have come!' Dark brown eyes lit up in delight and he held out his arms. '*Bienvenida*. Welcome!'

Madelina. The use of her full name brought a lump to Maddie's throat. Only her father and his family had ever called her that. To everyone else she was Maddie.

'Miguel!' Tears sprung to her eyes as they embraced then Miguel kissed her on both cheeks. 'It is so good to see you again.'

'You too, *guapa*. It has been so long. And you have brought a friend with you!' His English, spoken with a thick Spanish accent, was good and the use of *guapa*, beautiful, a typical Spanish endearment, made her smile. She remembered that she and her cousins had communicated using their own form of 'Spanglish' and gestures, that had never deterred them from having fun. 'Yes, this is Sophie.' She turned to Sophie. 'Sophie, meet my cousin Miguel.'

'Come in, come in, both of you. My mother is waiting.' Miguel opened the door wide.

As she walked into the little town house, memories flooded into Maddie's mind: running down the long hall with polished decorative tiles on the walls, into the spacious living room on the left, and then a long kitchen. On the other side of the hall was another huge room and at the back of the house was a beautiful courtyard with colourful plants and a fountain.

'Oh my goodness, it doesn't seem big enough for all this,' Sophie exclaimed, looking around in wonder.

'I know, it's like a Tardis, isn't it?' Maddie agreed.

As Miguel led them into the kitchen, a woman got up from her chair. She was smaller than Maddie recalled, and the hair she remembered as long and flowing was now up in a bun. But there was no mistaking the nose and the eyes, so like Maddie's father's. It was Tía Valeria.

'Madelina. Is it really you?' Her eyes raked Maddie's face then broke into a big smile. 'Oh *querida*, it is so good to see you.' *Querida* – darling; Aunt Valeria had always greeted her father this way. Tears sprang to Maddie's eyes as her aunt enveloped her in a big hug then kissed her on both cheeks, as Miguel had done. Maddie returned the greeting, then she introduced Sophie and Aunt Valeria kissed her on both cheeks too. '¿*Qué tal?*' she asked. How are you?

'*Muy bien. Y tu?*' The reply came to her easily. Very well, and you. She had learnt a few basic phrases during the holidays she'd spent with her cousins. 'I am so sorry about Tío Juan,' she said gently.

Her aunt put her hand over her heart. 'He is in here, always,' she said. 'Now let us have lunch and talk, Madelina. It has been too long since I've seen you.'

So, over crusty bread, thickly buttered, huge slices of jamon and a bowl of mixed salad, Maddie, Miguel and her aunt talked, with Miguel translating now and again when necessary, and addressing Sophie too sometimes. Maddie glanced over at her friend, hoping she didn't feel left out; Sophie smiled reassuringly back and looked as if she was enjoying herself.

When the meal was finished, Miguel got to his feet. 'I have to go to work, Maddie. It has been good to see you again – and to meet you, Sophie. Luis and Eliana would like to see you too, but Luis is in Barcelona and Eliana in Nerja. Maybe you can come over again and we can all meet up.'

'I would love to,' Maddie told him.

'We will arrange something; we will message each other.' Kissing first Maddie then Sophie on both cheeks, Miguel left.

'And Sadie, is she well?' Aunt Valeria asked.

Maddie nodded. 'She's married again and lives in Wales,' she said.

Aunt Valeria nodded. 'That is good, I don't blame Sadie for the divorce, it was tough living with your father when he turned to the drink, but he wasn't always that way. The Thiago I remember, he was kind, friendly, would help anyone. It was the accident that changed him.'

'Accident?' Maddie was about to put a huge chunk of bread into her mouth but paused and looked at her aunt.

'You don't know about the accident?' Her aunt looked astonished. She pulled herself together and continued. 'Your father and mother, they come to Spain to visit me, you are maybe five. One night they are driving back when a car comes shooting around the bend, your father, he tries to swerve but the car, it comes off the edge of the road, down the embankment. You and Sadie, you have bruises but your father hurt his back badly. He suffers a lot of pain and over the years he turns to drink to block this pain.' She let out a deep sigh. 'Thiago, he was a good man, things change people.'

Maddie was stunned. 'I had no idea that they'd been in an accident or that my father was in so much pain.'

Aunt Valeria poured them all another cup of tea. 'I do not excuse the things he do, or blame Sadie for walking away.' She passed Maddie a cup. 'But maybe if you understand why, you can forgive him?'

Maddie sipped her tea thoughtfully. She was pleased that they'd come to visit Aunt Valeria. She was a link to her father's family, and learning about her father's accident helped to bury the ghosts a bit. She hadn't known about the accident, hadn't realised her father had been in so much pain. It didn't excuse his behaviour, he should have sought help, but her aunt was right, knowing how he had suffered did help her come to terms with the man he had become.

'Do keep in touch, Madelina,' Aunt Valeria said when they left. 'Come and see me again.'

'I will,' Maddie promised.

'Bring your friend too. There is much room for you both to stay.' The kind woman hugged Sophie and they both left.

'How do you feel?' Sophie asked as they walked back towards the car park.

Maddie thought about it. 'I don't know. I mean, my dad was in pain, but he made it worse by drinking like that. He hurt us, me and mum.' She shrugged. 'I guess at least I know it wasn't just because he didn't care about us any more, he was struggling to cope.'

'Do you think you'll come to see your aunt again?' Sophie asked as they got into the car.

Maddie started the engine as she considered this. 'I might. It would be good to catch up with my cousins again and redis- cover my Spanish heritage.' She put the car into gear. 'Talking of catching up, what do you think of Josh knowing that waitress last night? Do you think he's gone to see her today?'

Chapter Sixty-four

Josh

He'd tossed and turned all night, wondering whether to take River up on her invitation to go and talk to her today. It had been such a shock seeing her, and the last place he'd expected to find her working was waitressing in a bar. More like the flamenco dancer, or a travel rep, teaching English maybe. She hadn't changed much, a little older and less fresh-faced, as he was too, but the same auburn hair, full lips, bright eyes. How he'd loved her. And thought that she had loved him too.

When he got up and made a strong coffee, still tired from the restless night, he decided that he wasn't going to visit River. There was no point in dragging up the past and no need for an explanation. River left because she loved the idea of travelling more than she loved the idea of staying in a small town with Josh. And she'd been right to go. They'd been too young, they'd have outgrown each other eventually, he could see that now. He downed the thick coffee. He wasn't going.

But a couple of hours later he was in his car, on the way over to the restaurant again. He wanted to hear her explanation, to find out what she had to say, why she had left him waiting for a phone call, a letter, anything to say that she hadn't forgotten him.

River was sitting outside, smoking, her face pensive. She raised her eyes to his, watching him as he walked towards her, pulled out the chair next to her and sat down.

'Hello, Josh.' Her eyes held his.

'Hello.' He could feel old memories stirring – her mouth on his, both of them lying in bed, kissing and caressing.

'So you came. I wasn't sure if you would.'

'Neither was I,' he admitted.

The man who had shown them to the table last night, the one he'd thought was the manager, came out. 'You would like a drink? Claro? Coffee?'

'Claro, please, *media*.' The light beer was so refreshing and low enough in alcohol for him to have a half.

'*Gracias*, Franco.' River smiled at the man and his face lit up. They love each other, Josh realised. River had found her match.

'Yep, I thought it would be good to tie up some loose ends.' He nodded towards the door where Franco had just disappeared. 'You and Franco are together?'

She nodded. 'We've been married almost eight years now.' She gazed silently ahead of her as she took a puff of her cigarette then turned to face him. 'I owe you an apology. How I left. It was hurtful.'

'What, without saying goodbye, you mean.' He tried to keep his voice level, not sound accusing.

She took another puff on her cigarette, a longer one this time, and blew out a spiral of smoke before replying. 'It was selfish of me but I thought you would try to talk me out of it again. And I was desperate to go. To spread my wings and see the world.'

286

'You never contacted me again. I thought we'd meant more to each other than that.' Now he was sounding like a petulant teenager.

She took a final drag, inhaled deeply, then stubbed out the cigarette in the ash tray on the table. 'I loved you, Josh, but I loved my freedom more. I wasn't the right woman for you.'

'I know,' he acknowledged, taking a sip of his beer before asking, 'And have you seen the world?'

She nodded. 'I worked my way around Europe, serving in bars, teaching a little English, then I met Seth and we went to Thailand. He got arrested on a drugs charge, I was lucky to get out. I decided to choose my men more wisely after that. I met Franco when I was working in Spain, we opened this bar, we have two young children who my mother-in-law looks after when we work. Life is good.'

So River and her husband owned the bar. And she looked happy. He was glad about that.

'What about you? You're an engineer now, I expect. Are you married?'

He shook his head. 'Nope.' He wasn't going to confess that she had hurt him so much he had vowed never to get involved with anyone again. It sounded so stupid and immature now. 'I quit engineering after a few years and have a motorbike work-shop, repairs and renovations. I've travelled a bit too, I'm over here for Steve and Kate's wedding.'

'Ah, your brother. And the beautiful blonde woman you were with last night? Is she your girlfriend?'

'A good friend,' he told her, finishing his drink. He had no wish to carry on talking. The past had gone, as had his bitter-ness. River was correct, she hadn't been the right woman for him. Looking back now he realised that it was more the devastation that she had simply walked away without saying goodbye that had hurt him. If they had remained together they would have split up sooner or later. They had wanted different things even then.

'I think she is more than a friend. I saw the way you looked at each other.' She stood up. 'It's been good to see you, Josh. I've felt guilty for some time about how badly I treated you and am pleased to have the chance to apologise.' She leant forward and kissed him on both cheeks.

'Don't. It's all in the past. It's good to see you too, to know that you're happy.'

'You be happy too.' She gave him a hug and he returned it. Then Franco came out, wrapped his arm around River's waist and they both smiled as Josh waved and walked away up the street.

Chapter Sixty-five

Sophie

When Sophie and Maddie arrived in the entertainment lounge that evening, Steve and Josh's parents called them over to join them, Steve, Kate, Peta, Billy and Art. They were all going home tomorrow, Sophie remembered, so probably wanted to make the most of their last night. Kate's parents had only stayed for the weekend, but Peta and Billy had booked for the week and become very friendly with their new 'in-laws'. There was no sign of Josh at the table though. Was he still with River? she wondered. Had he spent the day with her?

What if he has? It's nothing to do with you.

'Grab a chair, you two, it's the last night for the Henderson clan,' Art said. 'You've got me for another week though.'

'Where's Josh?' Maddie asked the question that was in Sophie's mind. She sat down next to Peta, leaving the chair by Art for Sophie.

'I haven't seen him all day, I think he's gone to see River. Put the past to bed maybe.' He picked up his drink. 'Or revisit it.'

'I can't believe that woman is living here in Spain. I hope

she's not going to wreck Josh's life again.' Anita's lips were pursed in disapproval.

'Now, Anita, Josh is a big lad now and he got over River years ago. They're probably having a catch-up for old time's sake,' Clive told her.

'They had a thing going then?' Maddie once again asked the question that was on Sophie's tongue.

'Yeah, love's young dream. They were only late teens though, almost ran off together. In the end River ran off by herself in the middle of the night, Josh never heard from her again. He was devastated. Almost quit uni. Was in a right mess,' Steve replied. 'You can't imagine it now, can you? Mr non-commitment Josh being besotted with someone.'

'He was young,' his father reminded him. 'It's all in the past now and I don't think we should be discussing it like this. We all have a couple of failed romances behind us.'

Steve immediately looked abashed. 'Sorry, Pop, only chatting. And talk of the devil, here comes Josh now.'

Sophie fought down the urge to turn around and watch Josh walk over to them. She waited until he sat down in the chair next to Steve, almost opposite her, then smiled a greeting.

'Wow, you were all here early,' Josh said. 'Can't wait to have your last drink, eh?'

'We've just had a chill day,' Steve told him. 'It's been good to spend some time together as a family, hasn't it?'

'It certainly has. And talking of family,' Josh turned his gaze to Maddie. 'How did it go today? Did you find your aunt's house?'

'I did. And she made me so welcome. My cousin Miguel was there too, I might come back again and have a catch-up with my other two cousins.' She grinned cheekily at him. 'And did you have a catch-up with your old girlfriend?'

Trust Maddie to come straight out with it. Sophie cast a furtive look at Josh, but the question didn't seem to have bothered him. He returned the grin. 'I did. She's married to the guy who showed us to our table last night and it's their bar, would you believe? They've got a couple of kids too.' He took a sip of his beer then shifted his position so he could talk to his parents. 'Can you imagine that, River running a bar? It seems so conservative for her.'

River had been a bit of a wild one then, like Maddie, Sophie thought. No wonder Josh was so attracted to Maddie.

'We all grow up. But now maybe you have met up again you have both cleared the air and buried a few things?' Anita asked.

'They were buried long ago, Ma, but it was good to see her again.' Josh turned his attention to Billy. 'Well, mate, back to work on Monday for you.'

'Don't remind me,' Billy said with a groan. 'It's all right for some: two weeks in the sun.'

Steve tapped the side of his glass with his fingernails. 'While you're all here, can I have your attention, please?'

'Here comes a big announcement. Is it the patter of little feet?' Billy teased.

'Not for a few years yet, mate.' Steve stood up and took a deep breath. 'My wife and I . . .' he began and was greeted by a roar of laughter.

'You sound like bloody royalty, mate,' Art told him.

'Cheeky bugger.' Steve gave him a mock-glare then continued. 'What I wanted to say – before I was rudely interrupted – is thank you all so much for coming to Spain and at such short notice to celebrate our wedding with us. We really appreciate it, don't we, Kate?'

Kate's eyes were sparkling. 'We certainly do.' Then she stood up too. 'And massive thanks to Sophie, Maddie and Josh for all your hard work in helping Steve plan the wedding. I know I thanked you on our wedding day, but honestly, I dread to think what it would have been like without your input.'

'A disaster, that's what!' Art quipped and everyone chuckled.

'It was a pleasure,' said Sophie. 'We're just glad it all worked out OK, aren't we?' she looked to Maddie then Josh, who both nodded in agreement.

'I'd like to say it was a pleasure, but actually it was a pain in the backside so if anyone else is planning a secret wedding, please don't call me,' Josh jested.

'Oh, that's a shame. I was hoping to call on your services now you're an experienced wedding planner,' Art bantered.

Another roar of laughter.

Sophie grinned. This was going to be a fun evening. And it seemed that Josh's past relationship with River was definitely that, past. Like Maddie, he had probably put a few ghosts to bed. She was pleased that he and Art were staying for another week, they were good company.

She was so pleased that she'd taken Maddie's advice and come for the two weeks. This holiday was exactly what she needed. And when she went back home she was going to find a new flat to move into, with a garden. And she was going to ask Pat if she could work a three-day week so she could start her own business, as Janine had suggested. She was changing her life and looking forward to the future.

Chapter Sixty-six

Josh

Sunday

Josh looked up as he heard Sophie's peal of laughter. She was playing beach basketball with some children, her blond hair tied up in a ponytail and the poppy-red short-suit she was wearing showing off the tan she'd got while they'd been here in Spain. She looked so alive – she'd really let her hair down and joined in the fun this past week. She and Maddie were great company. He could see that his cousin Art thought so too. The four of them had been hanging out together, and Josh couldn't remember the last time he'd enjoyed a holiday as much as this one. It was a shame there were only a few days left.

The ball hit him on the back and he turned around to see Sophie laughing at him, her ponytail swinging behind her, eyes dancing with mischief. 'Come on, lazybones. Don't just sit there, join in the game.'

'OK.' He scrambled to his feet, picked up the ball, walked nonchalantly over the sand to the rolled-up beach towel a few metres from the net that marked where they should stand and tossed the ball in to the hoop. The children all cheered.

'Bet you can't do it again,' Sophie challenged.

'Challenge accepted.' Josh had two more goes and both times the ball went through the hoop. 'Now it's your turn. Best of three,' he said, handing Sophie the ball.

She took it off him and walked over to the beach towel marker then paused, balancing the ball on her hand as she eyed up the hoop, her tongue peeping slightly out of the corner of her mouth as she concentrated. Then she stood on tiptoe and aimed the ball. Everyone cheered as it went through the hoop. She grinned triumphantly at Josh.

'Best of three, remember,' he told her.

'No problem.' Sophie had two more attempts and both times the ball went through the hoop. 'I think that's a draw.'

'I'd say best out of six but me and Art are planning a ride out to Benalmàdena today. Do you fancy going with us?'

'Sure.' Sophie tossed the ball back to a young boy. 'Got to go now, sorry.'

The boy grinned good-naturedly, and turned to aim the ball at the net.

Sophie and Josh headed for the car park, where they found Maddie and Art already waiting by the car. They piled in in their usual order, Art in the front by Josh and Maddie and Sophie in the back, and set off for Benalmàdena.

They had a lovely day walking around the marina, then after lunch on the harbour front, they went for a ride on one of the yachts.

As they all sat at the front of the yacht, looking out to sea,

Josh thought how much he'd enjoyed the past few days, so much that he didn't want the holiday to end. Sophie suddenly roared with laughter at something Art had said, her eyes sparkling, her whole face alive, and as he watched her Josh realised how much he was going to miss her.

Chapter Sixty-seven

Sophie

I can't believe that I'm going home on Wednesday, Sophie thought. The days had sped by and she'd had the time of her life. It had been a long time since she'd had such a carefree holiday. She felt renewed, ready to go back and face life again. Except for one thing. She'd be saying goodbye to Josh.

She gazed out at the ocean, knees bent, arms wrapped around her knees, bare feet buried in the sand, her discarded sandals beside her. She'd come down to the beach early this morning, leaving Maddie to recover from the night before. She should be tired too, they were dancing until the early hours of the morning, but she couldn't sleep. All she could think of was that she was going home in two days and would miss Josh terribly.

She had no idea when her feelings had changed from ones of warm friendship to something stronger. *It's the holiday atmosphere*, she told herself, *I'll be fine when I get back home. I've got my new flat to sort out, and my business to grow.*

'Morning.'

She looked over her shoulder at the sound of Art's voice. 'Morning.'

'You're up early.' He sat down on the sand beside her, his legs brown and toned. Like her he was barefoot.

'So are you.'

He nodded. 'Couldn't sleep. Can't believe how quickly these two weeks have gone.'

'Me neither.' Sophie watched as a boat came into view in the distance.

'It's been fun, hasn't it? I'm glad I met up with you and Maddie.'

Sophie turned to him and smiled. 'It's been the best holiday I've ever had.'

'Does Maddie think so too?' Art asked casually.

Sophie nodded. 'She's loved it. We both have. You and Josh, you've been great company.'

'Do you think she'll be sorry to say goodbye? I know she won't want to keep in touch. She doesn't do commitment, does she?'

He was trying to sound as if he didn't care, but Sophie could hear the emotion in his voice. She had wondered if there was something between Maddie and Art, had seen the way they looked at each other sometimes. She recalled how she'd seen them laughing together on more than one occasion, their whole faces wreathed in joy, how they had often danced a smoochy dance, their bodies completely in tune.

'No, she doesn't, but there's no reason why you can't keep in touch. She might like that.'

'What if I want more than that?' Art's voice was low.

Sophie reached out and touched his arm. 'Maybe Maddie does too. You won't know until you talk to her. What have you got to lose? We're going home on Wednesday so you probably won't see her again anyway. Not unless you tell her how you feel and find out if she feels the same way.'

Art's eyes met hers. 'I'm scared she'll knock me back. Could you sound her out for me? Find out how she feels?'

Sophie hesitated for a moment then nodded. 'OK. I'll try.'

'Thanks,' Art said, kissing her on the cheek. He got to his feet and walked off, leaving Sophie staring out to sea. So Art was interested in Maddie, and wanted to act on those feelings. She had an idea that Maddie was interested in him too. What about Josh? She liked him, really liked him, she thought. Did he like her too in the same way? Should she try and find out or walk away? If he did return her feelings, did she even want another relationship yet?

She sat there, gazing out to sea, trying to figure out what to do.

Chapter Sixty-eight

Josh

Josh stopped in his tracks and stared at the two figures sitting close together on the beach, facing the sea. Sophie and Art. So, this is why Art was up so early. He slid his hands into his shorts pockets and watched as Art turned to Sophie, his expression earnest. When Sophie reached out and touched Art's hand Josh felt as if he'd been punched in the stomach.

Art and Sophie. So he'd been right.

Thank goodness he hadn't made a fool of himself and told Sophie how he felt. He could walk away and she'd never know that he'd fallen for her. He had to turn away right now before they embraced. He couldn't bear to see them kissing, to see such an obvious sign of their attraction to each other, when he was the one who wanted to hold Sophie in his arms, to put his lips on hers, to ...

I'll forget her when I get home, he told himself as he walked back across the sand, away from Sophie and Art, his heart feeling like it had been trodden on and smashed into tiny pieces.

But he knew he wouldn't forget that easily. Sophie had snuck into his heart and he had hoped that she might feel the same way. How wrong he had been.

He turned away and went back to the hotel. They were all meeting by the pool later and he wanted to compose himself before they did that, prepare himself for seeing Sophie and Art all loved up.

As he passed reception on the way to his room a guest was handing in some tickets. 'Can you see if anyone wants to use these? It's four tickets for the Caminito del Rey walk for tomorrow. We booked them but have changed our minds about going,' he said.

Josh had often thought of going on that famous cliff walk on a narrow platform over the gorge of the Guadalhorce. It was said to be really breath taking. 'I'll have them,' he said, walking over. 'How much were they?'

'I don't want any money, mate, just glad you can use them. Enjoy.' The man handed him the tickets.

'Thank you, that's really kind of you,' Josh said. The man nodded and walked off.

Josh shoved the tickets in his pocket and made his way up to his room, wanting to compose himself before he met up with Sophie again. After drinking a strong coffee and giving himself a good talking-to, he went down to the pool, their usual meeting point. Sophie, Maddie and Art were already there. Sophie had now changed into a canary-yellow bikini and was rubbing suncream into her long, tanned legs. Josh felt his eyes drawn to them, imagining rubbing that cream in. *Stop it, Josh! She's not interested in you.* He dragged his gaze away. 'I've just been given tickets for the Caminito del Rey walk tomorrow. Anyone fancy going?'

Sophie looked up. 'I wouldn't mind.'

Maddie looked a bit worried. 'Isn't that the pathway across the gorge? It's dangerous, isn't it?'

'Not now. It was renovated a few years ago and is perfectly safe. Even kids can go on it,' Josh told her.

'I'm up for it,' Art said.

Maddie sighed. 'Go on then.'

'It's a morning slot, which is great as it gets too hot in the afternoon, but it's a couple of hours' drive, so we need to all meet in reception about nine to give us plenty of time to get there. Is that OK with everyone?'

They all agreed. Then Sophie, Maddie and Art went for a swim in the pool. Two more days, Josh thought as he watched them jump in. Two more days and they would be back home. He'd miss Sophie, he thought as he got to his feet and went to join them: best make the most of the time he had left.

Chapter Sixty-nine

Sophie

'I can't do it. I feel sick.' Maddie clung on to the wire running along the side of the cliff. 'I thought I could do this, but I can't.'

They'd been walking along the Caminito del Rey for about twenty minutes and Sophie had realised not long after they'd set foot on the pathway that Maddie wasn't very comfortable with it. She'd had no idea that her friend was so terrified of heights. Maddie had gone deadly pale and looked like she was actually going to be sick.

'Oh, Mad, why didn't you say you were scared of heights?' she said, placing her arm sympathetically on her friend's.

'I thought I'd gotten over it,' Maddie whispered. 'Besides, I didn't expect it to be this high. And this scary.'

'Neither did I,' Sophie admitted. She was finding it hard going too. The pathway was dizzyingly high above the gorge and she was scared to look down into the depths of the river lashing against the rocks. And even though she had a sun hat on she could feel the morning sun burning her head and back.

'Don't look down,' she advised Maddie. 'Focus on what's

ahead of you. And keep to the cliff side, holding on to the wire like you're doing now, then you won't feel so nervous.'

Maddie took a deep breath. Then another. 'Just give me a minute and I'll be fine.'

'Are you struggling too?' Art asked. He and Josh had held back to take some photos and had now caught them up. 'I was OK until I went to the barrier to take a photo looking down. It just suddenly hit me how high we are and now I feel all shaky.' He did look queasy, Sophie noticed.

'You'll all be fine once you get used to it. Just take it slow, there's no rush,' Josh said, walking beside them. 'Do you know the history of this walk? I looked it up. It's amazing.'

'I googled it last night too,' Sophie said. 'Apparently, it was originally built so that the construction workers of the hydro electric company could pass from one side of the gorge to the other for maintenance, wasn't it?'

'Yep, and it was much more scary than it is now. Did you see the photos of what it used to look like with its crumbling paths and broken boards? No wonder so many people died walking it,' Josh replied.

'I'm not liking the sound of this,' Maddie said with a shudder.

'No need to worry, it's been completely renovated. If you look over the barriers you can see the old path below.' Josh went to the barrier and peered over. 'See, there it is.'

'No, thanks,' Maddie and Art said in unison, both keeping well back. Sophie had to agree, there was no way she intended to peer over the barrier.

'If it was built for the construction workers, why is it called El Caminito del Rey? That means the King's little path,' Maddie pointed out.

'From what I read, it was called that because the Spanish king at the time walked along the path on the way to the Guadalhorce Reservoir to officially open the dam several years later,' Sophie said, glad for the chance to take her mind off the sheer drop below. She was sure that Josh had started the conversation to put them at ease, and it worked. Maddie and Art were now holding hands as they walked along, as if to support each other, always keeping close to the cliff wall.

It was a long walk, but a pleasant one as they all chatted away easily for the rest of the journey. When they all came to the famous glass walkway where you could stand and look down on the sheer drop below your feet, even Maddie and Art plucked up the courage to stand on it for a few minutes – but kept their eyes firmly ahead. So did Sophie – just long enough for a photo. Josh, of course, stood there for several minutes, taking photos of the surrounding cliffs as well as the gorge below.

But when they came to the suspension bridge across the deep gorge on the last leg of their journey, Maddie's courage failed her again.

'I can't walk across that,' she said, ashen-faced.

'It's perfectly safe, honestly. And once we cross the bridge we're on the way down,' Josh told her. 'Just hold on to the sides and don't look down. I'll go first and you can see it's fine.' He stepped on to the bridge and strode purposefully across, turning to wave when he got to the other side.

'He's made that look so easy,' Maddie said.

Art swallowed. 'We can do it,' he said resolutely. 'Come on, Maddie. We can do this. I'll go first.'

He stepped on to the bridge, arms outstretched, holding tight on to the sides. Maddie took a deep breath and followed gingerly, holding on to each side too. Sophie waited until they had both crossed over, then made her way across. Then she made the mistake of glancing down and immediately froze as it hit her that if the bridge gave way she would plunge below, smash against the rocks, then be carried away by the river.

Stop panicking! The bridge is perfectly safe.

'Hey, Sophie!' Josh called. 'You're doing well.'

Sophie looked up and saw him standing on the other end of the bridge as if he'd spotted that she was scared and was encouraging her to look at him rather than the gorge a hundred metres below.

She focused her gaze on Josh and carried on walking, concentrating on getting to the other side. 'Thank goodness it isn't a windy day!' she shouted.

'I know, I wouldn't fancy it either,' he agreed.

She took the last few steps off the bridge. 'Phew! I'm glad that's over with!'

'We did it!' Maddie flung her arms around Art and he hugged her, his face breaking into a huge grin. Josh glanced at Sophie and she grinned too. It looked like Maddie might have feelings for Art after all.

'Are you OK with that?' Josh asked as Maddie and Art went off hand in hand.

She threw him a puzzled look. 'Of course. Why wouldn't I be?'

Josh looked a bit uncomfortable. 'I saw you and Art sitting on the beach yesterday morning. You both looked very . . . close.'

'He was telling me that he had feelings for Maddie and wanted to know if she felt the same way,' Sophie explained. 'He wants to keep in touch with her when we go home. I promised

I'd speak to her and try to find out how she felt, but I guess I don't need to now.'

Josh looked surprised. 'I thought it was you and Art.'

Now it was Sophie's turn to be surprised. 'No, definitely not. We're just friends.'

It's you I want. The words popped into her head and she pushed them away.

Chapter Seventy

Josh

So he'd got it wrong, Sophie wasn't interested in Art. *That doesn't mean that she's interested in you,* Josh reminded himself as he sat in the bar later that evening, waiting for the other three to join him for the last evening of their holiday. He thought back to the scene on the beach that had seemed so intimate. He had no idea that Art liked Maddie so much, but then why would he? He hadn't told Art that he liked Sophie. But Art had liked Maddie enough to do something about it, to try and find out if she felt the same way. Should he do the same or was he going to let Sophie go without finding out how she felt? Maybe he should ask Maddie if Sophie was over Glenn yet.

Or maybe he should be a grown-up and talk to Sophie himself?

Not yet though. This was their last night and he wanted to enjoy it with Sophie, not spoil it by telling her how he felt then being knocked back. That would make things awkward. No, he'd wait until he got home and see if he still felt the same way after a couple of days. If he did he could pop into the florist where she worked, ask her out to lunch. Best to make sure he hadn't just got caught up in the holiday mood first; they'd spent so much time together over the last couple of weeks.

'You look miles away.' Art put his pint down on the table and sat down. 'The girls will be here in a few minutes, Maddie texted me to say they're almost ready.'

'So you two are definitely an item then?' Josh asked.

Art grinned. 'Yep. Maddie's great, isn't she? Gorgeous, fun, I can't believe my luck.' He shot a quizzical look at Josh. 'What about you and Sophie?'

'What about us?' Josh asked in what he hoped was a casual tone.

'Well, anyone can see that you both have the hots for each other. Are you going to ask her out?'

'I don't know,' Josh admitted. 'Yes, I do fancy her, but I don't know how she feels. It's not been that long since her ex boyfriend upped and left. I'm not sure if she's over him.'

'Then ask her. I was scared to ask Maddie because I thought she was into you so I talked to Sophie. Turned out I got it wrong. If I hadn't said anything we might never have seen each other again.'

Josh shook his head. 'Tonight's our last night. I'm not doing anything to spoil that. And don't you say anything to Sophie or Maddie, please. I'll handle this my way.'

'Handle what your way?' asked a voice behind them.

Josh looked up to see Maddie standing at the table. He looked around and saw that Sophie was at the bar. She looked absolutely stunning in an emerald-green mini dress that showed off her tanned legs to perfection.

'Just a bit of business,' Josh said as Maddie sat down and she and Art embraced.

Sophie joined them in a few minutes with drinks for herself and Maddie and they all started chatting about their Caminito del Rey walk.

'I can't believe I did it,' Maddie said. 'I am terrified of heights. I would never have gone if I'd known, but I'm glad I did it.'

'Me too. It's good to push your boundaries sometimes,' Sophie said.

The band came on to the stage then and both girls got up to dance. As Josh watched Sophie, he thought how happy and care-free she looked. Maybe Art was right and she had got over Glenn. But even if she had, that didn't mean that she fancied him.

Later when they were dancing a slow dance together, his arms around Sophie's waist, her soft hair brushing against his cheek, the sweet smell of her perfume stirring his senses, he desperately wanted to kiss her and tell her how he felt – and the way she was looking at him he wondered if, maybe, she felt the same way too. He was tempted to hold her closer, to kiss her cheek, but he stopped himself because he suddenly realised that he wasn't scared Sophie wasn't attracted to him, he was scared that she was. Because Sophie was different to all the other women he had dated. He had the feeling that if he started dating her he wouldn't want to walk away. And he wasn't sure if he was ready for a relationship yet.

Chapter Seventy-one

Sophie

Sophie watched as Maddie and Art hugged goodbye. Art lived in Manchester so was catching a different flight later that day. 'I'll see you soon,' Art promised and they kissed tenderly, then Maddie climbed into Josh's rented car, which he had arranged to drop off at the airport, and they set off. Kate and Steve had returned yesterday so Sophie, Maddie, Art and Josh were the last of the wedding party to go home. They'd spent a fantastic evening together yesterday then Maddie and Art had gone off for a moonlight walk. Sophie had woken the next morning to find Maddie's bed empty and guessed she had spent the night with Art. They seemed smitten with each other and were obviously intending to keep seeing each other. Maybe Maddie was finally ready for a relationship.

Maddie, Josh and Sophie were all going back on the same plane, but while Maddie and Sophie had seats next to each other, Josh was seated at the back. Sophie wished he was sitting in their row so they could talk a little more. She didn't want to say goodbye. She would miss him so much. She replayed memories of the holiday in her mind while Maddie slept all the way home. Sophie guessed her friend hadn't got much sleep last night.

If only she and Josh could have spent the night together too. Sophie pushed the unwanted thought from her mind. She didn't want a one-night stand with Josh, she wanted a relationship and it was clear that he didn't feel the same way. They had laughed and danced together, spent most of the holiday in each other's company, but with Maddie and Art too. At no time had he attempted to take things any further. He saw her as a friend and that was it.

She was just getting caught up in the whole 'holiday romance' thing, that was all. It was just because Maddie and Art had been mooning all over each other that she felt like this. She'd soon get over Josh once she was home again. He'd been such a big part of her life these past few months, what with planning the wedding, then these two weeks in Gibraltar and Spain – but that was all. Besides, a relationship with Josh would never last, he didn't do commitment, and she didn't want to get hurt again. She needed to forget Josh and concentrate on making a whole new life for herself that didn't involve compromising to please a man.

She looked out for Josh as they got off the plane at Birmingham International but there was no sign of him. They caught up with him again at luggage collection, waiting for his case. Sophie's pink and white case came along the belt first, then they spotted Maddie's bright yellow one moving towards them. They waited, chatting with Josh until his silver case came into sight. 'Right, I'm off to get a taxi now. How about you two?'

'Sophie and I are going to share a taxi, we only live ten

minutes from each other, you're welcome to share it as well if you want,' Maddie said. 'You live in Worcester too, don't you?'

'Upton-upon-Severn, so not far out. Thanks – if you're sure, it'll be a lot cheaper than paying for a taxi all the way from Birmingham.'

'No problem,' Sophie said, pleased to have the chance to spend a little more time with Josh.

They all sat in the back seat, Josh in the middle, and chatted away about their holiday as the taxi drove along the motorway to Worcester.

Sophie was dropped off first. Josh said a casual 'See you around' as she got out, and Maddie said she'd message her. Sophie fought back the disappointment as she walked into her flat. Josh hadn't even said goodbye properly, never mind suggesting meeting up again.

Don't be stupid, he's just Steve's brother. There's no reason to see him again now the wedding's over, she told herself.

She was due in work the next day and Friday, although thankfully she had the weekend off, so she unpacked, sorted out her clothes for work, then made herself a hot chocolate, scrolling through some holiday photos on her phone as she slowly sipped it. She paused at the photo of herself and Josh on the jet ski, both of them with their heads back, laughing. Maddie had taken it and sent it to her; just as she had taken one of Maddie and Art, too, sending that to Maddie. She scrolled to that photo, smiling at Maddie in the front. Typical Maddie, always wanting to be in charge. Art hadn't minded though, they were a good match actually, she thought, remembering how they had supported each other on the Caminito del Rey walk – and how

Josh had stood on the other end of the suspension bridge, talking to Sophie when she'd had an attack of nerves. It really had been a fantastic holiday. She finished the rest of her drink and went to bed. It took her a little time to drop off, thoughts of Josh occupying her mind, but finally she fell into a deep sleep and woke up the next morning feeling a lot chirpier.

She got out of bed, flung open the bedroom curtains and looked out at the blue, cloudless sky. It was a glorious day. She wasn't going to waste it moping over Josh and what could have been. Yesterday morning, before she'd left the hotel, she'd organised to view a couple of flats after work today, then on Saturday she was going to the garden centre to get some compost and plants to make some more terrariums. And she wanted to talk to Pat about her plans to work a three-day week. She was about to change her life.

She showered then pulled on canary-yellow cropped trousers and a white daisy-patterned T-shirt and made herself a cup of coffee. It was hard to believe that yesterday they had still been in Spain. If they were still there now, they'd probably be planning a day trip out with Josh and Art. For two weeks she had seen Josh every day; they had practically been inseparable and now he was gone.

She wasn't going to think about it. *Keep busy, that's the thing.* And she had plenty to keep her busy.

'You look amazing,' Janine said when Sophie walked into work. 'You've got a gorgeous tan and I love those trousers. It looks like the holiday did you good.'

'It did. It's just what I needed,' Sophie replied. 'How was Pat's daughter? Do you think she liked working here?'

313

'Zania? She was great. And yes, she seemed to enjoy it. Why? Are you going to do what I suggested and ask Pat if you can work part time?'

Sophie nodded. 'Do you think she'll let me?'

'I reckon there's a good chance. Go for it.' Janine patted her arm. 'Good luck.'

Customers came in and out all morning and there was no time to talk to Pat, but when things had calmed down, Sophie slipped into the back where Pat was doing the books. 'Pat, could I have a quick word?'

'Of course. Everything OK?' Pat asked, peering through the glasses perched on the end of her nose.

Sophie nodded. 'It's just, well, I wondered how you'd feel about me working here three days a week, so I could spend a couple of days at home making my terrariums and gift boxes? I thought maybe your daughter might want to cover the other two days?'

Pat sat back and pushed her glasses back up on her nose. 'I'm sure she would for a while, at least. And I'd like to give you the opportunity to make a go of this. You're very talented, Sophie. How long do you want to give it a try for? Shall we say the New Year? We can discuss if you want to make the arrangement permanent then. Oh, and I'd like you to still make the gift boxes and terrariums for me. How does that sound?'

'That would be perfect. Thanks, Pat.'

'Well done, you,' Janine said when Sophie told her the news. 'I'm glad you've got over Glenn and are getting on with your life.'

'I'm moving home too, going to get a place with a garden.' Sophie showed her the two flats she was viewing after work.

'Good idea.' Janine gave her a hug. 'Go, girl!'

Sophie was excited about the flat viewings, they had both looked perfect, but she was disappointed when she saw the first flat in the converted Victorian house. It had tiny, dark rooms and the garden was no more than a small communal lawn, it looked nothing like the images online. Her heart sank as she drove to meet the estate agent at the second flat, but to her relief she fell in love with it as soon as she walked in. It was on the bottom floor of a block of three flats, with a garage right beside it, and a small back garden which was completely hers to do what she wanted with. It needed a bit of updating but otherwise it was perfect. The garden was securely fenced and plenty big enough for flowerbeds, pots and a small table and chairs. Inside the flat were two bedrooms, one which she intended to use as a workroom, a separate kitchen and lounge. And the rent, if she was careful, was affordable without the need to take in a lodger. The drawback was that a few other people had shown interest in it. Sophie immediately said she'd like the flat and the estate agent promised to get back to her as soon as possible. Then she headed home, stopping off at the local supermarket to grab some essentials on the way.

She messaged Maddie to tell her about the flat as soon as she'd put away the groceries and put the oven on to warm up. She'd bought a readymade lasagne and salad, a quick and fairly healthy meal. Maddie texted back **Well done. You'll get it – I've got a good feeling about it.** Sophie smiled, put the lasagne in the oven and put the kettle on. Things were looking up. She hummed to herself as she popped a teabag into a mug. She really, really hoped that she would be accepted for the flat.

She'd just finished her meal when the intercom buzzed. Surprised, she got up to answer it. It was gone eight. No one ever visited her without messaging first. Unless it was Maddie, popping in to surprise her and talk about the flat. She went over and pressed the button. 'Hello.'

'Hi, Sophie. It's Josh. Sorry to call unannounced but it's important.'

'Josh?' Her heart lurched. What was he doing here? Had he forgotten something?

'Come on up.' She pressed the button to open the downstairs door then opened her own door and left it on the latch. There was a knock on her flat door a couple of minutes later and Josh popped his head around. 'Hi.'

'Come in,' she told him.

He pushed open the door and stepped inside, closing it behind him.

'I didn't expect to see you so soon. Is everything all right?'

'Yes. No.' He coughed. 'I ... er ... I hope you don't mind me turning up like this but I wanted to talk to you face to face, not over the phone.'

'What is it?' She was starting to feel worried. Had Kate and Steve had an argument? They'd looked so happy together when they were in Spain.

'Look, I don't know how you're going to take this, Sophie, but as Maddie said, if I don't say it I'll regret it for the rest of my life ...'

Her breath caught in her throat as his eyes met hers, held hers. She reached out for the back of the chair to steady herself. 'Maddie said ...?'

'Yeah, I talked about it to her when we dropped you off last night.' He paused, his eyes still holding hers. 'I like you. Really like you. And I don't want to lose touch with you. These months planning the wedding and getting to know you have been wonderful, and the last two weeks in Spain I've felt that we've got ... closer.' He moved a little nearer to her. 'So I wondered ... Well, would you like to come out for a meal or a drink ...?'

Her heart did somersaults in her chest as she nodded. 'I'd like that.' Then she paused, wanting to make sure that she hadn't misunderstood what he'd said, she didn't want to make a fool of herself. 'Do you mean as friends?'

His eyes seemed to get bigger, darker, and she felt as if she could drown in them. Tingles of anticipation spread over her body. He shook his head. 'Not friends. As a date ...'

She bit her lip, fighting back the smile that was forming there, the urge to throw her arms around him. 'I'd really like that.'

She paused. 'Do you fancy a coffee now? I'm about to make one.'

'That would be lovely, thanks,' he said.

'Make yourself comfortable,' she indicated the sofa.

She made the coffee and they sat down and talked. Sophie told Josh about her plans to work part time, and the new flat she was hoping to rent with a garden, and Josh was really interested. The time flew until Josh noticed it was almost midnight. 'Oh gosh, look at the time. I've got work tomorrow. Have you?' he said, getting up.

Sophie nodded. 'Don't worry though, I never go to bed earlier.'

'Me neither. Fancy meeting for a drink after work? About eight?' he asked.

She nodded. 'I'd love to.' She named one of the pubs in the town. 'I'll see you there.' He leant forward and kissed her briefly on the cheek. Their eyes met, and her heart stilled as his lips moved closer to hers. It felt like every nerve in her body was waiting for his next move.

His lips met hers and she returned his kiss with a passion that took her by surprise. She stepped back while she still could. 'See you tomorrow.'

'Looking forward to it,' he said.

Chapter Seventy-two

Josh

His date with Sophie was on Josh's mind all the next day. 'Calm down, she's agreed to go on a date with you not be your girlfriend,' he reminded himself. He felt ridiculously excited though, like a young lad going on his first date. He hoped Sophie felt the same way.

He went shopping straight from work, buying a pastel green T-shirt and white shorts, then he showered and changed, arriving at the pub early, not wanting to keep Sophie waiting. He sent her a text to say he was there, and did she want him to get her a drink in.

White wine spritzer please, she replied.

She arrived five minutes late, a vision of loveliness in a red and yellow maxi dress. He waved to her and she almost did a double-take when she saw the T-shirt and shorts. He grinned when he saw her expression.

'Like the new look?' He pointed to the T-shirt. 'Green for renewal and freshness. I looked it up. I'm a new man.'

'So I see.' She looked amused. Then spotting her drink on

the table she smiled. 'Thanks, just what I need.' She picked up the glass and took a long sip. 'That's better. Now tell me about your day,' she said brightly.

The advantage of planning the wedding together over the past few months, then the time spent in Spain, was that they were already friends. There were no awkward silences, no wondering what to say. They chatted easily all evening, laughing, sharing news. Josh didn't want the evening to end.

'Do you want to meet up tomorrow evening for a meal?' he asked as they left.

Her face lit up. 'I'd love to.' She smiled. 'I wonder what colour you'll turn up in tomorrow.'

'There's another reason I chose this pastel-green top today,' he said softly.

'What's that?' Her voice was little more than a whisper, her topaz eyes staring into his.

He reached out his hand and ran his finger gently down her cheek. 'It means optimism.'

'What are you optimistic about?' she asked softly.

His eyes held hers, his heart racing as they widened, her lips parting softly.

'I just want you to understand that I am serious about you.' His voice was thick and husky, his eyes still holding hers. 'I mean that.'

She licked her lips and nodded, unable to speak.

And then his arms were around her waist and he was pulling her closer, lips almost touching hers and she was leaning into him, as if she longed to feel his lips on hers as much as he wanted to feel hers on his.

And they kissed.

They met the next evening for a meal, Josh teaming a white patterned sleeveless shirt with beige chinos. Sophie rocked a red jumpsuit with a sexy strappy bodice top. *She really is gorgeous*, he thought again. 'Any news on your flat?' he asked.

'Yes, it's mine as soon as the paperwork is sorted out.' She smiled at him. 'Want to see some photos, or will that bore you?'

'I'd love to,' he said, thinking that Sophie could never bore him.

She was so enthusiastic about the flat, and he could see why; it had a lot of character.

'I'm only renting but it's got such potential and the landlord said I can do what I want to make it feel more like my home. I love doing up places,' she said enthusiastically.

'Really? That's something we have in common then.' He told her about his cottage. 'You'll have to come and see it some time. In fact, you could pop over tomorrow. I'll cook us lunch,' he offered. 'If you're free, that is.'

'That would be great. Shall I bring the wine? I can get a taxi back.'

Or you can stay the night. There was nothing he would like better but he wasn't going to push Sophie. She meant too much to him to do that. 'Good idea,' he told her. 'Do you like roast beef and Yorkshire pudding?'

Sophie's eyes shone. 'I adore it. But I like my beef cooked really well, not pink.'

'Then that's how I'll cook it.'

Sophie turned up at lunchtime the next day, dressed in yellow shorts and a white top, smiling as she noticed the light blue T-shirt and black shorts Josh was wearing. 'Still the new man, eh?'

'Yep.' Josh wound his arms around her and they both kissed. 'Come in. Dinner's almost ready.'

'It smells lovely,' Sophie said as she followed him into the kitchen.

'Fancy eating out in the garden?'

'Sounds great.' She took a bottle of red wine out of her bag. 'Shall I open the Merlot?'

'Please. You'll find glasses in the top cupboard on the left.' Josh opened the oven door. 'Take them outside if you want, I'm about to dish up.'

After a delicious lunch, and two glasses of wine, Josh gave Sophie a tour of his house.

'You could do such a lot to this,' she told him.

'I plan to.' As they sat in the garden drinking another glass of wine he told her his plans and she listened as if she was really interested.

They went inside a little later to watch a film, curled up alongside each other on the sofa. Josh put his arm around Sophie's shoulders and she snuggled into him. He looked down as she looked up, topaz eyes meeting his, red rosebud lips slightly apart, inviting him to kiss them. So he did. Then they were caressing, stroking, kissing deeper, lying in each other's arms on the sofa, bodies pressing against each other and Josh felt like he was exploding with desire. He lifted his head and looked in Sophie's eyes that were mirroring the desire he felt.

'Fancy taking this upstairs? We'd be more comfortable.'

Her tongue moved over her lips, then she nodded. 'Sounds a great idea.'

Chapter Seventy-three

Sophie

*W*ell, *that was definitely the best sex I've ever had in my life,* Sophie thought, when what seemed like hours later she lay in Josh's arms. It hadn't just been about the sex though. She really liked Josh – more than liked him. She hoped it wasn't just about the sex for him.

He kissed her tenderly on the forehead. 'I've been dreaming about doing that for a long time, and it was even better than I imagined.'

'Really?' She propped herself up on her elbow and smiled down at him. 'And exactly how long have you been lusting after me?'

He pretended to think. 'Let me see. Probably since the first time I met you in here,' he placed his hand over his heart, 'but my head,' he touched his forehead now, 'wouldn't admit it because for one you were in a relationship . . .'

'And two?'

'I didn't want to be in a relationship and I guess that I knew I'd want us to be more than a casual fling.'

She stilled, her eyes searching his face. 'And now?'

'And now a relationship with you is what I want more than anything.' Then he frowned. 'Unless that's not what you want? Are you more interested in a fling to get Glenn out of your system?'

'Glenn was out of my system weeks ago and I don't do casual flings.'

He wrapped his arm around her neck and pulled her to him, kissing her soundly. 'Neither do I any more,' he told her. 'I'm a reformed character. You've seen the T-shirt.'

He pulled her in for another embrace. 'Now, do you want me to get you a taxi or do you want to stay the night?' He kissed her on the nose. 'I'm in the garage for eight so you'll have plenty of time to drive home and get changed for work.'

'Stay the night,' she told him, snuggling up to him, tiredness overwhelming her.

Sometime in the night they both reached out for each other and made love again before falling back to sleep. Sophie woke in the morning to find herself lying on Josh's chest, his arms around her. It felt good.

His eyes opened and he smiled up at her. 'Morning.'

'Morning.'

'Shame we both have to go to work, but do you fancy meeting up afterwards? Going for a meal or a drink? Or you can come back here and I'll fix us something,' he offered.

'That would be great, but you come to mine. It's my turn to do a meal,' she told him.

'Deal.' He kissed her on the nose. 'Now, do you want to shower first while I fix us coffee and croissants? I remember you liking them at the hotel.'

She raised herself up on her elbow. 'Are you saying you got them in especially, hoping that I would stay the night?'

'I like croissants too, remember.' He smiled. 'But it's always good to be prepared.' His lips caressed her face, then her neck. 'I have a confession to make.' He leant down and murmured softly. 'I think I love you.'

Happiness flowed through her. She wound her arms around his neck and whispered, 'I think I love you too.'

They left the flat together, embracing before they got into their respective cars. Sophie hummed as she drove home to get changed, memories of last night with Josh flitting through her mind.

'Well, you look cheerful,' Pat said as Sophie came almost skipping into work a little later. 'I take it one of the flats was OK?'

Before Sophie could reply, her phone buzzed. She glanced at the screen. It was a text from the estate agent. **The paperwork has been approved. Please let us know what date you would like to move in.**

She smiled. 'Yes, and my offer's been accepted. The flat is mine!'

She went through to the back and put on her overall, thinking how much all their lives had changed since they started planning Steve and Kate's secret wedding. Steve and Kate were married, Maddie was actually dating properly, and she was with Josh. She had a good feeling about being with Josh: he was kind and considerate, and had such a zest for life. She was happy. And looking forward to the future. The Spanish Wedding hadn't been such a disaster, after all.

End

Acknowledgements

Everyone loves a wedding, don't they? And a surprise wedding sounds so romantic – but is it really? How would you feel if your partner organised a wedding for you, and you had no chance to decide how you would want it, what dress you would wear or the venue? I would hate it, and many people I've spoken to have said the same. So I thought writing a romance novel about someone organising a surprise wedding for his partner might be fun. Especially if the wedding was set in Spain, meaning that the legal ceremony would have to be conducted in the UK or Gibraltar (for UK residents). I know several people who have been married in Gibraltar, and was a witness to the wedding of two dear friends over there. The wedding dance scene in the register office in this story was actually taken from their wedding – thank you Rich and Annie for letting me use it. I knew the basics but am also very grateful to Leanne Hindle, Wedding Consultant from *Marry Abroad Simply* (www.marrya broadsimply.com) for her help and advice regarding the legalities.

Many thanks to Headline for contracting me to write

another romance novel for them, and to the editorial team of Rosanna Hildyard, Eloise Wood, Elspeth Sinclair and Jill Cole for their advice and expertise. Thanks also to Phillip Beresford for designing the gorgeous cover.

As always, I am indebted to the bloggers and authors who support me by hosting me on their blogs, reviewing my books and sharing my posts. Particular thanks to the members of the Romantic Novelists' Association who are always willing to share their writing experience and advice and to the lovely Rachel of Rachel's Random Reads for organising my blog tour. And massive thanks to you, the readers, for buying my books and allowing me to live the dream of being an author. Thank you all so much. I hope you've enjoyed reading about Sophie, Maddie, Kate and Josh.

Finally last but not least, everlasting thanks to my lovely Dave for his constant support and encouragement, and who thankfully knew better than to organise a secret wedding for us. ☺ And also to my family and friends who all encourage me and support me so much. I love you all. xx

Addictive thrillers. **Gripping** suspense.
Irresistible love stories. **Escapist** treats.

For **guaranteed brilliant reads**
discover **Headline Accent**

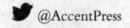 @AccentPress